YOU HAVE THE WRONG MAN

Also by
MARIA FLOOK

Family Night
Open Water

Stories by

MARIA FLOOK

YOU HAVE THE WRONG MAN

Pantheon Books   New York

Many of the stories in this collection were originally published in the following: Agni Review: "Rhode Island Fish Company" · *Bomb Magazine:* "Riders to the Sea" (also reprinted in *The Pushcart Prize Anthology, 1995*) · *Michigan Quarterly Review:* "Asbestos" · *Northwest Rieview:* "Lane" · *Playgirl:* "You Are Here" (originally published under title "Clean") · *Ploughshares:* "Exchange Street" (originally published under title "Cheaters' Club") · *Triquarterly:* "Prince of Motown"

Grateful acknowledgment is made to the following for permission to reprint previously published material: Jobete Music Co., Inc.: Excerpt from "Too Busy Thinking About My Baby," words and music by Barrett Strong, Norman Whitfield, and Janie Bradford, copyright © 1966 by Jobete Music Co., Inc. Reprinted by permission of Jobete Music Co., Inc. · *Jobete Music Co., Inc., and Stone Diamond Music Corporation:* Excerpt from "Let's Get It On," words and music by Marvin Gaye and Ed Townsend, copyright © 1973 by Jobete Music Co., Inc., and Stone Diamond Music Corporation. Reprinted by permission of Jobete Music Co., Inc., and Stone Diamond Music Corporation. · *Hal Leonard Corporation:* Excerpt from "Sexual Healing," words and music by Marvin Gaye and Dell Brown, copyright © 1982 by EMI April Music Inc., Bug Pie Music Publishing and EMI Blackwood Music Inc. All rights for Bug Pie Music Publishing controlled and administered by EMI April Music Inc. All rights reserved. International copyright secured. Reprinted by permission of Hal Leonard Corporation. · *Melody Trails, Inc.:* Excerpt from "Turn! Turn! Turn! (To Everything There Is A Season)," words from the Book of Ecclesiastes, adaptation and music by Pete Seeger, TRO—copyright © 1962 (Renewed) by Melody Trails, Inc. Reprinted by permission of Melody Trails, Inc., New York, N.Y.

Library of Congress Cataloging-in-Publication Data
Flook, Maria.
You Have the Wrong Man : stories by Maria Flook.
    p.   cm.
  ISBN 0-679-43184-5
  I. Title.
PS3556.L583R48   1996
813'.54—dc20   95-26156

Book design by M. Kristen Bearse
Manufactured in the United States of America
First Edition
9 8 7 6 5 4 3 2 1

❖ ACKNOWLEDGMENTS

My thanks to friends who have encouraged me in the writing of these stories: to Kim Witherspoon and John Hoberg, to Claudine O'Hearn, to Lou Papineau, to Kate Flook, for lending me her copy of J. M. Synge, and for her confidence, and to Judith Grossman, for her kinship and faith. My full gratitude to Daniel Frank, my editor, who opened essential windows in this text, from which I saw deeper and deeper.

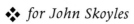 *for John Skoyles*

NORMA

I want the coffin to be white.
And I want it specially lined
with satin. White, or deep pink.

She picks up the shawl to make up her mind about the
color. From under the shawl flops down a dead arm.
Gillis stares and recoils a little. It is like a child's
arm, only black and hairy.

NORMA

Maybe red, bright flaming red.
Gay. Let's make it gay.

Gillis edges closer and glances down. Under the shawl
he sees the sad, bearded face of a dead chimpanzee.
Norma drops back the shawl.

NORMA

How much will it be? I warn you—
don't give me a fancy price just
because I'm rich.

GILLIS

Lady, you've got the wrong man.

—*Sunset Boulevard*
Charles Brackett, Billy Wilder, D. M. Marshman, Jr.

❖ CONTENTS

YOU HAVE THE WRONG MAN

❖ RHODE ISLAND FISH COMPANY

I have been losing sleep because of a fish truck parked outside my bedroom window. The cooling unit on top of the cab makes a constant hum. The hum itself isn't too bad, I could have adjusted to that, but the pulse of the freon varies in tone. Low gurgles and sudden surges, an almost moody mechanical tempo that is ruining my nights. It's important to me to keep on top of my fatigue. My twenty-year-old niece has come to live with me for a semester. I'm happy to have someone in the house again. I might have sold it after the dust settled and my husband moved to Denver. My sons were grown. I stayed because I have always liked our street, which crests College Hill. Living on a hill is lucky; I look down at the city and see the metallicized glass and rosy granites of the New Providence. I still like the ashy façades of the old buildings, the chalky dome of the State House upon its brilliant marble plinths. The light here is constant; it enters the house early, arcs across, and in the evening it's on the other side with nothing to obstruct it.

My sleepless nights worry me because I need to be fresh in order to remain level. I wanted to maintain my initial "openness," which my niece seemed to appreciate from the start. I have grown to enjoy her company, although she is mercurial, unpredictable, dewy, then full of bile. I try to comfort her, but sometimes I cross a line and I can't tell until I'm over it and she has already retreated.

I enjoy opening my closet so she might have something "on loan," and I'm never shaken if she's slow to return it. My boyfriend, Garland, insists it's vanity itself that I encourage Pamela to wear my clothes and give her carte blanche with my hundred-dollar shoes. He says I *put* her in my wardrobe as proof to all that I have kept my figure. He is right. I am pleased that at thirty years her senior, my pinstripe Capri pants, my kitschy pearled sweaters, and a gorgeous rubbed-silk Italian jacket fit Pamela as if she were me. We are similarly svelte, narrow-waisted. My curves have held up. Pam sometimes rifles through my lingerie drawer since we are the same cup size. Not overly buxom, but lord knows, not flat. I found her in my bedroom and we shared the tight oval of the antique pedestal mirror. Reflected there, we discussed what we thought was the sublime optimum. What was perfection? We made our lists and briskly concurred—the ideal was early Loren.

"She's completely drenched, you remember? Her shirt

is clinging," Pamela said. "She walks out of the water onto the beach in that scene from *Boy on a Dolphin*."

It was remarkable to me that my niece should identify that particular Sophia Loren movie. I watched the film with my husband twenty-six years ago in the basement of the university here, when I was eight months pregnant. My ankles were swollen. I suffered from mild toxemia and held an amber prescription bottle of diuretic pills, which I swallowed on the half-hour with a cup of tepid cola. I was disappointed to learn that Pamela had never actually seen the film but only a poster of the starlet in her soaked jersey.

I sometimes recognize a familiar male scent on my sweaters when Pamela hands them back. It's the rich smoke from unfiltered cigarettes and sometimes the crude, slightly sweet odor of shucked oysters. A briny residue which adheres to her boyfriend, Leon, long after he's washed up after work. I think Pamela hoards my clothes on purpose, a signal of protest when my warmth becomes too much for her. Yet, when it comes, I like the way her gratitude is expressed in quick, astonished whispers, which she checks.

Sitting across from her at the table, I notice her thick chestnut hair is the impenetrable red of Renoir's women. I mentioned this to Pamela because she was enrolled at Rhode Island School of Design and she should know the reference. She looked at me, nodded. She stabbed a green bean and moved it like a push broom over the plate before she put it in her mouth. She kept her left arm in her lap so I couldn't see the persistent blemish of a tattoo she had recently removed, inexpertly, with a surgical razor. The sore was still raw. I made her go to the doctor and he told her to apply Silvadene Cream and a loose dressing, but Pamela believed that a wound needs some air now and then. Dinner time was the only hour she could squeeze into her schedule to air it.

At the School of Design, Pamela had a rich social life which carried her from one day into the next. Her rituals of health and hygiene, and, in this case, wound-dressing, were always pushed back to suit her schedule of excitements.

The tattoo was a leftover from her teen years in Philadelphia, when she joined a girl gang. The gang was called the Fem Fatals. The name lacked the French pronunciation. The gang had shortened their name to just the Fatals, then they called themselves, quite simply, the Fates. I remember discussing this with Pamela at the time. She must have been fifteen when I asked her about the three goddesses, Atropos, Clotho, and Lachesis. I wondered if her group of girls had known about them. Pam had said, "Three fates, really?" She had looked quite skeptical. She said, "Don't we just have one fate? The thing is, you buy it. Right? It's just a matter of when it's going to happen. It doesn't matter how."

Pamela was more sophisticated since she had started college, and she didn't like to talk about the years she roamed with the girl gang. Most of all, she seemed embarrassed that her gang had been all of one gender. She wore long-sleeved sweatshirts over her tattoo, and finally she decided to rid herself of the actual mark. Pamela said, "You have to remember, it was the early eighties. We didn't have anything to do but hang out. Tattoos were the hot thing, they were contagious. Like a spider's web."

I said, "How is a spider's web contagious?"

"The idea. The *idea* gets on you like a sticky web. It trapped all the girls in the neighborhood. Maybe it was because of Cher, I don't know. Cher was a curse on us."

"Cher was?"

"Yeah. She was, like, a hero at first. She was cool, at first. But it wasn't like the sixties when people knew how to go about it."

"Go about what?" I said.

"You know, change the world. Don't you remember, didn't you try it?"

I told her I was busy raising my baby sons, though I was sympathetic and wore black armbands on occasion. I wasn't trying to rile her, but she looked at me in astonishment. She was trying to picture me pushing a baby stroller in the park while the war raged in Vietnam. "You had your babies in the sixties?" She stared at me hotly. She couldn't believe it. She hit the saltcellar against the palm of her hand. Nothing.

"It's the humidity," I said. I apologized for the saltshaker; I wasn't going to apologize for the other.

She told me she didn't think a black armband would be much help then or now.

Pamela's teens had been hardest for my brother, who didn't have the gift of flex. I hated to watch him square off with Pam. It was like looking at a flood on the television. The news footage shows the muddy current plunging through a town, taking everything, but there's always a big tree standing against it. Pam was twenty now, and going to school. I was pleased to have her stay with me during her first semester. Then it was up to her and her father to figure out where she would go. Dormitory, apartment, loft. There were many reasonable options.

"It's better to be scarred than to have a tattoo," Pam was saying.

"That's a doozie of a scar," I said, eyeing the sore patch on her forearm.

"I just hope I got all the ink out," Pam said, "it looks pretty awful. At least you can't read what it says." She studied the place on her arm where the deep writing had been. "Illegible," she said, "thank God."

Her arm looked like the fell on a leg of lamb, the blotted violet ink of a meat inspector's stamp beneath a yellow scab the size of a small wallet. "It will heal," I told Pamela. "You didn't want the word *Fatals* written there forever. You were right to remove it. I'm just glad you went to see the doctor. Your arm could have become infected."

Pam said, "The doctor was okay. He didn't ask me about it. He knew I made a mistake, but he didn't grill me."

"He didn't ask what the tattoo had said?"

"No, he was cool about it," Pamela said.

I was happy my doctor had behaved himself. It felt strange to have someone in my charge again. My two boys were grown and thousands of miles off. I tried to remember the last time I had driven either one of them to a doctor. It was David with a split lip that wouldn't heal. The physician sprinkled graphite powder or something just as sooty on his mouth, and after a time the crack disappeared. Then, David was gone to college in Denver to be near his father. Denver. What a place to go to college. David just had to leave New England. New England can be suffocating to some. My oldest son, Michael, dropped out of college.

He was running a healthy business writing and printing résumés for law and medical school graduates and for hundreds of others whose impressive fields I had imagined my own sons might have pursued.

Pamela, sitting across from me, dabbing her arm with a two-ply napkin, was an absurdity, really. But I welcomed her. She was always changing her appearance; her lovely hair was fluffed one day and gluey the next with a hair dressing that smelled peculiarly familiar, like diaphragm jelly. "Don't knock it," she said. "It works like Dippity-Do." Her clothing was sometimes too tight. Her jersey leggings exposed both curves and muscle, the taut fabric exposed a clenched tendon or shimmied over a hollow dimple, made evocative creases at her pudendum.

I too wear running tights, but I make sure my oversized T-shirt falls past my hips.

Pamela was immersed in contemporary culture, but she at last had a focus. She was studying graphic design, something for a career in advertising. She could never make it all the way through her explanation of what she planned to do. I knew she hadn't really decided on a final goal; it went against her grain to do so. At least she went to class every day. I trusted something would emerge. I was nosy and I once opened her portfolio to find it empty except for a book of wallpaper samples: daisies, fleurs-de-lis, imitation marbles, paisleys, and washable vinyl plaids. I couldn't resist asking her about it, and she told me these books of wallpapers gave her ideas. "Design breeds design," she told me. "One curlicue leads to another more defiant and ultimately awesome spiral. Curves and planes, everything has to oppose or relate."

I started backing out of her room, but she was smiling, teasing. If she was bluffing she wasn't trying to hide it, and this made me believe she wasn't bluffing after all.

My friend Garland wasn't pleased to hear I took her in. "You never mentioned this niece," he said, as if to accuse me of conjuring up my niece out of the thin air. I assured him that Pamela was never around in the evenings and we could still have our privacy. I told him perhaps he might invite me to his house for once. I could bring fresh linens over there. He always said his own sheets were soiled and rumpled and he didn't want me to have to rough it. "Now's your chance to tidy up," I said. I was tired of Garland's "I'm an old recluse living amidst towers of old newspapers and crusted sardine tins" routine. Garland was a poseur. He was theatrical, phobic, but only to a degree that enabled him to avoid a full-blown obligation. His house at the university was a rather calculated mess. It was meant to ward off all but the most undiscerning strays, graduate students who came and went, unafraid of Garland's three-day-old coffee and greasy glassware. Garland's apartment sported a door-length poster of a bullfighter and a few faded Chinese lanterns strung from the ceiling fixtures with nylon fishing line. These eyesores were leftovers from previous tenants, from the pre-Beatles era, and yet Garland had lived there, in that one apartment, for twenty-two years, more than two decades, and with two different wives. The lanterns, the bullfighting poster remained. Certainly, these things were meant to imply he wasn't settling down yet; he wasn't a permanent tenant within any specific ethos, time frame, or any imprisoning building structure. He didn't wish to redecorate his surrounds; he didn't want furnishings and artwork that might accurately clock or log his existence. Therefore, he needn't knock down the fading paper scraps of the early dwellers; their imprint was still important to him because it prevented his own. Even the few souvenirs or relics left over from his two marriages were arranged here or there as if he had come upon them after the fact. I actually preferred my own house to his, but something made me want to assert my presence in his apartment, and I was always trying to do it.

"It's ugly now," Pam said, showing Garland the oozing strip of skin. "It will smooth out eventually. It has a few phases to go through. The doctor said it will get crinkly like a second-degree burn."

"A second-degree burn is not something to sneeze at," Garland said.

"Yeah, but at least it won't say 'Fatals' anymore," Pam told him.

"Praise the lord," Garland said.

"She's showing you something, you don't have to criticize," I said to him.

"Maybe I'm being churlish, but I just ate a heavy meal," he said.

"No sweat," Pam said, "it takes stomach to look at it for long."

"Why don't you cover it up?" Garland said.

"She does. She does cover it up. I bought her the gauze sponges and the tape," I said.

Pam held her arm extended so that it divided the room. "Men don't like this kind of thing," she said. She stood there and waited to see if I would defend Garland, who had moved to the leather sofa. I shrugged my shoulders, but I turned my back slightly on Garland and she was satisfied.

"Well, I'll see you later," Pam said. "I'm going downtown with Leon. Leon knows what I'm going through. He wrecked his mountain bike and skinned the meat off his elbows. It took a while to come back."

Garland turned to me and said, "The tone of the evening has been irrevocably set. Who can think of the flesh now?"

"Suit yourself," I said and I sat down in the firm captain's chair that always helps me face someone squarely. I leaned back in the deep seat, aligning my spine with the rigid center dowel. I cupped my palms over the smooth knob-ends of its arms. I was ready for the edgy debate that always took us into sex.

I didn't mind Leon coming to the house. Pamela and Leon were adults; I couldn't baby-sit them. I soon adjusted to seeing Leon coming naked from the bathroom, strolling down the full length of the hall.

The first night we met, Leon walked towards me, back-lit by the moon coming through the fanlight window. I couldn't avert my eyes in time. In that glimpse, I couldn't help but notice that his penis was still partially erect in its dreamy recovery from sex. He nodded to me and smiled and kept walking. He didn't cover up. He wasn't ashamed of his body and didn't turn his hip to hide himself. Why should he? My alarm was overcome by something stronger, an affection. A warmth so familiar and even, a level surge that I found pleasing. I thought of my own sons moving through these halls, and although Leon wasn't their double—he wasn't my sons' equivalent in any way—he looked too comfortable to be a mere guest.

I closed my bedroom door. Seeing Leon wasn't like seeing my sons, at all. I felt the current of heat that flows upward from the pelvis to the brain in an instant recognition. I felt its flashpowder aftertaste in the back of my throat.

My nights were altered after that. The kernel of my sleep disorder had germinated with my first glimpse of Leon. His lanky gait. His long strawberry-blond hair, newly shampooed, seemed quite lion-like when it fluffed in golden tiers along his shoulders. When I saw him again the next night, he mumbled, "Hello." He might have whispered something else. He stood still beside Pam's door and shrugged his shoulders, as if he couldn't decide if he should return to her bed or join me in mine. Of course, I might have imagined this. I told myself my sleep troubles arose from Leon's part-time job. Leon drove a refrigerator truck for Rhode Island Fish Company. Leon loaded the truck with fish in the evenings, sliding four-gallon plastic trays of whole flounders, cod, bluefish, and swordfish steaks onto galvanized racks like built-in bookshelves on either side of the truck. Then he stacked bushels of shellfish, quahogs and mussels, in the forward part of the truck, making sure the bushels were squared and wouldn't topple. The next morning, before rush hour, Leon would leave the house to deliver the fish to processors and seafood distributors, sometimes driving all the way into New York or over into Hartford. If he was going into New York City, he had to leave Pamela's bed at 4:00 A.M. in order to keep to his schedule. If he was delivering locally, he could sleep through until the morning. The fish stayed fresh overnight in the refrigerator truck. After 11:00 P.M., because of Providence's off-street parking ordinance, Leon had to park the truck in the drive, beneath my bedroom window. The unit on top of the cab was loud when it switched on and off, and it kept me awake.

My position lets me make my own hours, but I prefer to work mornings. I write press releases and public relations materials, myriads of simple three-page brochures for a large maternity hospital. A single pamphlet, written with sincerity, some *flair*, printed on good color stock, and distributed in the nick of time, can save the lives of a teenage mom and her infant. I never hold a squalling newborn, but I reach new mothers in the early stages with my pamphlets about back exercises, childbirth classes, nutrition guides, laundry instructions, crib safety, premature labor warning signals. Schedules, lists, tips, warnings.

There are occasional conflicts between the busy routines of the delivery rooms and the hospital's heavy abortion schedule at the out-patient clinic. My pamphlets cover these opposite extremes. I try to get information across in a nutshell.

My routine became thrown off when Leon started to park his truck outside my window. After a week of very little sleep, I couldn't get much done at work. I decided to talk to Pamela about the fish truck. I wanted to make sure she understood that it wasn't Leon. I liked Leon. He was agreeable, gentle, like one of those orange tomcats that seem so adaptable, eating table scraps on the stoop, then being invited into the kitchen, then finally taking full license. Garland laughed when he heard me; he reminded me that it was Leon's name itself that had tricked me into thinking of him as a tame cat. I protested; I reminded Garland that Leon was very sweet to Pamela and he was always courteous to me. I wouldn't say anything to Pam about Leon's nude prowls, his silky sex talk, clearly audible and more so as it neared its conclusion. His release, which he adeptly prolonged, shimmied through several octaves. It was quite a disturbance at first, but I might have been able to sleep through that after the first few times if not for the irregular blasts of the pumping freon. The freon was the problem. Leon would have to park the truck elsewhere, down at the harbor at Rhode Island Fish, somewhere out of my hearing.

Garland noticed the dark smudges beneath my eyes and he tugged me to him on the sofa. "You just have to put your foot down," he told me. "Leon can get the truck in the morning like anyone in his right mind, there's no reason he has to park it here for the night. You don't have to sleep with those fish outside."

I laughed about that. It was a local mafia joke, wasn't it? To "sleep with the fishes."

"That's Hollywood's golden days," Garland said. "Today's mob is all MTV punks; their talk is streamlined because of greed. They don't think in those lovely metaphors."

"But how would Leon pick up the truck? I'd have to drive him. It might be easier for me to sleep over at your place," I told Garland.

"That's avoiding the issue. You have to set some rules here."

"Yes," I told him, he was squirming so much I didn't push it further.

. . .

Then, for a week or more, there was no truck. There was no Leon. Pam sat across from me at dinner, her hands in her lap.

"Don't pick the scab," I told her.

"I'm not," she barked at me. "Christ—"

"I just mean, don't be tempted," I said.

"For once, can we forget about it?" Pam said. "It's all you think of. My fucking scab."

"It's almost healed, isn't it?"

"What's it to you?"

"You aren't eating anything tonight. Aren't you going to a concert?"

Pamela said, "I'm going to hear a band. It's not a 'concert.' There's a difference, you know."

"You should eat something before you go out drinking."

Pamela said she knew how to drink. We didn't talk about Leon. It was over with Leon or maybe it was just beginning. I wanted to tell her that love took many shapes before it gelled. Did I need to tell Pamela, former member of the Fatals, anything more about life's lessons? She liked to instruct me. Pamela told me, recently, that life was just one big pass/fail course. All these little tests were meaningless except for the distraction. "We all need our distractions," Pamela said to me with new acidity, as Garland arrived at the house.

When Pamela went out to hear the rock-and-roll band, Garland and I took apart one of my photo albums just to remake it in basically the same fashion. I had, years before, removed any photographs that upset me, photographs of my husband sailing a Sunfish in Newport, or steering a golf cart with a tasseled surrey; yet, even without his image, some of the remaining photographs recalled the ones I had destroyed, and these ghost pictures hung before my eyes. That week, I had received phone calls from both of my sons, one right after another, and I felt comforted that they had remembered, almost simultaneously, to love me. There was no official occasion, and their unexpected greetings warmed me for days afterwards.

During one of these surprise phone calls, my son heard Leon's voice behind me in the kitchen and my son was curious about him. I liked hearing the shy, tinny resonance of my son's uncertainty—perhaps his ranking was being challenged in his absence. "Oh, that's just Leon. He's Pam's squeeze," I said, aware of the complex fiber-optic braid of jealousies carried back and forth across a thousand miles, at a cost, by AT&T. I told my son I just loved having Pamela in the house.

"Here's one of Pam," I said to Garland when I found a snapshot of my niece photographed when she was a little girl. I hunted through my photographs, ignoring my own babies, and once and again I found a photograph of my brother's daughter. The little girl looked back at me, unexpectedly, from her place in those early years, years when I had hardly thought of her.

"She looks almost the same," Garland said.

"Oh, she's a natural, isn't she? You can see it, even then."

Garland said, "She's exotic, if you like that sort of thing."

This made me feel funny. Was he saying he didn't appreciate Pamela's beauty or was he saying that I lacked something, something exotic? I couldn't compare myself with a twenty-year-old girl, could I? His comment fired me up. I looked at the picture of my teenaged niece as if she were more to me than just my brother's child—but what? I looked at my lover, wanting his face to blur the other until I pinched the cardboard sleeves of the album together.

After that, Garland and I went to bed. Later, I left Garland in the bedroom and went down the hall. I saw Pamela's bedroom door open, so I stopped and looked inside. The lamp on her bed table burned, but she hadn't returned from the rock club. She had left the lamp on. I liked how Pamela had made the room look different. My son's furniture looked unfamiliar with her clothes and some of mine splashed about, her shoes paired at the foot of the dresser, and her electric hair rollers crammed on the bottom bookshelf. The bed was unmade, the floral sheets tugged high on the corners of the mattress as if ready to spring loose. She made love to Leon in these sheets, but never at the same time that I made love to Garland, so it didn't seem like a similar phenomenon. What I did with Garland was entirely different; the difference wasn't because of our ages or our particular status or file category in the "human condition." It was something else. Garland and I sought privacy upon privacy, yet Pamela and Leon seemed happy to have me, and even Garland, in close eavesdropping distance of their lovemaking, as if we offered some kind of moral support. Did we sanction their raw and sensuous improvisations as we imagined them to happen? Our quiet endurance might even encourage them. Then, afterwards, if I was still awake, I might heat steaming bowls of chowder for Leon before he went off in his truck or back to Pam's bed. I crumbled the oyster crackers over their plates, as if they were too weak to do so on their own. I couldn't keep from imagining Leon's phenomenal levels of expertise, which had left him looking so peaked.

Pamela never bothered to give me much support, to stick around when Garland and I were at it. Did she think I didn't need or require her interest, her acknowledgment of *my* intimate life?

As I reached to switch off her lamp, I noticed some of my brochures on the bed stand. She must have brought these upstairs from my desk. There was the new one about seeking proper channels of litigation for victims of the Dalkon Shield IUD. This, of course, was of no use to Pam, who had always used a diaphragm. Then there was the booklet on Creative Visualization, not one of my fliers but one from the Home Birth Association. Then, beside the brochures, I saw a large amount of money flattened beneath a hand mirror. I picked up the mirror to look at the cash. It was more than five hundred dollars in an even fan that suddenly undulated in the breeze from the furnace grate when I lifted the mirror. The bills fluttered strangely, like something you might see ruffling underneath the water in a coral reef. I wondered where she could have obtained that kind of money. Her father paid me directly for her household expenses and gave Pam a modest allowance for school supplies and recreation. He also allowed her to use a J. C. Penney credit card and one from Sears. She didn't often go down to the mall to shop at those stores and preferred to browse at Screamin' Mimi's, where everything was spandex and vinyl. Perhaps the money was Leon's;

it could have been his wages and she was going to return it to him.

Those days when the fish truck was parked outside, I some-times thought about the fish, the fishes themselves, chilled, layered, their eyes still clear and fixed on some last, wistful look into the deep. Now that Leon was nowhere to be seen, and the truck was parked in who-knows-whose driveway, I even dreamed about them. Perhaps it was their very form— elongated pods, seed-shaped, leaf-shaped—which made an attractive vision. I found myself comforted by the image of these netted creatures. Didn't these fish, when alive, move as a whole? Shifting in silky forward propulsion in shiny rows and layers. In Leon's charge, they again were grouped, resting one upon the other, gill to gill. I saw how I was again thinking about mortality. I often do in the horizontal station of darkness that mimics the last phase. We expect to reach this phase; small complaints provide a window on our de-cline, yet we constantly work to ignore it in our daily lives.

Once recently, when I was bathing in the clawfoot tub, I heard the hall phone jangle. Pamela went out to the land-ing and picked it up. The caller asked for me. I heard Pamela say in a slur, "Oh, she's decomposed, she'll have to call you back." Of course Pamela must have said, "She's in-disposed." The error, hers or my own, alarmed me. It sum-moned a picture of rot that I couldn't shake until I had rinsed, stood up, and dried off.

So there we were, on any given night, the fish and I, lying there on our chilly pallets. The fish were out of their element, that element which scientists assume was most likely everyone's first element and comfort, the sea. I was making a parallel, or contrast, I couldn't decide which—the fish with those flat dime-store eyes wide open, and I in stiff waves of bed linen. But, thinking of Leon's fish, I couldn't daydream with any reasonable purity.

Garland left me to go back to his apartment. It was trash day and he needed to discard the refuse he had forgotten the previous week. "I have to get home in time for the trash," he said every Wednesday night.

His various methods of escape, his ferocious plunge from me each night was impressive and I was wary. I never demanded he stay to eat breakfast just to prove something. After all, we weren't babies. I saw him off at a late hour. I touched the back of my hand to my lips, tapping back a rich yawn. I was still downstairs when Pamela came home. She crashed against the front door until it swung open. Immediately, I saw that something was wrong. Her coat was wrenched off her shoulders and trailing. Her face looked glazed and contorted. She might have been weeping, or retching.

"What's wrong," I said, taking her wrists to keep her squared before me. She twisted in my grasp, not wanting to meet my eyes. Then she leaned against me and shuddered. She felt like a bean-bag doll when I gripped her arms. I had seen something like this at the hospital, but, I walked away from the sight. I wasn't a physician. I was a writer of brochures. I didn't often feel ashamed of my profession until I watched others taking hold of a situation, what some people called "taking action."

With this in mind, I shook her and asked, "What's happened?"

Nothing.

I asked her again. I lifted her face to see her mouth was bloody, her lower lip swollen like a wide slice of plum.

"Are you hurt?" I asked.

"Look at this. Look what I have—" Pamela said. She stood up straight to plead with me eye to eye. "Look at this!"

"What is it?" I said. I didn't see anything.

Pamela stepped back from me and opened her fist. "I can't believe this is happening," Pamela said.

I looked into her hand. There was something in her palm, but it was so reddened with blood I couldn't tell what it was. Without thinking, I picked it up with my thumb and forefinger and immediately set it down on the kitchen counter. My knees locked, and I weaved slightly from the trunk. "My goodness," I told her.

"It's the tip," she whispered, then she exploded into sobs.

This surprised me. I had imagined something else. "What do you mean, 'the tip'?" I asked her. "This didn't come from you? I thought you might have passed it, you know—"

Pamela said, "God. You thought I passed it? Like I was pregnant or something? Are you kidding?" She looked intrigued, as if she might have liked to adopt the idea.

I was relieved that the reddened scrap wasn't the result of an unauthorized abortion. After all, if Pamela tried to remove a tattoo with a razor, what else might she try? Then it occurred to me that something equally bizarre was unfolding, and I tried to follow her explanation.

"It's the tip," she insisted. "He was on me, and I bit it," she said.

I sank down to the floor, my back against the refrigerator. I thought of the chapters of psychology I had read in college. Men feared one thing more than any other. I had always thought their fear outlandish. Then I considered Pamela, she must have been very threatened to do such a thing. I pulled myself up from the floor. "Are you all right? Did he hurt you?"

"My teeth are loose. I think one is falling out, I can push it back and forth. It hurts." Pamela showed me how she could wobble her front teeth.

I was having some trouble getting her to explain what had happened. "What is that?" I said to her. "What is *that*— on the counter?" I spoke with more depth and volume than I expected. I shouted. My confusion had loosed a basso profundo, to make up for my coming up blank. I still didn't understand what had happened.

"I told you. It's somebody's nose, just the tip. You aren't going to tell anybody. I mean, it's awful. Someone could take it the wrong way."

"A nose? Oh, honey, I thought it was worse."

Pamela looked at me. She made another double take, as if my ridiculous error in thinking had again outwitted her. My scenario appealed to her. She started to sputter. Her laughter came and went in maniacal waves.

Her laughter startled me, it seemed ghoulish. Of course—she was upset. Her reaction could be excused as hysteria. Finally, I took her shoulders and gave her a shake.

"He was forcing you, so you had to fight back? Is that it?"

"He was on me," Pamela said, her eyebrows were lifted high, arched in drunken mirth.

"You were attacked and you bit his nose?" I said, trying

to pinpoint the cause and effect while avoiding the tone of a legal technician.

Pamela went over to the counter and looked down at the knob of flesh, too casually I thought. "Shit, he was on me. He was just on me." Her words were comfortably slurred. She held her fingers against her upper teeth and wobbled them once or twice to show me.

I said, "He wouldn't get off of you even when you asked him to?"

"I didn't ask anything. I already had hold of him. It hurt to bite so hard. I saw cold stars behind my eyes. He was snarling. I couldn't let go. My jaw was locked. Then he hit me and my teeth clicked through like a stapler. He did it to himself."

I made Pamela rinse her mouth and then I gave her a cold washrag. She held the dripping towel against her lips. "Don't worry," I told her. I kept touching my fingertips to my temple where I felt a peculiar stabbing. Pamela sat down in a kitchen chair. She drummed her fingers on the table. This confused me. She seemed to be waiting for me to decide something. I had to consider my niece, and yet, I wondered about the boy. I imagined him stumbling through town in a bloody stupor. I asked Pamela, "Who was it? Did you know him?"

"Yes and no."

"Yes *and* no? This is important—did he know your name?"

"I've seen him at the bar. He was a creep. He pestered me when I came outside. It happened so fast. Please, I need to talk to Leon. Will you call Rhode Island Fish?" Her eyes were strange, bright with anticipation, almost like a child in the swell of pride that comes directly after a minor peril. She wanted Leon to know.

"Call Leon," she said again. Her request was chilling because its urgency seemed oddly programmed.

I ignored her wish to telephone Leon and asked her more questions. "Was he a big man, a heavyset man?"

"He was just some guy. A guy is a guy, isn't that right? Who cares which one? Maybe you can call Leon and tell him what happened to me."

"Okay," I told her, and I went over to the counter once more to see it. It looked suspect, this tiny leaf of tissue. It looked peculiar, too white and spongy. Like a sliver of tripe.

"We have to report this," I wanted to tell her. I wanted to go to the telephone and call the police just to see what her reaction might be. I told her the police would come over in an instant when it was a situation of attempted rape. I imagined the police, the social workers, the rape doctors, all the troops who gather after sex crimes.

I went over to the counter and looked down. The bubbly scrap in its congealing web made me reconsider contacting the police. Something didn't add up. I had to be firm and canny all at once. I had to be one step ahead of Pamela and one step ahead of my own first instincts. My first instincts keep me within the routine patterns of good deeds, indifferent allowances, and blank permissions that normal people live their lives by. Let the poor be poor, the murderers be jailed, the average citizens be left alone. If I wasn't always exactly innocent, I knew which side of right and wrong I was meandering in, and I knew something more. I knew about crimes of loneliness, and this was shaping up to be one. I could not be sure if my niece was justified in what she had done, but there wasn't any reason to call the authorities. This was a family matter.

I called the emergency desks at Rhode Island Hospital and at Miriam Hospital and asked the receptionists if anyone had come in. I asked them if a young man with a facial cut had registered to get care. Neither hospital would tell me if such a boy had arrived. One receptionist said that there were always a lot of nose injuries because of all the car wrecks. The nose was the first to strike the dashboard, it was the "pointer." "People are lucky if it's just the nose. A nose can be reconstructed." It's really just a decorative appendage, like an awning, and it could be reaffixed. I called all the hospitals. I interrogated the emergency-room receptionists for Pamela's sake. She watched me as I talked to the switchboard operators, the nurses, the interns. She looked very peaceful, pleased I was doing everything I was expected to do. She listened as I told one hospital receptionist that my son was supposed to be there, he had a bad laceration, a dog bite, and could they tell me his condition. The receptionist told me she couldn't give me the information I wanted, but just between her and me, there was nothing like that, no dog bites had come in for days. She asked me if we owned a pit bull terrier. The hospital had to report pit bull incidents directly to the Providence police.

I asked Pamela what she wanted me to do with the bit of flesh. I could wrap it in something and put it in the freezer or I could destroy it, I told her. Flush it like a goldfish with tail rot, a condom in its rumpled length.

"You decide," she said.

"The toilet," I said.

"Good," Pamela said, and she stood up to hug me. She went upstairs. In a few minutes I heard her dialing the telephone on the landing. She was telling Leon about the attack. Her voice was breathless, yet perfectly modulated as it expressed her alarm, her pain, her triumph. I put my face close to the gooey lump and studied the snip. I pushed it up and down the Formica, making sure. Pamela kept talking to Leon, explaining how her teeth were loose. There was something in her tone that made me shut my eyes and throw my head back. I listened to her talk to Leon, tell him how he never should have left her on her own. He should come over. She would forgive him. I took the piece of flesh over to the sink and pushed the faucet open. I rinsed it under the stream, passing my hand back and forth until it felt clean, rubbery, then I bounced it lightly in my open palm.

Tripe. I had thought so. It was a relief, but it was a sad confirmation.

I greeted Leon at the front door. He looked truly upset and I wanted to tell him what I knew. He shouldn't assume any responsibility for Pamela's performance tonight. When Pamela joined my household, I had felt such rich swells of a permanent kind—one might call it loyalty or love. Now I was forced to feel caution. Forced! I watched Leon climb the stairs. I studied his narrow hips, the hollow of his broad shoulders beneath his shirt, which suggested brute strength at rest. Brute strength looks vulnerable this way. I heard

Pamela lock the bedroom door after him. When I went to bed, the truck was going full swing outside my window. It had a new tic, an unmistakable gushing followed by a sizzle, then nine or ten drips slowing, until the last drip never seemed to come before the gushing started over again.

The next day I took Pamela to my dentist. The dentist bonded her front teeth together so they would stay in correct alignment as her gums healed over the jostled roots. She would not lose any teeth. She told the dentist she had had a fall playing tennis. He lifted his eyebrows, and I too wondered how she had been injured, since the rest of the story was a charade. Her teeth were indeed loose, but from what? Perhaps it was a self-inflicted injury, but I didn't hope for that. It was more upsetting to think Pamela had created her own assailant, imitated his anger, and invented his violence against herself. It was more likely that someone had become irritated with her and slapped her hard.

Pamela was lying on the sofa eating ice cream that I had bought for her, hand-packed, at the Portuguese grocery. She had not mentioned the bloody snip, and so I asked her about it. "Where did you get tripe at that hour?"

Pamela sat up straight. She put the bowl of ice cream on the floor. "You knew it was tripe?"

"Not at first."

"Shit. You're unbelievable, you know that?" Pamela looked at the floor and moved the bowl of ice cream with her foot distractedly until it was halfway to me. "You let me go on and on like this since yesterday? You knew it was bullshit? God, what is it like to be so *perfect*? You go around trying on other people's shoes? I guess you have so much *insight*. You're so sweet. Sweeter than sugar—"

"Where did you get tripe in the middle of the night?" I asked her.

"Where? Star Market. It's open twenty-four hours, remember?"

"You hurt my feelings," I told her. I picked up a magazine and fluttered the pages, to show her that I was living with it. I wasn't put off. When she saw this, she stormed out of the room. I must have appeared too much like one of those teachers who can't be ruffled by a spitball, and this infuriated Pam. Maybe she was hoping I would use the techniques from my brother's paperback book about "tough love." If I had followed those puerile hints, she could stomp off feeling justified. She was paralyzed by my cheery intrusions, by my unfathomable maternal impulses—loving shrugs, my shoulders shifting like downy wings. My tactics were for my own survival as much as for hers. Mothering someone helps keep me in line, but I couldn't admit that to her, could I?

In a few minutes, Pamela walked back down the stairs and straight out the front door. That night Leon showed up. He told me he didn't intend to stay long, just long enough to tell Pamela he wasn't interested in her games. I suspect he didn't know the whole truth about the "nose," but he told me he assumed it was bullshit or Pam would have opted for the extra publicity that going to the police would have brought into it. If there was an ounce of truth in it, she would have contacted the newspapers. He told me he had watched her tricks, several times, and he had had enough.

"She needs professional help," Leon told me, and I nodded. I felt sad that we weren't everything she needed. Why couldn't we be everything, Leon and I? I have felt powerless before. Several times in my life I have looked at my mirror and tried to gauge my level of psychic energy, how much was left? I've always wondered at the tiny ration of strength we all start with and how it either intensifies or lessens. Like with watercolors, a little bit goes a long way; diluted, it makes a wash that can cover a whole lifetime with one weak color, or you might use it in a concentrated dollop here or there. I suppose the way I have lived my life, my strength has surfaced as an unremarkable sky blue, a domestic sky with neither the exuberance of dawn nor the inky ritual of night.

Leon sat down across from me for a few moments. It didn't seem as if Pamela would be coming home soon. He said he wasn't going to waste his time waiting to say goodbye to someone a second time. He asked me to convey the message for him.

"What should I tell her exactly?" I asked him.

"Tell her she's immature. How about that?"

"That's a little harsh."

"Now, you. Why can't she take you as a model?"

I smiled.

Leon said, "Pamela better behave herself or she'll be losing something when you give her the heave-ho."

I won't give her the heave-ho, I thought to myself. Leon, of course, had already excused himself from any further involvement with Pam. He looked at me across the table. His eyes didn't dismiss me as we stood up. He took my elbow and tugged me around to face him.

"Where's Garland?" he said.

"Where's Pam?" I answered, as if our exchange had been rehearsed and cued, delivered with the bold alacrity of a witty stage production.

"I mean it," he told me. "Where are they?"

I walked ahead of him up the stairwell. I killed the hall switch and followed the moonlight's slack bed sheet across the old planking. I was first in my bedroom and I turned around in the doorway to greet him. Given his youth, Leon's perceptions of me had been accurate from the start, that moment when we maneuvered through the dark and were unmoored in a momentary swell which took these weeks to crest.

He untied the collar loop on my robe. The satin piping dangled, and then the robe fell. I pushed the heel of my hand up the tight trellis of his ribs, rotated my wrist at his shoulder, and coasted my fingertips down his spine. Despite a fear that Pamela would show up, our lovemaking was sweetly edgy, prolonged, and forgiving. Leon betrayed Pamela in each hesitant discovery and into the next. I sensed it was a slave's secret worship at the eve of his freedom, and he still thought of her. After all, it was she who led us to this union and she would serve to unlink us afterwards. Perhaps I am too seasoned, but her echo didn't spoil any of it for me. Leon endured the halting scrutiny in my touch, and, in turn, I indulged his playful, cantankerous urges, which he had not dared to introduce to her. How often would we come across these same luxuries?

In an hour, we dressed and walked out to the curb.

There was the fish truck, newly washed. Its silvery panels still looked wet beneath the street light, blue-white and iridescent as haddock skin.

"So, you're all loaded for tomorrow?" I asked him.

"It's all set," Leon said.

"The usual?"

"The same. The cod's a little ripped up tonight, weird. But, we've got some nice tinker mackerel, tiny as slippers."

When I told him how much I liked tinker mackerel he went around and opened the padlock on the truck. He hopped into the mist; his shoe slipped on the wet tread but he regained his balance and he pulled me up into the narrow aisle. I stood beside him, between the tiers of fish, as he found the plastic tray of mackerel and lifted the lid off. The fish were tiny, mottled with gold and silver dapples; the flesh along their spines was deep cobalt. "They're beautiful," I said.

"For breakfast?" he asked me.

"I can't wait until breakfast, maybe tonight." I said. We both laughed at my greed for the taste of the local delicacy.

Leon looked around the truck for a container, but there wasn't anything. I pulled out the hem of my jersey and we laughed as he stretched the fabric around a half-dozen fish. He was begging off, leaving just these fish as keepsakes. I forgave him. He got behind the wheel of the truck and rested his elbow out the window, showing his luxurious ease, which I still admired. He seemed to know it impressed me and he smiled. I waved to him with my free hand as I steadied the icy hammock of fish at my waist.

Pamela came home at midnight. I broiled the fish with mustard and vinegar and set it down in front of her. She was touching her nose with a wadded Kleenex. Her tears were real. "I'm not on drugs," she said.

"Of course you aren't," I said.

"It's usually what people think," she told me, "but it's worse than drugs. I get crazed for a while, then it passes. Can you forget it?"

"Sure I will. Don't worry," I said.

"I don't know why I do these things," she said.

"Your arm is almost completely healed," I told her. I lifted her wrist and stretched her arm out towards me. She tugged against my pull, but she relaxed as I cradled her elbow in my palm. The raw patch had calmed and a new field of pink had surfaced, hairless and glossy. I wanted to mention the ancient statuary in Greece. I had seen marble limbs discolored, worn concave at the wrist and fingertips, marred by centuries of human touch. Unchecked, these habits of adoration can wear away their subject. To tell her this might sound too much like a tour guide's expert monologue, and already Pamela had pinned her napkin beneath her plate and was standing up from the table. How would I say, "Sit down, let me describe these treasures"?

❖ LANE

It was the end of summer. I was living in a seaside town where the rent was cut to nothing during the off-season. I had a good part-time job delivering propane tanks. The tanks were heavy and I enjoyed the physical work. The truck was old and had character; I grew to expect its misfirings and to enjoy the low warble of its engine. I liked the people I saw on my job. They were busy hanging wash or shaving with cold water since their gas had run out, and they were always pleased to see me. I had much time to think about my life. Mostly, I thought about a woman. I saw how the end of an affair is an end to the suspension of disbelief, a lot like the close of a circus act when we see the sword swallower collect his array of knives. The lights go up and we see the nets and wires which we had not noticed before. The tent is dismantled, fluttering down, like the huge dusty petals of an inverted flower.

For the past few years I had been studying medicine, but I was dependent on financial aid, which had become increasingly difficult to arrange, and I decided on a year away from the university. It wasn't that I didn't fare well or didn't have the stomach for it. After working with cadavers, and having numbered and labeled their remnants, I was at ease with the great stillness they presented to me. Nothing upset me, really. Blood, with its broad spectrum of reds, from Campbell's soup to valentine satin, had become an ordinary sight. The abscessed sacs and tumors and the wild geometries of accidental lacerations could not unnerve me. Surgical instruments steamed and wrapped in sterile towels had once excited me, but they started to look like silverware wrapped in linen napkins at a place where I used to work as a waiter. Only once, when I was required to dissect a single hand, did I find myself skittish, unable to concentrate.

There is nothing that represents the soul more than the hand. To find the digital arteries and nerves I had to peel back thin, elastic ribbons of muscle from each finger: the "flexor profundus"; the "flexor sublimis"; the "flexor ossis metacarpi"; and so on. These strips of muscle, snipped and flayed open, gave the hand the appearance of a party-popper.

I felt uneasy, even in the glaring light. These shredded bands of muscle had once represented the human touch. But I didn't leave my studies over something like that. I thought that maybe I wasn't entirely interested in a medical career, and I needed some time to think about it.

Lane had invited me to spend another weekend with her. Our relationship remained undefined, and these weekends were nerve-racking to me because I never knew what to expect. Although on the surface it was casual, even comfortable in a disappointing way, I was edgy. It was like registering for the draft; I was pretty sure I wasn't going anywhere but there was always an outside possibility of something urgent occurring that would require my participation. It's funny how one word means more than one thing. In war, seeing some action was a bad thing, but it was different from *getting* some action. The latter phrase is something you might hear when you're standing five deep at the bar rail in the safety of your neighborhood tap. I have always disliked the swells and shivers of anticipation. Despite its great symptoms, it is a passive emotion. One can only endure it, drive faster, run up the stairs, move closer. It's a waiting game.

Lane had recently moved and was living in a second-floor apartment in a leafy, residential section of Cambridge. It was an exclusive area. I wasn't surprised at the high rent she was paying because she had confessed to me that she was doing pretty well. She was going to be able to make it through winter without getting a job. She had just published a popular novel that received enough attention to be optioned by a film company, and she was actually getting some checks from it all.

We had celebrated her good luck earlier that summer at my place on the sea. I was very fond of the cottage I had rented, a tiny Victorian built around 1910. It still had most of the original shingles, quite weathered, and the house was a salted, silvery color with a few asbestos patches.

"I could buy this place and fix it up. I could start all

over, from the floor on up," she said, and she waved her arms over the room to emphasize how she would have it demolished.

"It doesn't need that much done to it," I said. I was laughing, but I didn't see anything wrong with the place.

"I know an architect at MIT who just needs to have the square feet of a place and he draws up whatever you want done. Sunken tubs, skylights, waterfalls, wet bars, cathedral ceilings, anything. From scratch."

"You'd have it razed?" I said.

She said, "Two stories is plenty."

Lane had again misconstrued a rather basic vocabulary word. But I was happy to see her looking so thrilled with her news about her book. I didn't like to think it was just a matter of some money coming in. I wanted her to be pleased she was there with me, walking the narrow gangplanks that edged my lot and led us down to the sea. Then again, she was very excited about her book and didn't seem impressed by the rough blue presence, the ragged surf, which always made me feel raw and swooning—as if I might, in a spree, drink it all up or let it drink me.

She didn't acknowledge the first icy crescents of foam which touched her, the waves which rushed over her legs and rocked her backwards. She followed me into the water completely distracted by her thoughts. I found her very attractive in her preoccupied state, like a woman succumbing to anesthesia—giddy, dreamy, lips parted. One moment she was submerged and the next she was lifted by the waves. I truly believed she would allow herself to be carried out on a raft of amateurish sensations of greed and self-congratulations. I, too, was buoyed by my fascination with her new success. It washed over me as well.

I hadn't expected to see immediate rewards for her first efforts. I was surprised. Her writing was that sweet-savage stuff of the popular romance novel coupled with a new frankness and urgency to tell the truth about one's childhood and coming of age no matter who was implicated. The setting was the rural South, and the novel's title was *Southern Charms*. She was going to call it *Charms of the South*, but I reminded her of Disney's feature-length cartoon *Song of the South*, so she avoided that construction. She had tried to write more than a romance, using allusions to up-to-the-minute feminist discoveries and enough pop psychology that she should have included a glossary. She was naïve in her descriptions of sex, paradoxical in her use of muddied lace and bare skin sticking to vinyl car upholstery. But there was an abundance of entertaining childhood symbols: a doll's arm was twisted, a teddy bear smashed against the headboard in a love scene. Her publisher was a good publicist, making sure the book was noticed by the newspapers and by today's literary stars. They lined up on the book jacket like the principals in a shotgun wedding.

I was glad Lane didn't have to get a job. I'm forever aiming at that goal, but I'm not unhappy to do some manual labor out under the sun. I took my shirt off delivering the propane tanks and in a few weeks my skin deepened in correspondence to a color chart of wood stain preservatives that was left behind at my cottage. That was fine, because I have a severe widow's peak which suggests a vampire's if I get too sallow. Women have said it's the hairline of a tango artist, of a marquis, of a Casanova. A girl once told me, in her love talk, that I had the chiseled profile of tragic figures in history book block-print illustrations. I said, in reply, that the similarity resided in the fact that all romantic heroes died young, before they started to lose their hair. In fact, I know that women are intrigued by a rather dramatic scar that runs down one side of my face. It's a perfect line, carved like a seam of grout. In our idle games, once I even let a girl roll a tiny BB or ball bearing down its track.

I was able to get the Friday off and I was glad to be driving north, into the city to see her. It was good to breathe the impurities and diesel fumes of the Southeast Expressway and to inch along with the back-up on Storrow Drive. That carbonized perfume and oily aftertaste was fine with me after too much salt air and the overwhelming scent of hot scrub pines that had intoxicated me all summer.

That evening we were going to a book-signing party. After the party I would take her to some bars where we would get drunk. Lane was an easy drunk, as some men say about innocents, and I liked to think of her that way too. With a few rounds in her, I could have a little height over her, I could graduate to the head of the class. In daylight hours she was often too bossy with me. She confined me to a mild-mannered, superficial behavior which irritated me the way wool slacks can chafe the inner thigh when you're walking in a direction you don't want to be going.

She sometimes made me feel like a boy climbing the narrow stairs of a choir loft.

I looked forward to the dark of the coming night. I thought of it this way—I wanted an asphalt-and-glass situation after the white light of the seaside, I wanted to get her immersed in darkness and in the loud music of the times.

When I arrived at her door, she was dressed in a flowery kimono. The robe was torn and unraveling at the shoulder. This, I can tell you, was completely calculated. She said she was getting into the bath or out of it, so I turned around and went down the street to a Store 24 for a carton of cigarettes, which I knew I'd be ripping through in two days. She already had me biting the nail off my little finger and flicking it into the gutter as I walked back to her place. The sun was heavy and dripping through the leaves like a form of coy lava—I knew it was going to be hard for me to keep calm, the façade was rippling, yet not falling away. I kept saying to myself, this might be the time I get my way. I might be rewarded for my utter patience, but not unless I was able to contain myself. I must continue to relate to the world as mouse to lion, as flea to dog. I had to go on that way just a bit more. I took a deep abdominal breath, like a pearl diver or someone standing below a window starting his serenade. Even breathing had become a secret chore. With Lane, I practiced the nonchalant sigh, the easygoing exhalations of someone trying to go with the flow. In truth, I was fighting against an internal current, a carnal river rising. I could no longer outsmart it with intellectual patter between drags from my Winston Kings. Being with Lane was like doing the crawl in a Swim-Ex, battling the mechanical waves in a bathtub-size stationary swimming pool. You keep swimming and never reach the shore.

Inside, she showed me a few crumpled pages from the new novel she was working on. She said she had been working poorly because of the humidity. The humidity in Boston was much worse than the humidity below the Mason-Dixon line. "One is oppressive, the other is sultry," she explained. The Boston kind was taking its toll on her. Then she blamed her dog. The dog was whining all night. "Masha's in heat again. I've cleaned it up but you might find a trace I didn't see," she said.

"A trace of what?"

"You know."

"Oh, Christ." I didn't know what else to say. Lane had named the dog after reading a few paragraphs in *The Portable Chekhov*. Whether Masha was one of Chekhov's greedy serfs or a member of the aristocracy, Lane couldn't tell me.

"You should have her spayed," I said, although I had said it before.

"If *you* had a dog, would you have it altered?" Her voice exaggerated the word *altered*, as if she were speaking of torture situations involving the canine psyche.

"This is all hypothetical, but, yes, I say it's less cruel in the long run."

"And what about lobotomy?" she asked. "Is that a merciful procedure?"

How she made these leaps I can't say, but they amused me. "Except for a few important chemicals, the brain is not the essential organ in reproduction. We're talking about an overpopulation of mutts."

"Is that what we're talking about? Pedigrees?"

I went along with this initial babble, though this was a playful uneasiness, a relentless back-and-forth I wanted to avoid.

She jumped in and said, "Let's go shopping, I need something cool to wear."

"Talc is nice," I said. My voice was strong, still wry, without a desperate edge.

The shopping idea seemed all right—I needed to get outside to get some air. I wanted to breathe the good dust of the automobiles. I stood on the sidewalk as she searched through racks of cheap Eastern sundresses which were arranged in tight rows in front of a shop reeking of incense and herb oils. She chose some shifts and went inside to try them on. In a few moments she came back to show me how she looked in one. It was "like a bandana," I said, and she frowned. She purchased a plain white dress. "An anorectic's wedding gown," I said. "Nurses' wear at your basic Roumanian hospital," I told her.

She frowned again.

"An *angel's underthing*," I said, and one side of her mouth lifted in a crooked smile. She liked what I was saying. Her smile was disturbing. I felt the first, tiny pinball of optimism shooting around in my belly.

We met in a college town and came to depend on one another without the fulfillment or debt of admitting our love. We never assumed appropriate roles. From there we continued our friendship, wrote letters about our work and about our lives, our landlords and lovers, those kinds of predicaments. She put it this way: "We are cut from the same fabric. If I never see you again, in fifty years we'll probably end up in the same rag heap." I didn't like the metaphor. She seemed to be saying we would never unite in our lifetimes but that at the end of our days, as castoffs, we would find one another in our solitary tatters. But I was encouraged to believe that we were inseparable in some way. She came through the towns I lived in and stayed for a few days here or there, she slept near me, sometimes in the same bed, her bitch Masha lying at our feet, a swirl of red fur, tail knocking.

After buying the dress, we walked over to the river and sat on a bench in the shade. The park was busy with couples—college students, accountants on their coffee breaks, lovers in difficult stages of reunion or flight. These various pairs were immersed in small games, shoving one another or embracing, flirting, frowning, exhibiting all the comical gestures and little threats of new or steady romances. What these enviable matches did together, in public view—even those couples snoozing on car blankets—amounted to something. I let my imagination walk a straight line from where Lane and I sat to some distant point, but I was walking there alone. The funny thing was, Lane was always holding my hand or shining her huge, flat turquoise ring on the knee of my pants. She put her arm through mine, and we walked along the river. I saw our reflections momentarily sketched and then erased, smeared across the graphite surface of the Charles.

I was curious to watch what was happening to her as the novel kept selling. She adopted mannerisms and styles from different literary grand dames. She tried to copy Virginia Woolf's eye makeup from an early photograph of the novelist. Woolf had worn a thin smudged line in the hollow of her eyelid, where the delicate membrane meets the bony socket. The line helped to dramatize her sunken look.

But Woolf's cosmetological method was hard to employ. Lane's face, no matter how she tried to embellish it or shade it, was too fresh, expectant, blank.

Yet, she was publishing's new pretty one with a knack for fancy phrases. Her imagery and metaphors made readers want to scratch their heads, but a smitten public forgave the numerous incongruities in her prose. The text didn't matter. Her looks were the whole package. People said, "Look at that *face*," when they saw her picture. Lane had a face that made you think a child was staring, homesick, out of a woman's eyes. For a few weeks, her photograph was everywhere.

In one picture, Lane was walking away from the photographer, her face tilted, turning back to look over her shoulder in shy gratitude. It was a come-on. Her eyebrow was lifted in submissive wariness. Lane melded the prim and the sexual with angelic perfection. Yet, don't angels, especially those ones painted on cathedral ceilings, dressed in their gauzy bolts, just look like whores on Sunday?

During this time of celebration about her book, she often called me to complain about her situation. With all the distractions, she was not able to work on her next novel, and, then, could she actually write a novel any better than the first? When I tried to encourage her, she changed the subject abruptly. She just wanted me to listen as she listed the obligations and burdens of sudden fame. I told her she looked beautiful on the cover of the novel. She said, "I think my hair is too full."

"Sphinxlike," I reassured her. "You look like a sphinx."

"Doesn't it stick out like a shelf?"

"No, really. You're just a sphinx."

Several months ago, in the dead of winter, she called me in a frantic mood. "I need your advice," she told me. "I really don't know what to do." Her voice was breathy, humid as if from tears.

I was lonely those days and I was greatly warmed by her voice. Her apparent confusion and neediness activated my numbed-up charms and ignited the braided wick of all my complex humane impulses. After weeks of poor-me solitude, I was happy to offer my support, if I could. When she was off-balance like this, I felt stronger on my own legs. I was reminded of my talents and abilities; I could feel my height and weight as a man; I would test the fabric and flex of my character. It was good to entertain these ideas of myself against the backdrop of her frailty.

"What is it?" I asked. "You can tell me—"

"*People* magazine," she said,

"*People*?"

"They want to do a thing on me. Should I go with it? What do you think?"

Her news felt like when I took some buckshot; a row of burning cinnamon Red Hots had been grafted to my thighs and buttocks. I had wanted her to admit to a station of lone-liness that might have paralleled my own. By comparing our trials we might have engendered a mutual sympathy which in turn could have ignited a further commitment, a reciprocal desire.

"*People*?" I told her. "Hell, why not *People*?"

"Oh, great," she said with exaggerated relief. "I thought it might be, well, sort of tacky. But they say it sells books."

"Sure it would," I said.

"Well, should I wear my hair up for the picture? I could

leave it down, but up looks better. Won't I look more serious if I put it in a french braid or something? I mean I don't want to look like just anybody."

"Up is good," I told her. Then I told her that I had a medical problem. I said I might have found a lump somewhere, and maybe it was something. She paused, she seemed truly concerned. She asked me if I was certain it was cancer and shouldn't I go to a doctor despite the fact that I was almost a doctor myself. I didn't actually say it was cancer. Later that night I called her back, I said I had lied, but I couldn't say why. I didn't know why. It wasn't because of *People* magazine. It was a lie that assumes its position in desire. It appears suddenly, without rehearsal or further explanation. It swells up like a physical hurt, a nodule, an unnameable lump, a lie. I've studied some research that proved that *loneliness can kill you*. Lonely people are more likely to have infections, kidney stones, even fatal illnesses. People living alone get three times as many cold viruses and are more likely to develop digestive ailments and skin disorders. Perhaps this was happening to me.

I wasn't irked by her success. I was happy for her. I cringed when a critic called her book, "Fantasy Tales of Daisy Mae and Li'l Abner." It was true, she had a white-trash background that she exploited mercilessly. She knew the speech patterns, the drawls and twangs of the West Virginia mining regions. Even when her prose was tangled and purple, she had learned to exploit her native communities, the destitute Appalachian landscapes, the tar-paper shacks and abandoned rail yards, body and soul.

. . .

She was in the small kitchen, spooning out ice cubes from an aluminum pitcher and filling our glasses with tea and shaved lemon slices cut so thin they looked like the gills of a fish. I would have preferred a little of the bourbon that I had remembered to bring with me. Lane was satisfied with fruity wines or syrupy brandies. I had learned to look after my own thirsts. I went into the bathroom to find an unpleasant scene. The floor was smeared and there were dark paw prints everywhere. I was used to a little mess now and then, but this could have been cleaned up before my arrival. "Expecting any guests?" I called back to her.

"Oh, God," I heard her say, "I forgot. The dog was in there last night. I had to lock her up and I haven't tidied up yet."

"Didn't you say you took a bath in here today?" I was looking at the dog hair and red smears in the tub where the dog had scratched the porcelain. "Masha must have had a bad night," I said. Lane came into the bathroom with a bucket of Spic and Span and two new sponges. I started on the tub and she went to work on the floor.

"I gave her my Valium," she told me.

"How much Valium do you give to a dog?"

"I must have given her too much, because she seems real sleepy."

I walked through the apartment to find the dog. She was lying quietly at the foot of the bed, wearing men's underwear.

There are many ways to react to the harsh sights of our times. We can laugh at six people in wheelchairs crossing a busy intersection on an icy day, or we can feel miserable about it. I have learned to embrace the grimy little mysteries I come across, giving full rein to my sense of humor. My sense of humor has saved me on every occasion. But I felt distressed when I found the dog in the bed of a woman whom I've wanted for a long time, and this dog is wearing some man's underwear. I reminded myself that it was common to put underwear on dogs in heat. The ASPCA didn't have to learn about Lane's bitch, in its pathetic, biannual phase of receptivity. The dog was drugged but not stuporous.

"It will be a while before the Valium wears off," I told her, "and please, no tea for me," I said to her. "I'm starting now." I made no small production of pouring myself a real drink.

It was around dinnertime then, and Lane took a carton of jumbo shrimp in black bean sauce out of the fridge. How long the carton had been sitting there, I didn't know. We ate it cold, right out of the box. I liked dipping my fork into the carton and stabbing randomly at its fleshy contents, biting a tangy pink crescent right off the fork; it mirrored my mood somehow. I started to feel better from the bourbon. I was going though my carton of cigarettes, and nicotine surges pulsed in both my wrists, dancing up one arm and down the other.

We had to be in Brookline at the house of a small-press publisher. It was a book-signing for Lane's friend who had written a group of stories about Vietnam. Lane had written something for the sleeve, some patriotic phrases. I read the blurb and saw that Lane didn't have any idea about that war.

She took a few extra minutes putting a line along her eyelid with a sharp, waxy pencil. She scolded me for watching her as she applied her makeup, and for a minute I was bored and edgy as I stood beside her; she treated me like her handmaiden or a younger sibling.

"The smeary look is in," I said. "You put on your makeup like you're working on a drafting board; that lip liner is thin as a blueprint. Why don't you muss yourself up some?"

"I don't tell you how to zip your pants," she said.

"Unzip them," I said. I stood directly behind her as she leaned into the bathroom mirror. There was a hairsbreadth between us, yet I did not fit myself against her. I just dropped my face to her hair, my lips to her shoulder. I stood behind her and faced her face in the mirror. That was all.

I never really liked these book events she took me to. The poetry readings in coffeehouses and college libraries were bad enough in the dark months of winter, but in summer they were a crime. Who wants to think of the printed word on a humid evening, when clothing feels unnecessary, when my shirt, itself, by its own accord, wants to peel away from my shoulders. My belt buckle unclasps, like the head and tail of a snake. My pant legs roll down until I can walk right out of them. Even a mosquito, its pulsing proboscis inserted somewhere along Lane's alabaster neckline, reminds me of sex. Clouds of gnats emerge from the hedges and suburban lawns like swarms of tiny, impertinent phalluses.

I opened the refrigerator again for another look.

"Oh, no you don't. They're waiting for me," she said.

She was wearing her new white shift and I made a bet

with myself that she'd spill some wine on herself before the night was out. I put her in the car and we started out peacefully, but after a few miles I stopped on Massachusetts Avenue at The Plough and the Stars. I heard her saying, "Not this place again." I was getting out of the car and leaving her where she sat. I knew she didn't like the idea of keeping her seat warm, and she accompanied me into the bar. She pouted, lifting her chin to such a degree she looked as if she were going to apply some eyedrops.

I was pleased to be in the Plough again; I loved its smoke and clatter and the smell of beer-splashed concrete. It was home to me, like someone's worn-down basement rec room. The glasses were large and open-mouthed like vases or the bases of lamps. Everyone held his beer level with his breast pocket, always at the ready to greet a friend getting off work. Anyone uncomfortable in his own rank or social standing would dislike the place, thinking it too dim and plain. I liked the clientele here; all had the rich background of daily work and the earned pleasure of time off. The men greeted the weekend oasis at the conclusion of their forty-hour routine, which would start again in just a couple more revolutions of our planet, but for now, it seemed as if an eternity separated us all from a huge collective Monday. A girl like Lane, uppity in her new freedom from her coal-town upbringing, fancied to think the place a dive. She preferred a fern bar or a lounge with a white piano. I was feeling my first orneriness of the night. I could make it a lot worse for her if I wanted to. She wouldn't drink a beer with me. She took a ginger ale and complained that its fizz was gone. "Nobody drinks Shirley Temples in here," I told her. I hadn't laid a finger on her yet, but I wanted to do one thing, a first thing. I wanted to release the full heavy twist of her hair from its red plastic clasp, yet I didn't touch a strand.

Thirst is a funny thing. If it's for a certain taste, and that taste is not on the shelf, not in this bar or the next bar, you keep trying all the bars until closing time. This has happened to me a lot. What I wanted was standing next to me, undrinkable like a stone bottle, solid fossil from a precious excavation site, like an item placed on a pedestal within a circle of electronic sensors at the Museum of Fine Arts. Something both vulgar and beautiful, suspended in time, petrified, like a tiny spider or a tree frog frozen in amber.

Being with Lane gave me the sensation of standing at the lip of a public swimming pool after hours. The lane demarcations are perfectly straight, the surface of the water is tight and quiet, like a sheet of polyethylene. I can see every speck on the bottom, the circular trowel marks left on the smoothed blue concrete. I'm looking for a tiny object, a hairpin lying on the submerged stairs, an earring where the floor slopes down, a red barrette where it's twelve feet deep.

The next best thing is the bitterness of ale, and I had a couple before we left there. By this time she was getting mad because we were late for the book bash in Brookline. She was wearing her white child-bride chemise, and I couldn't help noticing how it fit. It was making me feel unsteady and so I teased her and said she looked like "a flower girl for Phyllis Diller," but she didn't think it was funny. Some people have said Lane's hips are too wide, disproportionate to the rest of her. This is probably true. She's small-waisted, like a wasp, and this makes her back end twice as apparent. I like it. It's a simple matter of taste. A man has to walk through every door of a house and decide for himself how to arrive at home.

I put her back in the car. "I'm raring to go," I told her, but I drove off in the wrong direction.

She looked back over her shoulder at the opposite traffic heading on towards Brookline. "What are you doing! I'm already late," she was yelling.

"There's a band I want to hear."

"You have to hear music?"

"My ears are ringing. I need to unclog them with some rock-'n'-roll."

"Turn around! Turn, turn—" she screamed at me.

"Actually, the song goes, 'To everything, turn, turn, turn, There is a season, turn, turn, turn—' Pete Seeger pinched that off the Bible, did you know that?"

"Shit. Will you just slow down? This is a hospital zone—" She was reading the street signs for the same reason Hansel had dropped his crumbs.

I said, "It's just a mental hospital."

"How can you tell?"

"Those galvanized screens on the windows. They're not for the mosquitoes. This is where you can get your lobotomy, double coupons."

She laughed. I was driving over a row of potholes, and it had a sudden, wonderful affect on her. If only I had known the advantages of these neglected streets, I would have mapped out a more arousing route. I went around the block and took the potholes once again at a greater speed. The leaky shocks squawked, the bad suspension rolled the chassis seconds afterwards, the reverberations bouncing through the bucket seats. I remembered an erotic story about a woman riding a buckboard wagon in the Old West days.

I started to tell her.

"You'll blow a tire," she told me.

"I will for you, baby. Yee-hah—" I joked, but I meant it, and I wanted to.

A few years ago when she was out in California, I cashed in my only stock, Texaco—the man who wears the star—and it was just enough to fly out there. She had promised to pay half my fare, but it never materialized. In fact, she ended up using my traveler's checks like play money— "They don't look real," she said, as we moved up and down the San Francisco streets, eating Chinese pastries and buying loud kites and paper dragons with which she decorated her bedroom.

I suppose it was during that visit that I started to crumble. By this time, my desire for Lane had gone through its gawky stage, it had matured and had all its whiskers; it was none too pretty. I felt it when that 747 shuddered into motion and ascended through the first powder-puff cloud. The itchy titillation I'd been coping with for months had waned, and in its place was the constant whine of a revving engine, a huge McDonnell-Douglas without a wing span or any method of lifting off. When she met me at the airport, I was encouraged by her gypsy-like attire, a cheap leather jacket and her hair held off her neck by a ribbon that looked stolen from a caravan. Also working against me were the everyday tourist attractions: the throbbing climb of the cable car we rode with sightseers. Its gears meshing with the pinion dog teeth made an audible straining; its brakes screaked as it crested the hills, a momentary caution before its plunge downward. The trolley ride matched the rise and fall of my panic reactions.

It was difficult to stand beside Lane in the way she wanted me to, as an old college chum, a neutral alliance and witness to her gaiety and brief intellectual sprints of mind. She wanted me almost in the same way that gay men desire female confidantes with whom to share their most cherished secrets about their conquests and worries. She told me I was more beautiful than I was handsome. Once, sitting at her cluttered vanity, she painted my lips with a small sable brush, which she kept wetting on her tongue to taper it.

What kind of man would allow this?

I sat still as a post as she outlined my mouth, following the curve of my lips. I tried to concentrate on circus clowns, Indian braves, mime artists, greased wrestlers, any of several masculine performers. But these minstrels and vaudevillians would not excuse my passivity during her ritual. At last Lane stopped teasing my lips with the tiny brush. She said, "I knew it. You'd almost pass. You really almost would."

"As a woman?" I asked.

"As *me*," she said with increasing awe, and she seemed overcome by the idea of it.

That year, she had rented a little cottage north of San Francisco while she taught composition at an agricultural college outside Arcata. Her house faced the water, where we could watch sea lions bumping up and down in the surf and fighting for purchase on a single large stone. The house was one of those small Craftsman bungalows, extremely run-down but charming in its airy resemblance to a house of cards. It was January and chilly at night. We kept the wood stove going, using wood she had stolen from her next-door neighbor. At first I found this acceptable, one or two logs wouldn't be a crime. Soon, I saw that she had her thieving down to a routine. Waiting until night, when the other cabin's lights were out, she would edge across the wet lawn in her fluffy slippers and take the newly split logs. "Those are green," I told her, but she said that her neighbor counted his seasoned wood and it was better to take the green. Every night she would take enough wood for the evening and the following morning. I didn't think about it until I saw a teenaged kid out there swinging a maul and stacking the split wood under his father's directions. I saw the boy working hard. The maul hit a tough knot and bounced up, just missing his teeth.

Watching that kid, I thought of my own father. Once, my father had me dismantle a stone wall on the east side of our property and move it over to the west side of the house. It took a week to move all the elliptical stones to the other side of our lot, and then it was impossible to figure out how to rebuild the wall. It wasn't as easy as piling stone upon stone; I had to choose the rocks individually for correct balance and extension. There must have been some kind of mathematical pattern to follow and I didn't have the knack for it. I even stopped in the middle of the job to go the library to find an architectural text about building stone walls. I read a passage that claimed that because of "the whims of the glaciers," every Yankee landholder owned acres of melon-sized stones, too small to use as lookouts or landmarks, too large to ignore. As a result, there are crooked stone walls everywhere in New England, even in the heart of Boston. I couldn't get the hang of it.

My wall kept lurching to the left or right and when I had a few feet of it, the whole thing toppled. My father kept swearing at me. When I saw the boy outside Lane's cottage, splitting and stacking the new wood, I told her not to add so many logs to the stove. The place was sweltering.

That was the week we slept together in the same bed. I kept far over to one side of the mattress and tried to imagine lying between railroad tracks like I did when I was a kid. We lived a half-mile east of the B&O, and my friends and I knew the schedules pretty well. We counted the whistle blasts to determine if the train was coming fast or slow, if the boxcars were empty or carrying a load. If it was a heavy load, the engineer would lay on the horn extra time, a few shorts and then the long. If the string was too long to try to stop, they gave good warning, repeating the long phrases. We would lie there between the rails as if stretched out on our own living room sofas. As the train approached we could feel the vibration; we watched the grit on the tracks start to dance, but we were always seen in plenty of time. That was the whole point. To get the train to brake and come to a full stop. As the train slowed, the diesel chugged haltingly, as if remarking on the nuisance we created. The brakemen would shoot down after us, but we would be gone. Once, we had the idea to lie in the shade of a highway overpass where the trainmen couldn't see us in the darkness and we were further obscured because of the bend. This was the way we dared one another for weeks, and finally I took my turn. I didn't stay put between the rails, but I leapt to my feet so near the last, fatal instant, I could feel the breath of heat panting off the engine. It was one of those stupid moments of childhood, but I knew I would think of it often in my later years. Here

I am again, using it as a metaphor for a greater stupidity—lying here, playing dead beside Lane.

We were in the double bed, surrounded by the new paper dragon and kites I had tacked to the ceiling. I hadn't done a very good job, and the room had an anticlimactic feel, like a ballroom at the end of the night when the crepe-paper decorations begin to uncoil from the rafters. I felt lonelier than ever with her so near, inches away. She stretched beneath the sheet and sighed; she turned over with a luxurious rotation of her hips. She faced me and smiled. "You don't really mind, do you?" she asked. "That we don't do it?"

"No problem," I said, something beaten. Shouldn't these small, sour moments be questioned, rebuked? I was fully awake, as if a snowball rested on my forehead. No matter how I tried to separate my impulses from my actions, it was impossible to ignore my own needs. I recalled an iron lung I'd seen on display at a medical library and I tried to imagine I was encased in its rigid shell.

"You're full of shit," I told her, at last, and I got up, dressed, and went outside. I can fake many things—greetings, farewells, I can chuckle on cue, but I can't fake a good night's sleep. I went out, walked around the hem of the sea and up and down the one road I knew.

When I came back inside, she was at the door. She kneeled down and untied the wet laces of my shoes. "I'm sorry," she said. "I'm sorry." I lifted my feet, one after the other, so she could peel off my drenched socks. I pulled her wrist until she stood up. I steered her down the hallway. She tripped and fell to her knees. I yanked her to her feet again. She was limp, insubstantial as a scarecrow. I hooked my elbow around her neck, tightening my hold. I dug my other forearm into her shoulder blades to guide her. In the back room I shoved her onto the bed. I snapped her bikini underpants off her legs and tossed them. She started stuttering elementary words, fearful words, which sounded so clean and genuine, I was impressed. Her honesty aroused me. I fucked her the way I wanted. I can only describe it this way: I fucked her keenly. Then I started over. She sniffled at penetration, during, and in between. If it was rape, Lane never said so, but I guess it was. She cried out throughout our soulless endeavor. "Oh, God," she said, then she just said, "God," without any recognizable inflection, without faith or blame or surprise.

I pulled the car into the crowded parking lot of a small rock-and-roll club that looked like an old Esso station with the garage bays cemented up.

"I'm not going in there," she said. "I'm late for a party. They sent invitations."

"I'll engrave you one now," I said. I took my knife out of the glove box, a small blade I used for gutting and scaling fish. I saw it impressed her somehow. She didn't know the difference between a weapon and a utensil. I put it in my pocket beside the exiled king, the unknown soldier. I told her she would like the band, the Swimming Pool Cues. "Now that's a band with a sense of humor," I said.

"Only for a while. Then you promise we'll go straight to the party," she said.

Lane knew that the party depended on her presence. She was happy to be a little tardy. She would enjoy their notice upon her arrival, their relief and excitement at seeing her. The pages don't turn without her.

The place was thick with smoke, as if Hollywood had placed its smudge pots and dry ice in all the niches. The band was loud, clean, using the same four chords to enhance the heartfelt in everything. I was suddenly happy just about the music, and, for a few blesssed moments she didn't figure in it. As usual, men gawked at my scar. I was competitively handsome until they noticed my disfigurement, then I was a curiosity, a shock. Soon they saw Lane. The crowded tables, the men pinched against the horseshoe bar, dropped out of their conversations in a hushed, spasmodic response to her beauty.

Lane was with me.

People couldn't ignore us, one on one, and coupled we really buzzed the crowd. It was a gut reaction sort of thing. Tonight she had tied her hair up and it made her look like every guy's favorite grammar-school teacher. And who is teach's date tonight—a *GQ* Frankenstein's Monster.

That night must have been hard on the band; the crowd seemed irritable and unwilling to follow their ideas. "Is this the Swimming Pool Cues?" I asked a man at the bar.

"Beats me," he said. He noticed my face, the deep line running down my forehead, through my right eye, down my cheek and jumping two inches to begin again at my throat. "Hey, Ron, look at the scarface," the man said.

I was turning away, but the patron was drunk and his curiosity had him. He wouldn't let me get back to where Lane waited and watched. I was quite familiar with comments about my scar. It was a provoking sight, a perfectly straight line, almost a cleft, that halved my face and intensified its features. The scar made me appear twice as hard, twice as edgy or sly, twice as hungry as an ordinary man, and this was intriguing to other men. My scar always seemed to create a mini-dilemma at whatever primitive soirée I might intrude upon. The man pinched my shoulder and wouldn't let me go before his friend had a good look at my scar. "Where did you get it?"

"Born with it?" the other man asked.

I said, "Sure, that's right," because I hadn't even had a beer yet and the music seemed to be fading. I worried it might be my luck to come in at the end of the set.

"He's got his mother's slit on him," the first man yelled.

This was an interesting perception and the whole bar turned away from the tight little stage to locate the target of the strange remark. Even the guitarist, who couldn't have heard it, looked out into the darkness before him, resting his wrist on the neck of his guitar.

Not even a second passed and I'd thrown one. The first blow to come my way connected and put me off balance, the next got me square. This had me doubled up, but it was just a momentary thing. The men didn't follow through and I couldn't believe it when I saw that Lane had stepped into it. Lane was trying to pull somebody off me, someone who wasn't even part of it. It was so dark in there. She was like one of those little birds which peck at the shoulder of a rhino, and at first nobody noticed her. Then she got a good one, an elbow or the back of someone's hand which opened a little cut below her eye. I tried to push her out of the way, before she got roughed up. "Jesus," somebody said when at last they saw her, "what's she doing?" I shoved Lane ahead of me and we took our leave. Nobody cared. The men were laughing; I was bashed up enough without their help. I pushed Lane outside and up under a lamp where I looked at her bruised cheek. She seemed small to me then, familiar but unreadable, changing before my eyes.

I've lived behind this perfect line since I was thirteen, when I ran through a plate-glass window at a department store. The window was cleaned to a perfect invisible gleam. They had just removed the annual "Price Breaker" signs after a store-wide sale and there were no stencils or decals to inform me of the dangerous sheet. The scar runs down my face and throat and continues through my pectoral muscle, over the small brown plateau of the nipple, down the short ladder of my ribs and it ends below my waist where the hair at my pelvis begins to increase and obscures its path.

My parents were given five thousand dollars in insurance, which was to be saved for my college education. My father squandered the money before I was out of high school. He used to say, "Life is an education, and you've got living expenses to cover." So the cash went for rent and for a used car which still sits out in back of the house where I grew up. Its windshield sports a crack right down the center where I tried to kick it with the steel toe of my boot. I was standing on the hood to face my father who was behind the wheel, driving away, going ten, then twenty miles an hour until I slid off the hood making sure I landed on my feet. I straddled the white line of Route 138, waiting for my father to turn the car around. When he did, he was screaming at about seventy miles an hour, coming straight for me. It wasn't a simple test. I lost my nerve and dived out of the way when there was still a little time left, I'd say less than a few seconds, but I was too shook up to take advantage of it. When he passed by, I saw he was way over on the opposite side, nowhere near me. I was ashamed of my cowardice, ashamed of my gratitude.

I put Lane back in the car. "You could have lost some teeth," I said. She curled her tongue up over her front teeth at the idea. Her eye was a deep half-moon, but there wasn't much swelling. The tiny cut was *below* her eye so I knew that her eye wasn't going to close. I told her, "Never get between two goons going at each other."

"But they were all after you," she said, and she sounded like she'd been heroic instead of plain stupid.

"I take care of myself," I told her.

"Not too well," she said in a soft, regretful voice, imitating a mommy.

"I'm not the one with the banged-up eye," I said.

"It's always terrible for you, isn't it? I mean, that remark—" She couldn't hide her fascination.

"He's got his mother's slit on him" was new to Lane, but to me it was nothing. I went across the street to a soda machine and bought a can of White Rock ginger ale for her eye.

"For my eye?" she said.

I held the icy can against her cheek. We sat in the car for a while and she kept twisting the rearview mirror to study her puffy wheal. Jesus, she *likes* the shiner, I thought. She thinks it's romantic like Van Gogh's ear, or Ahab's wooden leg, or Quasimodo's hump. I could see she was thinking of the book-signing party. She would explain how she broke up a gang fight down in the red-light district.

Lane didn't care that it was just Chelsea, and that the night hadn't even hit its low point yet.

She had not talked about my scar since the first months I knew her, but tonight she was back on the subject. She was saying how impressed she was with my attitude about my disfigurement. She said that I was well-adjusted and *so very* tolerant of other people's feelings about my scar.

"Actually," she was saying, "I've always found your scar to be sort of attractive. It's Clint Eastwood or Burt Lancaster. I can picture them wearing it."

"I don't exactly wear it."

"We all do. We wear our misfortunes." She was joking, but I could see she really felt something, felt desire for those actors. It shouldn't surprise me. Sometimes I feel a whip cracking, herding my secret thoughts out in front. I can feel the oiled leather unravel from its coil and snap the air in front of my face.

I guess I told her all my scar stories. I told her about a teacher in tenth grade who was appalled by my face. At that time, the sutured skin was newly reconstructed, swollen, oyster-colored and knotty, not the thin pencil gouge it is now.

Lane said, "But it's not really a pencil line. It's more like a seam in a paper bag, or a good crease in a pair of chinos if you turn the leg inside out." She touched the scar as I was driving, rode her fingertip down the indentation from my forehead to my jaw. Then she put her hand back in her lap, although she knew the line kept going.

I was telling her how this teacher was really upset about me. She bent over backwards to see I was doing fine. She drilled me extra when I flunked a test and she handed me the hall pass whenever I wanted it, instead of giving me the third degree. The thing was, she never could get my name right. She kept calling me the wrong name; she called me Mark.

Lane didn't seem impressed by this story, it didn't describe the bandages and the hospital room. But she said, "How weird. It's like Jung's synchronism idea."

Lane always had this maddening half-knowledge about everything. I told her it would be more like Jung if my name had really *been* Mark. In truth it was more like Freud that the teacher made this mistake.

"Oh, you mean a Freudian slip."

"That's right. Jung is something else." I gave her some examples such as a girl who worked for Xerox whose last name was Copy, and a horse trainer whose last name was Furlong, a child beaten to death by her father whose name was Brandy Mallet.

"Branded by a mallet. Oh, I see," Lane said. "Then what was the point of your story about the teacher?" She seemed a little irritated that she didn't have her psychological terms exactly right.

"The teacher was just nervous, a real mess. She couldn't handle my presence in her class. That's all."

Lane said, "I'd write this down for a book or something, but I guess it's your life, isn't it? So it's your prerogative."

I wasn't exactly thrilled by this observation. I said, "Use what you want, it's the point of view that matters. You ought to write about your black eye. That's a firsthand experience."

I saw her looking at herself in the side mirror. She examined her bruise and smiled the way a woman smiles when she feels pleased by her attire. She's wearing her virgin smock, her black eye, and an added touch—something to increase her authenticity—her grandmother's cameo.

There were a hundred paper sacks of light winding along the sidewalk of the Brookline Colonial when we arrived at the book bash. I peeked in one sack and saw that it was filled with fine white sand in which a votive candle was centered. "Now that took some tinkering," I said.

"I told you it was special."

"Looks like we're not too late, look at that table of food," I told Lane, but she had paused a few sacks back to embrace someone, a Lord Byron type, so I headed for the pyramid of cherry tomatoes and the dolphin-sized sculpture of tuna salad. The yard was illuminated by lanterns strung from dogwood to dogwood, and in a discreet corner I could hear the Bug Assassinator going full blast, removing the insect sector from that elite neighborhood. On the flagstone patio, I saw a table of hardcover books, and a little man was sitting on a lounge chair signing one. He must be the author of *The Five Lives of a Vietnam Vet.* I wondered at the figure, it seemed random, why not the classic number nine? Turns out the guy had been hit five times and lived to write a book about it all. He looked pudgy and tanned, as if he, too, might live in this neighborhood and sit out by his pool. I made a promise to myself that I was going to avoid the whole literary notion of that evening and stick to food and the friendly talk of some ladies nearby. I knew I wouldn't see much of my escort; she was in her own world, describing her new novel to some people, and then she was talking about her shiner as if it were her new creation, a result of her slumming muse. I could hear little snatches of her conversation in her aloof and dreamy southern tones, the drawl she had once tried to overcome and then had relearned to stupefy her publisher and fans. I heard her saying to someone that she was putting some Vietnam stuff in her new book, but of course she would be dependent on research. Then she was saying how she loved to go to the "li-berry," which seemed to charm the partygoers, though to me, it just sounded dumb blonde.

I was happy for a while. The caterer was running back and forth with trays which he continually placed near me as if I were his official taster. I kept nodding my approval to him, but once I had my fill of the basic four food groups, I went over to a table where the caps had been left off all the bottles of booze. This encouraged me to slosh as much as I pleased into a lone tumbler which was smeared with lip color. I do like the taste of their lips left on fine glassware— it's even better on a longneck beer bottle. Soon Lane brought some bright-eyed, nervous people over to me. I wiped my palms on my jeans, ready to shake hands, but I saw she had steered them over for one purpose only, to show them my scar.

"This is what started the fight," she said. "The amazing thing is that he didn't bleed to death right there at the department store. They ripped up a brand-new Ralph Lauren, all silk, right off the rack, to make tourniquets," she went on.

"Why is it such a straight line?" a fellow was asking *her.*

She didn't even look at me. She had made up the Ralph Lauren part, they didn't have shirts like that at Montgomery Ward, and the EMS personnel didn't use tourniquets. There weren't any arteries involved.

She was saying, "It's a straight line because he was stunned and didn't move out of the way when the whole thing cracked and came down like a sheet of ice right on him; he just stood there. He was in a state of shock and all. It was like a wave curling over, like the famous Pipeline. One edge sliced right through him."

I was tired of her poetry and I walked into the house to find the bathroom. I had an awful desire to brush my teeth as if I'd been riding a motorcycle all day and the wind had dehydrated my smile. I saw this dry smile when I looked in the mirror above two lavender sinks. The bar of hand soap was black. The hostess had left the cake resting on the glossy box it came in, like an objet d'art. The box listed the soap's ingredients: tar, honey, and the spermaceti of some kind of marine life. Who knows what the hostess was trying to get across to people? The black soap made white suds. I knew I wouldn't have studied these items, the soap, the silver filigree on the mirror, my petrified lips, if I wasn't so unhappy with myself.

We had a stylish couple in tow when we left the party. They wore the black leotard–look of the 1950s which they claimed was making its way back. They said they were returning to Zen, butterfly chairs, and the Beat poets. The girl wore novelty earrings, two plastic cherubs copulating. She could pull the tiny figures apart and reinsert them. "Who says angels can't have a fuck?" she asked me.

I observed that the earrings weren't "period." No, she agreed, these weren't from the Beat generation; they were the very latest. She had a high, squeaky voice instead of the husky, jazz-infused kind I always associate with beatnik women reciting poems in coffeehouses. They wanted to go roller skating at a rink in the city that advertised a rock-

and-roll skating party. I figured I would enjoy watching Lane on skates, wobbly and off balance for a while. But she wasn't in the mood. She told them we'd drive them there but then she and I had to go back to her apartment because her dog had to go for a walk.

"You mean you have to go walk your doped-up dog when I want to roller skate with you?" I said. She shot me her severe glance, the kind, I imagined, she would one day use against her offspring. Suddenly, I was dying to be skating in a room of swirling unknowns, bodies on wheels, with loud music and the submerged thunder of a thousand ball bearings.

"No," she said, "I'm not in the mood to roller skate."

"I'll get you in the mood," I said.

"We'll help. We'll skate in a chain," the girl said.

"Stay out of it," her companion said.

"Oops," she said in a small, high voice from the backseat, in recognition of our predicament. I kind of liked our hitchers, they seemed awake and still lively, ready to continue life after the sedative effect of the book party. I wanted to ask them what they thought of our Vietnam vet, but I saw Lane had her copy of his book on the seat between us and I didn't bother with it. I let the pair off at the skating club and from the street I could hear the roar of movement above some nice rhythm guitar. "You're a drag," I told Lane, but she wasn't paying attention. She was looking in the mirror at the rainbow slick beneath her eye.

"It's even bigger now," she said.

"Bigger is better," I said. "I could prove that concept to you. If you'd just let me." I hated myself when I started hinting around.

"The dog," she said. "The dog must be going crazy."

. . .

Her place was hot and I went around opening windows. The counterweights were shot and I had to prop the windows open with old books. For one window it was *The Magic Mountain* and for another an old copy of *The Three Little Kittens*. I took some ice cubes out of the freezer and tied them in a sock. I made her hold the sock to her eye until she could not bear the cold. "It works best when you keep it there," I told her, but she kept leaving the sock on the coffee table, where it left a misty imprint.

"I can't keep doctoring my eye, Masha has to go out," she said.

I saw that I should have put the ice in a hankie or a flowered pillow slip, Lane was put off by the sock. I saw that her new white dress was ripped at the hem. Clothes just couldn't stay on her, they seemed to disintegrate. Perhaps it was a chemical reaction of some kind. It reminded me of the story of the actress Merle Oberon. Merle Oberon was supposed to be extremely seductive and twice as erotic because her normal body temperature was two degrees higher than the average 98.6. Maybe Lane's clothes were melting off her.

Many times I have tried to explain to Lane what has happened to me, what she had caused me to become. In the off-hours and daily solitude of empty routine, the ragged feather of obsession floats down upon me. White, weightless. It touches my lips. There are no words for it. The perennial seed of my dementia, explosive as a milkweed blossom. After months of close study and examination, an insight awakens—I am gravely lovesick—but then something happens. A wind starts up, as if from an enormous fan, like those used in movie studios to direct artificial snow or rain. And suddenly, the truth of the matter, the revelation, like a downy speck, is blown out of my hands.

I might have turned to her right then, torn away her gauzy dress and crushed her with my weight, the weight which was her. Instead, I took her icy hand and lifted her up, whistled for the mutt. "Let's go," I said.

The dog was not one to run and find its own leash. After a search I offered my belt, but Lane decided to tie a scarf to its collar. I thought the accessory looked too flimsy for a shackle, it was just a chiffon streamer from somewhere deep in the closet. Then we were back on the street for a nice midnight stroll. Masha had recuperated from the Valium and strained against the scarf.

After going a few blocks down Mount Auburn, I stopped Lane and kissed her. She would accept an occasional mild demonstration. I kissed her for too long and she pushed my chin away with the heel of her hand.

Out of nowhere, rogue dogs appeared, circling our Masha. I picked up a stone from the crumbling curb and threw it at the largest beast. It hit him square in the nose but it had no effect. The stone dropped to the sidewalk in front of the animal and he sniffed it once dutifully. We kept walking.

"Puppies are out of the question," Lane was telling her dog.

"We better go back before they get at her," I said.

"Don't let them."

"I'm not a canine bodyguard. That costs extra."

"Oh, that's nice. Don't go out of your way or anything."

Another dog trotted towards us. He was exceptionally motivated and made a beeline for the bitch. In surprise, or defeat, Lane let go of the chiffon scarf and the whole pack of dogs took off after her pet. We could hear them barking up one sidewalk and down another block as we ran after. Then there was silence. I imagined her dog and another locked together, the chiffon ribbon ruffling in the wind.

"Isn't there some sort of leash law in Cambridge? Dogs shouldn't roam the streets like that." I tried to sound indignant, but I was weary. "Oh, well. She'll come back when she's knocked up."

"Are you crazy? We have to find her. Don't just stand there like that."

I got the car and we patrolled the neighborhood blocks. We found a mangy convention of canines and Masha jumped into the car, still sporting the chiffon scarf.

"She's dog-tired," I said.

"Oh great. Now you're a punster," Lane said. "If this dog gets pregnant, I'll kill her!"

"Spay her. She needs a breather."

"But the money," Lane said.

Like Cagney, I wanted to rotate a grapefruit in her face.

"Have you got an extra pair of underpants?"

"No, not for a dog," I said. I fell on the sofa, and stretched out my legs. I shut my eyes the way I do when I feel like making a point while still holding my tongue. Then I removed my boots, heel to toe, without using my hands. That's another good one. "What's on TV?" I said. I really wouldn't have minded watching something.

"Didn't you bring any underwear?"

"I don't wear shorts in the summer, I put 'em in mothballs." I pulled the palm of my hand over my face. I followed my scar with my index finger, a mannerism I no longer tried to restrict.

"What have you got against me and my dog?" she said, but she wasn't serious. She came over to the sofa with some microwaved food. We sat together and ate.

"You go to a lot of trouble," I said.

"Cooking is for housewives," she said.

"You can't be bothered with simple domestic courtesies," I said.

"Exactly, but you don't believe me. You don't really think I'm an artist, that I belong to this world."

"Sure, you belong. There's room for one more."

She looked worried that I might not have understood. "I don't mean museums," she said. "I don't mean one specific place."

I looked around the apartment. I saw nothing but junk. One time a renowned painter had offered her a painting. He must have been campaigning for her when he gave her one of his better pieces. She accepted the painting but later returned it saying it wouldn't fit in with her "decor." She had initially thought the colors had matched her slipcovers, but the art wasn't suitable. It was abstract art. Lane couldn't understand the picture. "Doesn't it look like a huge molar? An X-ray of teeth?" She was thinking about buying some Audubon prints. Birds, insects, flowers.

Most of all, Lane was fond of photographs. The walls of her apartment were ruined with industrial-size tacks and masking tape which she had used to arrange pictures of her friends and family. She had enlarged the prints until everything looked grainy. She had pictures of me. Pictures of Masha. She had very little talent as a photographer, but she had learned how to read the light meter and to adjust the focus in Photography 101 at college. Since then, she seemed interested in documenting her life in an offhand, confused way. She took her own portrait when she had dressed to go to her father's funeral. There she was, sitting on the mortuary stairs, her white gloves in her lap. She had taken her self-portrait every day during the weeks following an abortion. "I have to remember how sad I was," she said. She didn't look very sad at all. She had just permed her hair and it extended over her shoulders like heavenly froth.

"I *was* sad. I was devastated," she told me. "That doesn't mean I stopped shampooing my hair." These details made me think there was something more to her. Was this darkness contrived? It continued to puzzle me. It was the same feeling I get when I search my house because I think I detect the smell of smoke, perhaps I've left a butt in the sofa. I walk through every room expecting to find something smoldering, maybe blazing, and I can't find anything. In one way it's a relief not to find a fire, then again it's a matter of concern, I keep thinking I haven't looked hard enough and the place will go up in the dark of night.

Every girl I have ever known has had some nude photographs of herself. A nude series taken by an old boyfriend, a college roommate, a brother maybe. It's not just vanity, but plain curiosity. Women like to know what they look like front and back. Lane had cheesecake pictures of herself and she gave me my choice of them. A student photographer had taken a series of her in an old garage. Lane tried several poses which even the mainstream girlie magazines would have considered cornball. In almost all of the shots she held a Mae West parasol or a fake revolver. Wild West–style. One of these pictures interested me, though. The photographer had asked her to hold a junked windowpane. She cupped a large piece of glass in the palms of her hands; its two thick edges crossed her at the waist and thigh and magnified her pelvic terrain, the slope of her belly, the smoky triangle I had seen only once before in true life. There it all was. Behind glass. I chose that picture, but she refused to give it to me. She said she wanted me to have the one where she's holding the ruffled parasol.

Lane had been taking a photography course when we first met. I'd seen her at different events, and at the Health Center when she came in for a ringworm infection that she had contracted from her dog. Then she called me one evening to ask me if I would like to be her "subject." "Would you mind?" she said.

I didn't know what she meant. I thought maybe she was conducting a sociological experiment or one of those tests where you're asked to avoid sugar or required to take massive doses of vitamin A while they test your urine or they see if your lips have developed fissures and cracks. When she mentioned pictures, I figured it was something to do with my scar. I'd had a number of medical photographs taken over the years. It's funny how scar tissue can draw medical interest years after the initial laceration. Once or twice I was paid for some photographs, but usually the doctors had said it was just for my chart. I have since learned how patients are exploited in a thousand ways like this.

Lane told me she just needed to take some portraits for

her photography class. She said, "I think you'd be interesting." I figured she was flirting with me then, and I agreed to meet her the next afternoon.

My girlfriend at that time was in the process of leaving me for another man, but she couldn't resist hanging around to see what was happening with this photographer. I had spent the morning in a chipper mood, enjoying the second thoughts of my girlfriend. The photo session was spoiling her plans. She had wanted to leave me "high and dry."

I expected Lane's camera to be large, perhaps the kind that required a tripod. It was a tiny Rolex, the size of a cigarette box. Lane held it before her eye as if she were reading the *Surgeon General's Warning*. I couldn't hear the shutter. My girlfriend was getting pretty irritated; she didn't believe that there was any film in the camera. I, too, had wondered about that—how often do you load that camera, how many shots on a roll? Lane seemed to be snapping a thousand shots, but after a while I started to like it. She bossed me. She told me to sit where the light edged my profile. She had me stand against a white wall; then she made me stand beneath a small arch between rooms. Lane took me through all the rooms of my apartment, as if she were looking for a place she had seen before. "Here," she said, "stand here at the foot of this rumpled bed. Now sit down. That's right. Now get in."

She came back into the living room wearing her tattered robe. I saw I was on the money about the sock, because she had exchanged the sock for a velour facecloth and she was dutifully pressing an ice cube against her eye. "How did you rip your kimono?" I asked.

"It's a thrift-store thing. All the stitches were rotten, and when I washed it—poof. It's ninety-nine years old to begin with."

"Why do you girls like that sort of thing? You hunt around until you find something another woman tossed out and you think it's the greatest."

"I have an interest in the unknown past," she said.

"Whose past?"

"The person who owned this robe might have been spectacular. I like to think so, anyway."

"Did you have imaginary friends when you were a child?"

"Yes!" She was laughing, delighted I had brought this up. "They were the best friends of all. I was totally at ease with them," she said.

I thought she certainly must be joking. She wasn't.

She turned to me and said, "You know everything about a woman's body, don't you? I mean, you studied everything, didn't you?"

I answered yes, of course. I had studied it all.

"I thought you would know."

"Don't you feel well?"

"It's just on my mind," she said.

I had told her before that I never wanted her to ask me for medical advice. It's funny how medical students are burdened by their friends coming over to show them muscle strains, skin rashes, sore throats. I had refused to look at her ear when Lane had a fullness sensation and she heard clicking. The symptoms were related to common hay fever, I was sure. It was a cranky Eustachian tube, but I didn't have the right instruments, nor did I want to make an incorrect diagnosis.

"Female troubles? What is it?" I asked, but I could not look at her. "A sore? Cramps? A burning sensation? Abdominal tenderness?"

"No, nothing like that. God, is that what you say to patients?"

"I don't have patients. I'm not a doctor. You're being unfair asking me these questions."

"Sorry," she said.

I didn't want to know what ailed her. I was banging an ice tray at the kitchen sink. I hated to have to drink something, but suddenly I had a weak sensation in my knees and at the base of my spine like the feeling I get when I've slammed on the brakes to avoid an accident and it takes a few moments for the adrenaline to melt away. I poured bourbon into a glass until I remembered to stop pouring.

Lane said, "It's some kind of blister."

"A blister?"

"Yes." She was sitting on the edge of the sofa. She looked embarrassed, but she also looked incredibly relieved. She was beaming at me.

"I'm not looking at your blister."

"Why not?"

"You better go to a doctor if you think you've got a problem. That's what they're there for."

"Can't you check it?"

"I'm not looking at your blister. That's final." How could my love object detail her imperfections with such aplomb?

The breeze was coming in the window behind her. I noticed the skin on her arms was raised with goose pimples. I went around behind her to shut the window. I wasn't paying attention when I removed the musty volume of *The Magic Mountain* and the upper sash slammed down. My fingers were caught between the two tight sashes and I couldn't free my fingers. I couldn't jimmy either window. She was at my side, trying to lift the bottom sash, but it didn't budge.

The pain was immediate, hot, increasing.

I had yelped when it happened but I was quickly moving beyond verbal complaint. I began to feel lightheaded. My fingers were squashed and I could feel the digital arteries pulsing to the second knuckles where the blood couldn't flow to my fingertips or properly return. The pain crested and subsided, crested again, and almost took my legs from me. I even stopped to consider it, passing out might be the answer. Then I used my brains and asked Lane to get me something—a screwdriver, anything. She returned with an iced-tea spoon. I pried it between the window sashes and tried to use it for leverage but it bent in half, fragile as a daisy stem, and my fingers remained caught. I repeated my request for a screwdriver. She returned with a letter opener which fit easily between the two frames, but it slipped and fell onto the external sill.

"You're turning white," Lane remarked. She was quite alarmed, being that I was pretty well bronzed to start out. At last, she came back with what I wanted, a Phillips-head. With my left hand I pried the sashes apart and released my fingers.

My right hand was squashed across the second knuckles, changing color in front of my eyes, but I saw that my fingers weren't broken. "Ice," I said. "Did we use all the ice?"

"Oh, God, I think it's gone. I'll ask next door."

"Take this with you." I gave her a wastebasket.

"That's an authentic Cherokee basket," she said.

I couldn't believe she was stalling over some moldy trinket from a reservation.

When she returned with ice, I put my whole hand in a bowl of it and tried to ignore the throbbing. It was difficult not to think of everything in bad terms. I wished I had not taken the day off nor left the seaside town. I imagined that my delivery job might be in jeopardy without the use of one hand. Then I saw I was feeling sorry for myself. I knew the fingers would be sore for a period of time, worse if I allowed any error in lifting and unloading the tanks, but I would be able to keep working.

Lane's shiner was in full swing, a crooked Ferris wheel of broken blood vessels. I let myself imagine that her robe, its rotten seams, might dissolve and fall from her shoulders as the night wore on.

"I could read to you from my new novel," she said. "It might relax you and take your mind off your hand."

"That would be fine," I told her.

I stretched out on the sofa. The pain was lessening; there's a threshold which is met, and then a steady retreat from it. I was learning to live with it. But I couldn't stop imagining Lane's blister. Who had she dated who might have given her a virus? "Maybe too much masturbation," she had admitted with a shrug, but I didn't want to explore her secret lesions, those raw spots that had occurred with no impulsion from me.

She began to read from her manuscript. I wasn't surprised to hear that the main character had quite a sizable scar. I didn't really follow the story, I was drifting. It started to rain. I heard the heavy droplets brushing the leaves, too weighty to cling. I could smell the dust of the streets as the rain stirred the litter and tapped the metal awnings.

Lane put down her pages and asked me again, "Can't you look at it, please? It's stinging."

She lifted her threadbare gown and opened her knees. I adjusted the gooseneck lamp until the brilliant cone fell directly on the subject. She pulled my fingers to the flaming spot, a tiny oblong sore spoiling the silky vestibule below her clitoris.

I wanted to kill her.

I split my time between MCI Framingham and MCI Cedar Junction in Walpole. Walpole is off the beaten path and I guess I can't expect her to visit me here, although I keep inviting her to come. I want her to see my arrangements, but Walpole gives Lane the drears and makes her jittery. She would have to endure walking through several electronic kiosks to get back to my unit, where I'm set up.

It isn't your glam slot at a major hospital. My work here, as a physician for the Department of Massachusetts Correctional Institutions, is mostly HIV housekeeping and stitching torn lips and ears after everyday brawls in the yard. I do my fair share of hemorrhoid operations and rectal suturing due to the violent lifestyle in here—the general stasis encourages a high rate of consensual sodomy, and then, of course, it's often rape. A few catatonic inmates require tube feeding, and I dislike the wretched task of tube insertion and squeezing a plastic bulb of high-protein glop directly into the patient's gut. I have come to see how the catatonics are wise fools. It's a natural reaction for the body to shut down in prison. Why force these men to continue to ingest a superficial sustenance? Bread isn't everything.

When an inmate's catatonia becomes too severe, I am required to administer electric shock treatments. I perform the procedure routinely. I carry the compact machine, the size of a laptop computer—I call it, excuse the pun, my "powerbook"—back and forth between Framingham and Walpole, according to jottings on my weekly planner. I had the machine in the trunk of my car the last time I went to see Lane. Imagine what I might have done? Today, I have an appointment with a firebug at four o'clock in Framingham. I'll zap the remorseful goon and he'll get his appetite back in time for dinner.

Acute AIDS patients are sent to Mass General when they're just about dead. I am pressured to keep them in the system as long as I can. The infirmary is a death house.

I see men after they have been raped. I see them transported on gurneys to "chapel" for their state-funded last rites. Sometimes, a man comes to me for a minor ailment, perhaps right after visiting hours if his girlfriend complained of his halitosis. I give him a tube of baking-soda toothpaste. These individuals are mobsters, baby molesters, cold-blooded killers. It still surprises me that they should tell me their stories and want to hear mine. My scar is an icebreaker. Yet, I believe they see it written elsewhere across my face: Here's a man, a free man, still in harm's way.

"You got trouble at home, Doc?" "Does the bitch be bitching?" they try to get alongside. The other day, I examined an inmate whose persistent jock rash presented like a rust-corroded chastity belt. He tugs my hand and says, "What's the daily mail? What bad deeds she be doing now?"

I talk about Lane. I hope to expunge her with each installment of my narrative. As I pump a rubber syringe of Hi-cal All-in-One Diet or I'm giving some hunger-strike zombie a Com-Electric cocktail, as I reposition a prolapsed colon, feeding it back through the traumatized sphincter, as I exfoliate bedsores, peeling scabbed doilies from the tender living cells—her story goes on. Every word rewords itself. My wind-and-piss monologues have earned their audience. She wouldn't like to know it, but Lane is famous across these secret tiers. From our hallmark mafioso all the way down to some pimply JD, and in the teeming holding tanks, everyone knows what she's done to me.

❖ YOU ARE HERE

Ronnie left a small coastal town after ending a two-year romance. She moved back to Providence, safely inland, and started a day job as a receptionist at Swan Point Cemetery. Visitors came into the office to ask for directions to their distant ancestors' monuments. Even the newly bereaved became confused in the huge network of cinder paths and had to return to the office to get their bearings. Ronnie looked up names of the deceased in a ledger and then she marked individual maps for the visitors. The illustrated sheets had a tiny ruby arrow pointing out the building where she handed out the maps. Beneath the arrow were the words YOU ARE HERE. Ronnie thought that this was a silly error. Shouldn't such notations be placed only on stationary objects? Once the map was removed from the office and consulted in the complicated twists and turns of the cemetery, the defining words, YOU ARE HERE, would have no meaning at all.

There were small, colored markers at the cemetery intersections and Ronnie told visitors, "Go left at the blue dot, right at the green dot, and then it's straight ahead. It's the black granite one between two old Victorians." Ronnie had memorized the monuments when she took inventory walks with her boss, who was resizing plots on a master blueprint, trying to squeeze new sites next to the antique markers whenever there was a bit of extra space. Every square inch would be sold. There was nothing to read in the office besides the maps of the graves, and Ronnie learned the layout pretty fast. The regulars didn't need directions to the graves, but they sometimes stopped in to say hello to Ronnie or to ask for keys to the mausoleums. They would tell her one thing or another: the grass was cut too short or burned from too much fertilizer. There was new evidence that local gangs had duped security again and bursts of chartreuse spray paint highlighted the erogenous zones of a white marble angel.

Several times a day, the office telephone jangled, but when Ronnie picked it up and said, "Swan Point," there wasn't anyone on the line. People often had difficulty making arrangements for a loved one's memorial service. A new widow might weep uncontrollably, or a husband, simply planning ahead, might feel uncomfortable asking for the price list. But when the phone rang and it was dead, Ronnie wondered if it was Roger. Once Ronnie thought she saw her old boyfriend driving around in the cemetery.

It can't be him, she thought, but it was just like Roger to take a pleasure drive through a place like that. He had often stopped with her in graveyards to smoke a little crack. He made a production about lining up the little rocks across his knee, like baby teeth, before choosing one for his pipe. Then he would try something with her. She didn't imagine he would be looking for her now. Yet, at odd times during her shift, a car pulled into the gravel circle outside the office. It looked like Roger's car, but she couldn't see the driver's face. The driver steered away. It was like a ghost car, because she could never identify who was driving, although she thought she recognized Roger's plaid flannel shirt-jacket. Maybe the whole scene, car and driver, was a materialization. Then again, it was more likely that Roger himself was trying to stalk her.

Roger had suffered an unforeseen reaction to her abortion. He had accompanied her to the clinic, where he sat in the waiting room, reading the whole newspaper. When she came out, he dipped his chin to look at her. He eyed her. On the way home, he bought her an ice cream cone. Yet she saw his disturbance as he watched her lick its drippy chocolate crown. His grief wouldn't wash away. "How can you eat that?" he told her. She took comfort in the dairy treat, but to please him she tossed the heavy cone out the car window.

Ronnie had endured the suction procedure, and she allowed herself some weeks for the spiritual adjustment. Guilt can be a strengthening fiber woven into the big fabric, or it can weaken its seams until the garment falls apart. Ronnie understood that the abortion resulted from their careless act, but she was getting on with her life. If she sang in the shower again or whistled while at her chores, Roger glowered at her. Roger let his symptoms balloon. Then Roger found God.

God happened to Roger in the same blind way Roger's seed had stolen into her.

His swerve to organized religion was the last straw.

For months Ronnie had been keeping to herself. It was a relief to go home after work to nothing. She had a small black-and-white TV. She preferred black-and-white; its chalky monotones seemed more generous and forgiving of the little flaws in Raymond Burr's aging profile. She liked the old monochrome *Perry Mason*s. Black-and-white film seemed like a convincing reenactment of the truth. Her mother sent her several women's magazines, which brightened the rooms. She slept well. She dreamed. Her thoughts were large, steady examinations of the past. If her mother called and asked her about her arrangements, Ronnie would say, "No current dilemmas, no impending dramas."

Then Ronnie met a man. She first saw him at Leo's, the restaurant where she worked a few nights a week. He began to joke with her in a friendly way. She laughed and let her receipt pad drop to her side. She would stop writing the order and laugh, but the woman who came with him didn't like it very much. Ronnie pulled the pad up to her chin again and concentrated on the point of her pencil; she waited. The man always ordered bourbon, but the woman said nothing. The woman looked at the man. Her big, haunted eyes didn't seem to disturb him. He sat attentively on the edge of his chair, like a musician in an orchestra pit performing the same notes he had performed many times before. He ordered a glass of white wine for the woman. It was always this way. The woman, looking straight at him, would let him order her drink.

Ronnie could identify the chink of ice cubes in his empty glass when he needed another round. It was more difficult with the woman's glass of wine; she had to watch the bowl to see its pale level slowly receding, as if time stood still, until at last it was empty. The woman drank in small, even sips. Her conversation didn't accelerate in the usual way. She waited for Ronnie to set her new glass on the table before she continued talking, and sometimes Ronnie took her time about it. Then the woman drifted forward in her chair; she locked her wounded eyes on the man. She whispered inaudible words, the way that people admit facts in a courtroom.

He was different. His voice was consistent and sincere in its commitment to keep going, to get through the night in a moderate and sociable way. When Ronnie placed a napkin on the table and centered a new tumbler of bourbon on it, he started to gab to her directly. He told Ronnie that he was a professor at the university.

"Is that right? What do you teach?" she asked him.

"Political science."

"Really?" Ronnie said, but it wasn't a question. She knew very little about his field and she didn't have anything more to say about it.

"I'm teaching a seminar in the First Amendment."

Ronnie nodded. She tried to remember which amendment was first. It might be the one about carrying firearms, but then she was certain it was the law about speaking your own mind in a public place.

"It's the question of our age," he said.

Of course, Ronnie knew he meant it was the "topic of our era," but the woman stared at Ronnie as if trying to figure Ronnie's whereabouts—late twenties? Maybe the third-decade mark had been struck with a gentle thump. Again, the woman lifted her face and stared at Ronnie, trying to oust her from the conversation.

Ronnie moved away and listened to the man's voice over the loud talk of the sports teams who came into the tavern to celebrate. His voice seemed to steady her even as it excited some part of her, and she believed he was aware of his effect. Of course, the young woman must be his student or perhaps a new colleague unsure of her standing in the department. Something was off. Their tilting situation distracted Ronnie from her other customers; if her regulars got chatty with her, she begged off. She preferred to get a rag and wipe the tables, concentrating her attention on the woman's glass of wine until it was empty. Then she went to get her a new glass, each time, perhaps at twenty-minute intervals, and this is how the nights went.

Then one evening he came alone. He took the same table in the corner. He ordered a drink from Ronnie and he joked with her in the way he had before. She smiled at him, keeping her pad close to her face. Something made her feel shy and nervous—a suspicion of love or the end of love—and she was guarded. He came back for a few nights and it became easier with him. He learned about her daytime job and he made jokes about her routine at the cemetery office. He said her job was really not much different from his line of business, teaching bored coeds. He told her, "We're both in day care, however you look at it." It was a funny idea. He asked her about her coworkers, her "skeleton crew." His silly puns echoed in her head while she worked at the cemetery until she met him again each night at Leo's. Sometimes she sat down beside him for a moment, mopping up the beery circles on the next table as he joked with her in his friendly way.

He gave her the key to his apartment so she could use the bathtub. Her place didn't have a bathtub, only a fiberglass shower stall. Since they were lovers, she figured he was making an affectionate gesture to let her bathe in his home when he was at work. She left the cemetery after her morning shift and went to his building. He was actually quite gallant and had purchased a new yellow towel for her use. He placed an ashtray on the windowsill especially for her. She always remembered to rinse the tub, and she cleaned the ashtray with a tissue. Often the yellow towel would be dry before he came home.

When she let herself into his apartment, she could hear the steady ruffled notes of an aeration filter from an aquarium in the dark living room. A woman he had lived with had given him two tropical fish for Valentine's Day. The fish were iridescent and billowing. Ronnie purchased a third fish on a whim. It was a long, spotted loach. Its length undulated and flowed as if it were a liquid within a liquid. The strange fish kept low in the tank, against the dunes of gravel, and it hurried away from the other fish who shifted back and forth in perfect tandem.

Ronnie grew fond of the loach. She moved close to the glass to greet it. She believed that its forlorn motions, its nervous prowling through its cloudy environment, hinted at its superiority over the other pair, which flurried about the tank as frivolous as ribbons.

"Poor fish," she said, addressing the single fish expressly.

The telephone was ringing. Ronnie went over to the desk and lifted the receiver. "Hello," she said.

Nothing.

"Hello," Ronnie said again. The person on the other end didn't respond. She thought she recognized Roger's fretful exhalation. A ragged, unhappy release of breath before she heard the receiver clunk into its cradle. Then, the dial tone returning. "Roger? Roger, is that you?" Ronnie said after the fact.

She thought about her mystery caller. The tiny hairs on the nape of her neck tightened. She told herself it was vanity itself to imagine she was being stalked by Roger. She went into the bathroom and found the little radio on top of the medicine cabinet. She flicked the dial to find her favorite talk show. She lit a cigarette and exhaled with force. She opened the tap full blast and snapped the window shade until the room was washed with light. She spilled the mineral salts into the tub and the water churned a violent, oily green.

It was a bachelor's bathroom; there was nothing frilly, no glamour magazines crinkled and swollen from the bath, no scented soaps. Shelves along the wall were half-empty, as if someone had just removed some items. All that remained was a smear of red powder on the glass shelf in the medicine cabinet and a tube of mascara which had rolled under the claws of the tub. Ronnie disliked bathing in a place where another woman had so recently departed. Yet the artifacts of other women intrigued her. As Ronnie undressed, she snooped through the medicine cabinet to find further evidence. She pulled open the vanity drawers and shifted the contents. Containers of disposable razors, old prescription vials, and a few chalky stubs of broken styptic pencils. Something caught her attention and she lifted it out. It looked like a sex toy of some kind. She examined the length of fleshy foam. She saw the word *Duromed* embossed on the rubber. Ronnie thought she recognized the item. It was an armrest cushion from a pair of crutches.

A foam crutch pad. It kept her interest. Its taut symmetry, its neutral shade had a comforting familiarity. It was the empty middle of the day when she wanted sex most. She didn't think twice about it and slicked the foam cylinder with a few drops of lotion and pressed it inside her. Its dense, alarming circumference was too harsh and stinging, but she moved it the way she wanted. It took less than one minute. She swayed forward with the sensation. Then she rinsed the foam rubber and put it back in the drawer.

She sat down in her bath. She listened to a talk-radio program called "Ask Joy." The host managed the phone lines and made on-the-spot analyses of dreams and arguments. She told housewives to be "sexual, not sentimental."

"For wedding anniversaries," she told them, "don't make cakes, make love. Light one candle. Light it at least twice—"

Ronnie tried to memorize the most ludicrous moments of Joy's shows, thinking her new boyfriend might like hearing these snippets as Roger would have. But she soon found out that her new lover had a different sense of humor. Her remarks were taken for their face value. He didn't seem to know the difference between her tender thoughts and her jokey details. He sometimes laughed at the wrong moments and didn't respond to the witty lines

or outrageous similes she fashioned in their bedroom conversation. He did want to hear about her bath. She was expected to comment on the water's temperature—quite
hot—and the yellow towel—neatly folded on the toilet
seat. It seemed to delight him that part of her day had been
designed and awarded to her by him.

As she soaked, Ronnie listened to the despairing phone
calls. The telephone lines were burdened. "Keep trying,"
Joy said. "You'll get through." Women complained about
their husbands and accused their lovers. Despite their
anger and humiliation, the callers sounded bright, excited
by their moment on live radio. They lost all fear of men-
tioning names, and even threatened their lovers. A caller
said, "There—I have witnesses. I swear, if he ever comes
back, I'll kill him."

When Ronnie had left Roger, there wasn't all this fan-
fare. She hinted around for a week that she had had
enough of his impromptu sermons, his dinner-table indoctrinations, which had robbed the last bit of cushion from
their relationship. She packed her car and said, "It's been
real." *It's been real* was Roger's typical comment on everything—until recently, when Roger had started to say, with
rhythmic authority, "Thank you, Jesus." Roger said *Thank
you, Jesus* after any little event. He said it at a sudden crack
of lightning, at the conclusion of a routine bowel movement, at incalculable moments during sex.

"It's been real," she said when she left him. Using his
old words against him in her final assessment was the most
cutting remark she could have made, but he nodded his
head and chimed in with the same.

A few months before she packed up, Roger had taken
her to a revival meeting. There was a new church right on

the highway. It had a big meeting room, a Kingdom Hall or some such thing with big plate-glass windows that were always blazing. Behind the new glass there was always a good crowd of people mingling, everyone holding white paper coffee cups. It always looked like something was happening, and Roger was interested. For more than a week, Roger cruised past the church, looking through its huge window. Then he made a U-turn, and rolled past again. He said, "That big window there makes me feel on the outside looking in."

"Well, that's just what you're doing. You're spying on those believers."

"That's what they want us to do. They make themselves a spectacle to recruit rubbernecks."

"Ignore it," she told him.

"Shit, it's a crowd, isn't it?" Roger took his foot off the accelerator as they drove by the new church another time. The people inside the big glass room looked animated in their conversations, standing in pairs and clustered in small groups, committed to their social hour before addressing serious matters.

Ronnie said, "It's an AA meeting."

"Nope. These are not mere friends of Bill, these are children of God."

"Maybe it's Mothers Against Drunk Drivers or one of those victim organizations. What's it to you?"

Roger steered off the road and into the asphalt lot. The cars in the diagonal spaces were economy compacts and several clunkers just like Roger's. Roger said, "We've got to check this out."

"Are you kidding? You want to go in there? We're not members."

"No membership required."

Ronnie said, "How do you know?"

"Sign says."

Ronnie looked at the signboard: *5 p.m. Revival Ev'ry Nite. All are Welcome.* She looked at her watch. It was four-thirty.

Roger said, "Look at this place fill up. That's proof enough for me."

"Proof? What proof do you mean?"

"These folks must be getting something out of it. All it costs is a little of their free time."

"I'm not going to any revival," she told him. She turned around in her seat to look at his face. "Roger? Just tell me something. What exactly is a revival?"

"It's an hour in which to reinvent God's love."

"You want to do that? Reinvent it?"

"Don't worry, Ronnie, it's like riding a bicycle. You'll get right back on it."

"You get right back on a horse, not a bicycle."

"There's a table of doughnuts in there big as a double bed. Cake doughnuts."

"Cake doughnuts? So you're telling me you've gone in there already?"

"You know, cake doughnuts. And good coffee."

He stood outside the car waiting for Ronnie. She didn't budge. She crossed her arms. She pulled down the visor mirror and looked at her own face to avoid looking at the blazing tabernacle, or whatever it was. Roger went around to the passenger window and dipped his head level with hers, but she didn't respond. He shrugged and walked away. He waited to hold the door for another couple before he entered the big glass room where people were hugging and chattering as if before a wedding. Ronnie pushed the visor away and watched Roger sidle up to the refreshment table, but she couldn't see what he was choosing for himself. More cars pulled into the parking lot, and she watched the families file into the building. One woman was dressed in a cloth coat with big oversized buttons, big as vanilla cookies. Some of these cookie-buttons were broken in half. A young teenaged girl wore square-toed dowager's shoes like the out-of-date pairs sold in thrift shops. Ronnie understood that these were poor white people if she ever had seen poor white people. She didn't like being forced to watch this kind of parade. Then it occurred to her, she should go get Roger and make him drive her home. First she would have to go find him, and she recognized a familiar panic. She felt it the same way each time. The idea of God hovering, waiting to see what she decided. Her desire to be on the inside with Roger instead of on the outside was the reason why people fell into all kinds of strange midnight societies. This feeling of being left alone.

Ronnie found him in the second row of folding chairs. He had placed a doughnut, her doughnut, on a small square napkin and rested it on the chair beside him. He had saved her a place. His bold assumption, that she, too, would join the circus, made her angry. She sat down beside Roger and bit into her doughnut. The white sugar clung to her lips and she rubbed the napkin over her mouth. She thought she was going to choke on the dry cake.

Ronnie didn't know anyone. Yet she seemed to recognize faces, she felt as if she knew these strangers. She recognized that these men and women had lived in their world within her world, and were, of course, not strangers at all. They forced this idea into her head by the way they smiled at her, nodded, winked. They appeared to recognize her. She hated Roger for bringing her there, back to these relations whom she had ignored for years. A hot torch of song erupted, suddenly, from the makeshift pews. Ronnie recognized the hymn. The folding chairs with their cheap vinyl seat cushions did not have the comforting effect of the polished maple benches of her childhood church but seemed to mirror the working-world adult life in which her faith was lost. Her stunned face, as she avoided people's eyes, only seemed to perpetuate the group's collective desire to organize an intervention on her behalf. Roger was beaming. He opened his arms to present Ronnie to the onlookers as if he had just reeled in a beautiful fish, still writhing gloriously on deck.

If it really was Roger riding through the cemetery now and again, Ronnie was glad he didn't stop and get out of the car. If Roger was born-again, it no longer concerned her. The radio host, Joy, would say it was "a ghost. Love's ghost pestering Ronnie's workplace. A common occurrence." It didn't frighten Ronnie. Ronnie sat in the tub, her chin pressed to her knees, her arms hugging her legs. She remembered that this was the position she had used as a child when jumping from diving boards. The bath had made her nervous. It was the same anxiety she had once experienced when washing a stain out of her blouse in a public rest room. She had to pull the blouse down over her shoulder and reveal her breast, in order to scrub the stained lapel. She expected intrusions and the apologies or silences one receives when doing something that is not illegal but too oddly personal.

Ronnie flicked off the radio and drained the bathwater. She looked down at the tub and saw that the porcelain was streaked a deep green. Oily rings descended the sides in deepening shades. She left it that way.

She had to return to the cemetery before going to her job at Leo's for happy hour and she dressed in a hurry; drops of water bled through the fabric of her blouse. She had just pulled on her skirt when she heard the dead bolt on the front door. Someone was coming into the apartment. Her lover might want to surprise her, but she had no interest in that. Ronnie found herself imagining something wild, perhaps an unauthorized reunion with Roger.

"Hello—" someone said. It was a woman's voice, maybe just a girl. "Anyone here?" The voice came from the living room.

"Just a minute," Ronnie called through the bathroom door. She pulled her pumps on, but her feet were still wet and she couldn't wriggle into them. "I'm coming out. Just wait."

A girl was standing in the living room. It wasn't the woman she had seen at the restaurant with her lover. This one was very young, young enough to be his daughter. Ronnie wondered if her lover could actually have a daughter this age. The girl was tall with broad, level shoulders and an angle of black hair which curtained one side of her face. She looked like a model in a teen magazine. She stood before Ronnie as if waiting to be officially welcomed. She was holding a large pleated umbrella. She twirled the umbrella once before closing it.

"Is it raining?" Ronnie didn't know what else to say to her.

"This is Japanese. It's paper and not really for rain. I

take it when I'm feeling in a mood. It sort of hides me," the girl said.

"Oh," Ronnie said. She smiled at the girl, but the girl was looking around the room. "Well, what can I do for you?" Ronnie said.

"I just wanted to see this place. It still looks the same. It needs something. Maybe some ferns or spider plants. Something. Don't you think?" The girl sat down on the sofa and stared at Ronnie.

Ronnie told her, "I'm just on my way out, then the place is yours."

"I don't think so. But that's how the cracker crumbles."

"Shit. I don't want to hear about it, okay?" Ronnie said.

"I say no more," the girl said.

Ronnie wondered if the girl was there for any real reason. Did she come to get a sweater, a hairbrush? Ronnie saw that the girl cupped something shiny in her right hand. It might have been a little silver gun, but it was only a pack of cigarettes in a glossy wrapper. "Did you leave some mascara here?" Ronnie decided to ask her.

"Mascara? I don't know. Maybe I did. Let me see it," the girl said.

Ronnie went into the bathroom and got down on her hands and knees to reach under the tub. She came back with a tube of Blue Midnight mascara and handed it to the girl.

"Jesus. This blue stuff? Who would wear it? No, that doesn't belong to me." She gave the tube of mascara back to Ronnie.

Ronnie looked down at the girl sitting on the sofa.

"I'm still very unhappy," the girl told Ronnie.

Ronnie stared at the paper umbrella with its scores of sharp pleats.

"I'm taking the fish," the girl said. "Okay?"

"The fish? Does he know about this? His last girlfriend gave him those fish," Ronnie said.

"They're mine," the girl said. "I gave him these fish. I'm the one before the one before you."

"You're what?"

"The *one before* the *one before you.*" She laughed and rubbed the tip of her nose with her knuckle. "Sorry I'm so blunt. That's just me."

"Well, shit."

"It takes a minute to catch up, doesn't it?" She put a cigarette in the corner of her dark mouth and flicked a plastic lighter. The lighter wasn't sparking, but Ronnie didn't get the girl a light. The girl said, "I brought a jar with me for the fish. It won't take a minute."

Ronnie stacked some magazines while the girl chased the fish with a small green net. The angelfish swirled in one corner, butted the glass, and shifted direction. They moved swiftly, streaking back and forth; they seemed to dissolve like candy. But the girl was expert with the net, it didn't take long. Ronnie looked out the window as the girl screwed the lid on the jar. The sound of the metal threads was shrill.

"I'm leaving," the girl called back to Ronnie as she walked toward the door.

"So long!" Ronnie was embarrassed by the gleam in her voice.

The girl turned around. "You know, it's my anniversary."

"Your anniversary? It's the day you met him?"

"No. Not the day I met him. I figure that today is the day I will remember. I'll remember the day I really shook him. I'll put that in my birthday book. What about you?"

Ronnie was surprised to hear herself say, "Hell. Why *not* today?" She was already thinking of Roger.

"That's far out," the girl said. "Let's write a note. We'll sign it together."

"I don't know about that."

"Two signatures will give it some umph."

Ronnie stared at the willowy youngster who looked more and more like a young Mod from Carnaby Street every second, a Jean Shrimpton look-alike, and she was overwhelmed by the sudden feeling of solidarity she felt with the young castoff. Ronnie said, "I know, we'll make him a cake."

"A cake?"

They laughed in competitive octaves until their laughter combined, dipped, and flowered together.

The girl put down the jar of fish. "You're wicked, you know that?" she said to Ronnie as she followed her into the kitchen. They pulled open the cabinet doors looking for supplies.

"I thought he had a mix in here somewhere," the girl told Ronnie. "But that was months ago."

"It's still in here," Ronnie told her. "Duncan Hines."

"Devil's food," the girl said, and she grabbed the box from a high shelf and tapped it on the Formica.

Ronnie twisted the dial to preheat the oven while the girl found a bowl and a wooden spoon. They stopped to look at one another. "You're kind of young, aren't you?" Ronnie said to the girl.

"It's all relative," the girl said, a little stung.

"I mean, you're young to have such a clear eye. It usually requires some years."

"Well, I'm one of these people whose nine lives go really fast. I'm accident-prone I guess—"

"I was wondering. Isn't that a bandage on your foot?"

"This? I sprained my ankle last fall. I wear an Ace if I have to walk somewhere. I live ten blocks."

"You should ride the bus. Tell me, did you need to have crutches?"

The girl looked at Ronnie. "Crutches? Not me. Well, I tried it for a while, but they pinched my underarms."

Ronnie said, "You can adjust the height of those things so that they don't pinch at all—"

They saw it at the same time. Smoke was rising from the oven door. Ronnie pulled it open to take a look. There was something on the bottom rack, on fire. It was a pair of golden mohair gloves. The gloves had been left to dry on the oven rack and had ignited when Ronnie preheated the oven. Ronnie grabbed a tongs and she lifted one glove, a burning hand, and dropped it in the sink. The other girl turned on the tap, dousing the glove. Ronnie reached into the oven again and lifted its mate with the tongs, but the flames ate it until it was a smoky cuff. She dropped the remains into the sink and they examined the sooty mementos.

"Are these yours?" the girl asked Ronnie.

"Not mine."

"Someone else was up here, I guess."

"Seems so."

They walked around the island for a second, collecting their thoughts.

"Fuck the cake," Ronnie said. "I can't make a cake, I have to go to work."

"Where?"

"Swan Point Cemetery."

"You bury people?"

"Only the predeceased."

The girl liked Ronnie's humor and together their laughter sparked and exceeded what either one could have achieved on her own.

"The graveyard? No kidding? Ashes to ashes—"

"Dust to dust. You know," Ronnie leaned nearer, "I think my old boyfriend has been stalking me there."

"You're kidding. He's after you at the cemetery?"

"I guess," Ronnie said.

"If he can wait long enough, you'll be easy to find. How long you going to make him wait?" the girl said with the pleasure of a practiced trickster.

Ronnie told her, "You're a breath of fresh air, you know that?"

The girl's face smoothed, revealing a simple, remarkable joy in their alliance.

Ronnie said, "Shit, you know, we almost had a baby together."

"Seriously?" The girl's eye's were wide. She might have thought Ronnie was referring to their lover in common.

Ronnie didn't bother to clarify it. "I'm going to be late at the boneyard," she said. Yet she knew that afternoons at Swan Point were always slow. People prefer to visit graves in the morning light. Early sunshine looks nursery-pink on the monuments. Afternoon light is harsh, and in the evening the stones lose definition, their chalky outlines dissolve against a field of dark. "Can we forget the cake and just get out of here?"

"Shit, the cake was your idea. I don't need sweets."

"Let's just take the fish."

Ronnie went to the bathroom sink and took a plastic cup from its circle holder. She walked back into the living room and plunged the cup into the fish tank, holding it before the speckled loach. The fish swirled forward and she lifted it out. Inside the plastic cup the fish seemed magnified. Its gills lifted and fell in silky hitches. Next, she put the key he had given her onto his desk blotter. The key was wet from her hand and it darkened the paper. The girl put her key directly on top, flush with the other. The metal teeth were shiny where the keys were identically sawed.

The girl took her jar of fish from the coffee table and dropped it in her big, oversized pocket. She lifted her paper umbrella and pushed the clasp forward until the pleats opened. Ronnie waited for the girl to go first, then she let herself out of the apartment and pulled the door shut.

Ronnie heard the telephone ringing, but the girl didn't seem to notice. Ronnie was seeing a picture of Roger, his whiskery chin; his cleft was attractive accented with one day's stubble. Perhaps his flaw resided in his great capacity to love the unborn as if it were more than just the sum of its parts. Ronnie had asked to see it and the nurse revealed a pulpy knob in a stainless-steel dish. "That's it. That's everything," the nurse had said, tipping the shiny bowl so that Ronnie could see its contents. Roger had once told her, "Faith is the art of creative visualization." Roger had wanted to teach her. She imagined him circling the block, or waiting for her on the cinder path at the cemetery.

On the sidewalk, the women walked abreast into the crowds of people. They split up at the corner. Ronnie went to her car. She looked down at her exotic token, pulsing in just two inches of water. Before she got behind the wheel, she watched her young accomplice walking up the street. She tried to see if the girl was limping from her injury, but the girl took easy strides, spinning her parasol behind her shoulder. The paper cone twirled at a wild velocity until its ornate pattern bloomed into a single bright color.

❖ THE GOLDEN THERAPIST

The office was quiet. Everyone had left. His blithe, irreverent apprentices had one after another leaned into his cubicle, saying, "Too bad, fella, you're loaded down," and "Overworked and underpaid." "Quittin' time, asshole." The men left at five o'clock with the ease of some grammar school boys after snapping their cases shut, each with his own distinct flourishes. Selby didn't lock his top drawer or stand up from his desk.

He leaned back in his chair and watched the winter sun sink below the window ledge. Its violent shield was twinned when he closed his eyes. When he looked again, an ambulance strobed over the granite of an opposite building, a soothing focal point compared to the peppery dish of hot sauce on the horizon.

He had promised to walk Pauline outside but she hadn't yet returned from the ladies' room. For the past several days, she had complained of a man, an ousted boyfriend or common-law husband, who harassed her after work. That morning, the man had trailed her to her job, following her into the building. The man threw his shoulder against the elevator door as it pinched closed without him. He took the next express elevator, which skipped her floor, but he found the fire stairs and walked back one flight, right past the guard. He entered her offices. Pauline was at her desk. He upset her computer terminal and pitched it to the floor, tugging her keyboard loose and then the surge suppressor. He dashed the plastic components against the wall. He reached across her tabletop and grabbed Pauline by her sweater lapel, twisting the wool into a tight rosette beneath her chin. She pounded him with her pocketbook.

Security arrived, but not until the man had ripped Pauline's imitation gator-skin purse in half, spilling its contents everywhere. Selby found the torn pocketbook alarming, like a real animal hide in the aftermath of a predator's strike. The swiftness of the attack and its immediate climax echoed a wildlife spectacle on the Nature Channel.

Her ex-boyfriend wore long, tousled hair and was dressed in a familiar UPS uniform. His shirt's front plackets were quite rumpled, as if he had worn the same brown shirt for days and perhaps even slept in it. Guards collected at the office doors, resting their styrene coffee cups along the baseboard before they escorted her lover outside, where a police van had been rolled right onto the sidewalk.

He offered no resistance. Pauline sank to the carpet, plucking her possessions from the rug.

Selby stooped beside her, helping her collect her personal items strewn under the chair legs. Her makeup mirror was a tiny sliver with a beveled edge, and he examined its narrow slice. "Just for lipstick," she told him and she took it from his hand. He repositioned the computer monitor on her desk, and together they tested the system to see if it still retrieved files. It had survived the crash.

Pauline was in a state of exhaustion. She crumpled at her desk in full view of everyone. Selby felt sorry for her. Her desk was stationed dead center in their congested pod of narrow cubicles. Her face was already smudged with inky, dried watermarks from an earlier bout of tears, and again her shoulders started to heave with silent tremors. She seemed completely convinced of the magnitude of her dilemma. She wrung her hands, gripped her waist, or massaged her teary cheeks as if in an interpretation of the Stanislavsky Method. She was heroine, victim, and jaded antagonist assembled in one fretful mask. Selby thought that only Barbara Stanwyck could get this across. He had so admired her in *Double Indemnity*. He wasn't certain if Pauline was acting.

"Are you all right?" he asked her.

"It's just the dry heaves," she told him. "I've been swallowing Maalox by the handfuls. It's not helping."

"One of the girls might have Valium," he told her. He thought she might need a binding ingredient.

"Oh, God, no. I don't want tranks."

"It might calm you down."

She looked at him. "I don't like a chemical solution to a problem."

"One man's meat is another man's poison."

"I don't need that kind of love medicine yet."

Selby said, "I guess not. Not until you've tried everything else."

Pauline reminded him of pretty young women he'd seen behind the chain-link fences of private schools, those institutions for Quaker coeds, Communist debutantes, and out-and-out problem girls. These girls were the walking wounded from whatever war was in fashion. Pauline kept her face tilted in a cagey squint; her mock bravado was reminiscent of the visually impaired, as if she measured her surroundings by sensory clues and committed aural details to memory. When she settled figures or busied herself with work, she talked to herself. It was a crazy monologue, like a clumsy sister trying to learn how to swing. Her lingo seemed exaggerated; her words might have been translated from English into a foreign tongue and back into English again so that her slang, its pitch and syntax, seemed a decade or so behind. Her cornball swearing and her little repellent prayers began to charm Selby. Her comic features and sizzling effects seemed mounted only to correct a great interior doom.

After the events that morning, Selby believed that Pauline was indeed at the lip of a deep peril. She had not really made a "cry for help," but her ordeal with the man in the UPS uniform had released a trigger. If she was just acting coy, he would find out, but Selby told Pauline that he would see her home after work.

"Okay," she had said. Her eyes searched his face for a trick of expression, but his face was washed clean.

During the day, she performed her tasks at her desk, but she didn't seem interested in a career in precious metals. At least she didn't chatter on about her sad story or make an inventory of her boyfriend's detours into that domestic violence terrain. She didn't have a tract and didn't complain that she was both a victim at home and overlooked at work, as the other girls would say. Despite her situation after hours, she kept cheerful and expectant. Pauline seemed consoled by some singular hope or idea. She might be waiting for a "dream vacation" or looking forward to a long sunny ride in a convertible. Once or twice Selby saw her warring with her private thoughts—something or someone—a formidable absentee opponent. Her struggle fascinated Selby.

To check on her, he walked over to her desk. She was wearing a cassette headset; she wore it like electronic junk jewelry. She pumped her heel up and down to the beat of the music. Selby couldn't hear the song, but the casters on her swivel chair squeaked faintly with the changing rhythms.

"May I try it?" he said.

She removed the fragile headphones and handed them to Selby. He held one foam-disc speaker to his ear. "Not exactly easy listening," he said. "How can you settle with this rock-'n'-roll blaring? You might get the wrong figure."

"This monkey-work? Who needs to concentrate?" she said.

Now she came up to him, adjusting a mohair scarf around her collar, tugging it between her two white hands.

"All set?" he said.

"Look, you don't have to take me home. I'll be fine."

"Sure I will," Selby said. "It's on my way, isn't it?"

"I don't know," she said. "Besides, I'm just going to Filene's."

He agreed to let her do her shopping and she walked out. He tried to listen for her footsteps on the plush carpet; he heard the elevator doors close and the whine of the cable, the compartment sinking. Below his window, the ambulance continued, a methodical blue funneling. He wondered if it was serious.

The floor was silent. He heard only the air vents blowing the building's stale, systematized warmth over him. He peeled off his suit coat and opened his belt. He closed his door and switched out the overhead until his cubicle was illuminated only by the refracted city light. Its silvery-alloy tones gave an eerie cast to the routine items on his desk. From his briefcase he removed a small black plastic bag from underneath his folders and the heavy, bound copy of a prospectus he had coauthored. It was typical of sex shops to err in their lame attempts at simple discretion. Certainly, the odd black sack looked more incriminating than plain brown paper. He had quite often identified men returning from Columbus Avenue, where there was a cluster of porn outlets. Selby recognized the opaque handle-sacks the men carried, the tedious wrappers and blank imprints universal to that realm of commerce.

His purchase was neatly coiled in the sack and already it started to work for him. He shook the bag and the toy noose fell on his desk. The silky braid of nylon fiber had come with a sheet of instructions. Selby didn't need tutoring and he crumpled the page of directions and put the noose over his head. Its extra length dangled past his shins. He looped the cord through the steel pull of his top drawer and cinched it tight, leaving a moderate tail. He took his key and locked the desk drawer. Securing the slip knot just below his jaw and above his Adam's apple, he sat in his chair and rolled backwards on the caster wheels until the rope was taut.

He lifted his knees and pushed his feet against the desk drawers to increase tension on the cord. He was expertly tethered and felt the noose tighten with exact compression on his jugular. As the loop contracted, his erection was enhanced. His pleasure corresponded directly to his choking sensation; he controlled his ordeal until he felt nothing above the neck and everything in his cock. If he started to pass out, he fingered the knot, loosening the noose just enough to let the blood return to his head. He started again. Selby had refined his method and only once in the past had he completely lost consciousness, although he had read of these sorts of deaths in the papers.

Pauline could have found him there. His door wasn't locked. From a distance, he heard maintenance vacuuming the hallway out by the elevators. This usually took them a bit of time. Next they would scour the sinks and clean the coffee machines before collecting trash and combing the individual offices.

The streets were dark when he finally left the building. He walked slowly towards the garage where his car was parked. Once or twice he put down his case and pushed his hands up his cheeks and into his hair. There was nothing vain in it, it was really just a nervous habit. His thick hair assumed a ridiculous, on-end appearance and he walked on.

He stopped to get a drink at the Steeple Street Bar.

Without a drink Selby was flying under poor conditions, a low ceiling, a fog. He didn't wish to go home to attempt an instrument landing. Thaddeus saw him come in and poured two fingers and set it down. Selby sat in his every-day spot, the farthest stool from the buzzing TV that had a blown speaker.

Selby lifted his glass and held it at eye-level. He revered each tumbler, each flute, each vessel of his every replenishment.

"An inch of the old spinal fluid," he told the bartender. Thaddeus nodded and made change from a twenty. The television news showed video footage of his own building. A rotor from a rooftop exhaust system had broken free and glanced a pedestrian. "That's my address," Selby said.

Thaddeus told him, "Happened right next door, yes, in-deed. Makes you feel like Chicken Little."

"It does just that. Jesus, Doctor, you're right again."

When he left the bar he went into Woolworth's to buy a new handkerchief. His wife would never have noticed, but he wanted to return with everything he had set out with. At the cashier, he spotted a toy for his son, a colorless substance packaged in a plastic blister. The toy was called SLIME. He bought a container of it. He looked forward to giving the toy to his son. He relished a moment of unself-conscious relief which disappeared as soon as he noted it.

In the parking garage, he took the new handkerchief from its cellophane and he rubbed it over his face. He wadded it into a ball and bit down upon it. Then he folded it again, placing it deep in his breast pocket. It was almost seven o'clock, perhaps he could avoid the dinner. This would depend on his wife. If her day had gone well, if she had nothing grave to report and had no complaint against him, she might have already eaten dinner with their son. She might have gone ahead, and the dishes would be washed, the kitchen light turned off.

"Did you eat in town?" she asked him.

"Yes," he told her.

She watched him as he poured a scotch for himself.

"A little touch of the golden therapist," he said, but she wasn't watching what he measured. He was grateful for that. Yet, because of her kindness he felt he had to give a careful performance in everything. Her disappointment was deep. She seemed to savor each regret, doubling its strength, as if it were a morphine elixir, addictive and luscious despite its toxicity. Even so, she showed her best face, she gleamed before him. Her looks were unchanged, they had only seemed to intensify with the years. Her features were still sharp. She was like an edge of clear amber or petrified wood, a little sliver of another time, glittering there.

The length of the evening ahead seemed overwhelming. He felt the rich pulse of his Glenfiddich kick in, and to arrest it he waved his arm over the living room, directing his announcement to his son. His voice was too loud. "I have a surprise."

The boy took the paper bag and squealed his pleasure when he recognized the SLIME.

"My God," his wife said.

"It's what the kids like," Selby told his wife.

The package stated that the SLIME would glow in the dark, so the lights were switched off. They crowded together on the living room carpet as the boy tore open the plastic and the stuff dripped into his hands. But his hands were too small. Both Selby and his wife cupped their palms to catch the overflow. "Be careful," she said.

"It won't stick to anything," the boy said.

"It's awful," she said.

They all shared a portion of the stuff. The boy giggled and cleared his throat in private happiness and his wife groaned in an exaggerated way to disguise the truth that she, too, was pleased. Selby held his share of the formless gel; it did not glow in the dark after all. He could not see it in his hands. There was something both intuitive and lewd in its method of escape. After a few moments in the dark, he surrendered to the same heavy feeling of the night before, and the night before that. He withdrew from the small circle, but his wife was first to stand up. She regained her crisp posture and with her elbow flicked the wall switch until the room blazed.

Although Pauline had many duties, and there were others in whose offices she collected mail or delivered faxes and internal memos, Selby decided to assume a primary role in the situation of her current romantic dishevelment. He waited to hear the scratchy tones of her headset as she slipped it off, and then he went out to talk to her about her stalker.

He grew to anticipate the spicy smell of her smoke when he heard her hunting in her purse for a lighter. The other girls hated the smell. They called her "Orient Express" because she chain-smoked clove cigarettes. He liked its Eastern scent coming secondhand to him. There was a recent memo forbidding workers to smoke at their desks, but Selby didn't turn her in.

Pauline could look like a gymnast in shiny stretch pants gathered in tight wrinkles at the shins, a chorus-line dancer

in a feline production, a circus clown when she wore oversized polka dots. She never wore her camouflage overalls
without her plastic banana brooch. Once she wore a pair of
leopard sneakers with shark teeth on the laces. "Grrr," she
said, and she clawed the air with her hand when he admired these. Selby liked to believe she wore her thrift-store
costumes to hide a ballooning despair just like his own,
the same covert gloom that forced him to prowl Columbus
Avenue.

He scolded her for coming to work wearing clothes
he'd already seen. "A repeat?" he said.

"It takes time to shop for this stuff, you have to go all
over to find it," she told him.

Often he sat at his desk without a desire to do the
transfers before him. It was no longer a passing boredom or
frustration. He looked at the clock all day. The hands barely
moved. The clock looked like a photograph of a clock. He
searched in his drawers for a pen that didn't squeak. He
couldn't find anything. He started to stand up more than
usual. He walked around his desk, and then he would walk
past Pauline to the big east window. He asked her, "He
show up last night?"

"Nope."

"You know what to do if he comes around?"

"Yeah, yeah. I know. Nine-one-one. I promise."

"Good girl," he said, avoiding her eyes.

He liked leaning over her desk and letting her fasten
the tiny foam headphones over his ears. She would look at
his face and judge him.

Pauline knew nothing about music, he thought. Someone was leading her on a goose chase. Back at his desk, he
stared through the window at the small slot of city it al-

lowed him. Across the alley, a shade was snapped open which had remained cockeyed for over a year.

When the flower was delivered, the girls stood in a crunch around Pauline. As she opened the box, the women dipped at the knees and groaned with delight. "A gladiolus—" someone said.

Pauline shrugged.

"*One* means the beginning or the end," a woman announced.

"Lucky kid," another said. In turn, they all expressed their jealousy.

"It beats me," Pauline said. "I'm really not into flowers."

"Don't look a gift horse in the mouth," they told her. It was her bland acceptance, her innocence, which they mistook for an unwillingness to divulge intimacies.

Pauline asked the women if they knew how many flowers were put on Elvis's grave.

"Plenty, I guess," somebody said.

"It was millions," she told them. "It smelled just like heaven."

"That was years ago," a girl said.

"They still bring them to the house. It's got flowers there all the time. Like an endless wonder," Pauline told them.

Then she was alone again. Selby walked out, but it was just as a couple of workmen had come to spackle the wall beside Pauline's desk. The men were joking with her.

"A little home improvement?" was all he managed to

say as he went by. She smiled, lifting her face to him; it was pure tolerance, he thought, that was all.

The week before, he had been late for a company awards luncheon. They were handing out the knickknacks to "ten-year employees" and "five-year employees," and to Selby, who had been working at the bank for fifteen years. The gifts were humiliating. Cross pen-and-pencil sets and imitation Mont Blancs. Faux-leather desktop planners. Women who were honored were encouraged to take the floral centerpieces back to their desks. Selby had stopped to see Thaddeus before coming to the luncheon. When he finally arrived at the event, he was surprised to see a handful of VPs, and even the CEO. He stood in the doorway of the banquet room and shifted his shoulders under his suit coat—his shoulders felt disconnected from his spine. After three doubles at Thad's, his gait was altered, his posture shifted from one dubious alignment to the next. With all his might, he tried to walk with brisk informality around the huge oval conference table to the one remaining chair. In his nervous haste he walked right past the empty seat. He then had to decide whether to turn around and backtrack or circle the table again. Neither option could save him. He paced out the door where he came in.

Pauline was not at her desk. Gone, too, the workmen, who had finished their repairs. There was a sour odor of caulk and plaster, and the waxy perfume of the flower was lost. On the blotter he saw a single salmon-colored petal, but then he realized it was an artificial fingernail. He pushed himself away from the desk, but she came up to him.

"Did you see the flower?" she asked.

"Very nice." He nodded, examining the solitary stalk. It might have cost as much to send a dozen.

"He thinks I'm letting him come back just because he orders me a flower?"

"It's a reconciliatory gesture," he told her.

"No dice," she said, lifting the flower from its vase. A fine white powder covered it.

"That's some kind of instant plaster," he said.

"Yeah, they were mixing it out here by my desk."

"It's ruined. I'm sorry," he said.

She looked at him. Her eyebrows hitched a quarter-inch higher. "It's not ruined," she said, still eyeing him. She stood up and took the vase over to the sink. He followed. She turned on the tap and ran the flower back and forth beneath the stream. She rubbed its petals between her fingers, letting the water fill each floweret and overflow. She tapped the stalk against the sink to remove the excess water droplets. "There," she said.

His stomach roiled at the sight of the drenched flower. He had certain aversions and sensitivities to different phenomena without the cushion of alcohol. He shivered if he walked past a lawn sprinkler. He couldn't take a foot bridge over a busy highway without severe pain in the testicles, and he didn't ride escalators if by chance the rubber tread was white like jagged molars. Recently, someone had put a spindle on his desk. A spindle! It was just another stimulus for one of his attacks. He asked Pauline about it.

"That spindle? There was a whole box of them. I handed them out. Everybody got one," she told him.

Selby mentioned the spindle to Thaddeus who assured

him his random aversions and fears were universal. "We all have our fair share of the jitters," he told Selby.

"Good as new," Pauline said when the flower was rinsed. She went back to her desk and replaced the stalk in its vase. She pulled her headset over her ears. She did not look up as he walked back to his chair. He studied the dewy hybrid again; the bloom looked harsh, its color magnified by the beads of water that trapped the office light.

The next day the flower was gone and in its place was a small glass aquarium which held a speckled mouse.

"Isn't it cute?" she asked. "When I told my friend about the anonymous flower, he sent me this mouse."

"What friend? The UPS driver?"

"Not him. A real friend gave me this pet. It's against the rules, I guess, but I'll take it home tonight. It doesn't eat cheese, you know. It eats these pellets." She picked up a plastic bag of pet food and handed it to Selby.

"I guess it's more nutritious than regular cheese," he said. He put the rat food down on Pauline's desk. "Your friend is very imaginative," he told Pauline.

"Yeah," she looked at him straight in the eyes, and he stopped prying.

The afternoon went on. The sun moved downwards at a hard angle, then rested outside his window. It seemed painless staring at the dying thing until he closed his eyes and saw it stayed with him. Then he heard voices, and he heard Pauline laughing. Her laughter was airy, with a few throaty catches, like the sound of pastel tissue being torn into strips. With the laughter, he heard the short, high squeaks of the mouse. He went to see what it was and found three young men standing before Pauline's desk. One held the animal by its tail and dropped it into the palm of his hand; as the mouse walked forward, the man tugged it back by the tail. The boys were all dressed the same, in huge, baggy trousers. He saw it was the uniform of the day, something resembling North African pajamas made from one bolt of cloth tugged loosely between the legs and cinched imaginatively at the waist.

"These are my friends." Pauline stood up. "The City Editors."

"A group?" he asked.

"You must have seen the piece about us in *Boston After Dark*," one of the men said.

"I'm sorry to have missed it," Selby said.

"You didn't catch it?" the boy was incredulous.

"They're playing tonight at the Living Room," she said. "They're the greatest."

"It'll be packed," the boy said.

They leaned against the files and the office equipment. One took a Xerox of his hand. Another picked up Pauline's phone and punched through the lighted buttons. They gathered at the fax machine daring one another to try it.

"They like electric stuff," she told Selby. "Come on, guys," she said, but she was beaming.

Selby wondered about the young men. He saw Pauline, tilting her face from one to the other and even towards him as he was asked to agree about rock-'n'-roll—that it was finally an industry like any other industry; it had its tycoons, its slaves, its gal Fridays. The group laughed and hugged Pauline around the waist. One fellow grasped her by the hips and lifted her up, lifted her above their small circle as if she belonged to them all.

It was the end of the day. Girls drifted by in twos and threes, calling to their friends over the partitions that separated the desks. He had not been invited for a drink in quite some time. He didn't like to be surrounded and preferred to hide out beside Thaddeus when he indulged in his routine. They gave up asking and the girls started to call him "Mr. Gloom." He didn't mind their joke. He had once heard them call Pauline a name. They called Pauline "Miss Hopeless Case." Once he listened to the late afternoon talk and was pleased to hear the two of them paired. He didn't catch the explanation, but he heard one of the girls say, "Miss Hopeless Case and Mr. Gloom," as if, at least in the minds of the office girls, they were linked. So what if the others considered them outcasts? It only intensified and made bittersweet their unavoidable connection.

Soon the place was empty. He was sure of it. He hunched down in his seat, but he couldn't see any point in staying longer. He had avoided the chattering crush, that was it. At five-twenty Pauline came to the doorway. "Still here?" she said.

"What about you?"

She shrugged. He felt an odd lightness and he turned to look out at the sun, which was setting. He saw some spots before his eyes and he could not be sure if the sun he was facing was the real sun or just its savage aftereffect. He started to tell her that she had awakened his feelings, but she interrupted him. He thought he heard her saying she liked a clear conscience.

"I just wanted to tell you I found an item of yours—"

"You found what?"

She opened her purse and unfolded a crinkled piece of paper. She gave him the instruction sheet. "I saw it on the floor," she told him. "At least it was me. Imagine if some-one else came across it—"

"Who else?"

"Maintenance," she said. "They might have collected it. You know, same as every night."

She didn't paint the whole scenario; he was grateful for that.

She told him, "Don't think twice about it. It's got noth-ing to do with me. But since you're feeling so down, I thought you might like to go hear my friends tonight."

"It's ridiculous," he said.

"They are not. They're very serious artists."

"I mean the other thing. The fact is—" He pushed him-self back in his chair. "The thing is—"

"Please," she told him. "Don't say anything."

He looked at the printout that had accompanied the noose. It was a poor translation from the Chinese manufac-turer, but he guessed it explained itself. He was relieved to change the subject and said, "The City Editors? Tonight?"

"Do you want to go with me or not?" She shifted her weight from one foot to the other.

"Those fellows with the Arab outfits?"

"Yes." She was grinning. She must have seen it from his point of view. "It's true, they're pretty clothes-conscious," she said.

"Those fellows are creepy. They're using you. Maybe they're dangerous," he said.

The sun had liquefied and rested like a full saucer on

the horizon. The sky had neither the glare of day nor the rich substance of night. They stood for a moment outside their building, where the Astroturf carpet led to the curb and the taxis.

Selby saw him first. He was standing on the opposite corner.

"Oh, shit," Pauline said. "He looks worse and worse."

Her ex-lover had not yet changed his clothes, but this time he wore the short, quilted company jacket with the shipping firm's logo on the breast pocket.

Selby told her, "Look, we'll cross at the light. Just ignore him." He put his arm through hers and steered her to the crosswalk. They walked right past the young man. Selby could have reached out and touched him. The man stared at Pauline as if she were an apparition, a holograph image that he himself had conjured and therefore could not intercept. The man had emerged from the first phase of his grief, in which he had sorted his emotions by tossing electronic appliances around, to his new station, which seemed to be a fully paralyzed remorse. Selby was no longer frightened by the loner and he told him, "Go climb back under your rock."

They marched beyond the ruined soul and left him weaving behind them on the sidewalk.

"Let's go eat somewhere first," she said. He took her to the Steeple Street Bar. They stood at the rail and waited for a table. Thaddeus attended to Selby, but she declined a drink. At last, they shared a camel-humped booth, which pitched her close. She ate chowder. He watched her use the heel of her hand to crush saltines in the cellophane packet until it became a fine white powder which she then poured over her soup. Every gesture she made seemed to wait for his response. She wasn't testing him, it was her way of an exchange. Her small perceptions, her very mannerisms encouraged him to say something, and she in turn was pleased, assured by his flat remarks. He grabbed the waitress and ordered more scotch. He told Pauline, "Try it. A little budget psychiatry. The golden therapist."

She didn't like the taste. He strained her scotch into his own glass, leaving a tower of ice cubes in her tumbler. He imagined taking it further, then he thought about a time when he was traveling with his wife. He remembered a motel, its six yellow doors facing the highway. He left his wife in the car when he went up to ask for a room, but before he reached the motel office a neon sign flicked on at the window. The sign said *Sorry* in pink script. How far did they drive after that, and where did they sleep? He remembered their bodies entwined for hours in one sunken place. They hardly spoke then, as they never did now. Yet his wife liked to mention the story of the neon sign from time to time. Whether she thought it was a sad, foretelling detail or a simple amusement, he still did not know. Out of the blue, she would say, "Remember that motel?" and she didn't mean the motel where they had spent the night together, she meant the initial place, where they had been turned away, the motel with the sign that said *Sorry.*

They walked into the rock club. Its walls were draped with black velvet curtains. "For the acoustics," Pauline told him. He knew that, of course, but he was pleased by just the look of it. It had the aura of a wicked shrine or underground crypt. The City Editors climbed onto the stage. The music started. It's good, he thought. Even if he didn't know the standards, it was a wonderful sensation. The wall of noise created a mild pressure as in jet takeoffs, a resistance; then he was lifted, buoyed. The crowd was crammed in shoulder to shoulder, and the kids decided which way he should lurch and dip as everyone weaved forward and backward with the music. Pauline was jumping up and down to the bass line. "Cheer up, cheer up," she might have been saying. She looked content in that environment, but there was nothing heightened or alert in her face. Once or twice, despite the crowd, he saw his own face reflected in the mirror behind the tight stage. He expected to see himself as someone wedged between the furious energies of youth and an embittered calm ahead. The music penetrated like a microbe or bacterium pushing through a cellular membrane. He surrendered to its contamination, its primary symptom being a weakness in his knees. He began to enjoy the song. The rhythm guitar was wonderfully scratchy, slurring. The audience responded, breaking off into small, ragged clusters of movement.

In the mirror behind the band, Selby recognized the heartsick deliveryman standing not ten feet away from them. The man waited, ready to exchange his place each time someone hip-hopped and freed a space nearer Pauline. He wasn't responding to the hiccuping bass line but wiped his hair out of his eyes and stood like a pillar of stone waiting for his next opportunity to close in on his ex-girlfriend.

Selby considered the dangers of such a face-to-face in that crowd, perhaps precipitating a stampede situation. He begged Pauline to leave with him. They squeezed through the crowd and went outside. A light snow glazed the street. Her leather flats didn't grip and she was totally helpless if she didn't cling to him. He walked Pauline to her loft apartment in a renovated textile mill. He made love to her in her platform bed, fighting a sense of vertigo. Pauline sensed his discomfort and she lifted her hips and moved over to the side with the rail. "Don't worry. No one has ever fallen off yet," she told him. In the dead silence, after the act, he heard the mouse on its exercise wheel, a constant lisping complaint from across the room.

It was snowing harder when he went back to the garage to pick up his car. He drove home to his wife. He was only a half-mile from his ranch house when a big, buff-colored dog jumped in front of the car. The headlights scrolled over the dog and Selby braked hard, skidding on the snow, expecting to hit the animal. Then he saw it on the other side of the car, clear of him.

As he walked through the dark house, he noticed a perceptible veil of clove perfume rising off his shirt collar. He unbuttoned his oxford and tore it off. He padded around the living room in his socks. He went over to the sideboard and poured a drink. He swirled it around in his mouth. The spicy residue of his night fought with the alcohol's standard smoky taste, ruining its effect.

The bedroom was black as he climbed into bed. His wife pretended to sleep. The sheets were warm, as if his wife had recently rolled from his side onto her own. He decided this detail described her kindness and sorrow for their predicament. They were falling asleep when it was at the bedroom window, level with them. A bold snarl announced its presence, followed by a steady, angry barking. Selby got out of bed and folded the curtain back from the window. He recognized the buff-colored dog he had avoided hitting on the street. The dog barked in a hateful rhythm, the same one or two grim tones. Its teeth snapped at the end of every tearing phrase. It was not the sound of hunger, or longing, or pining.

"A stray," his wife said. "I've seen him prowling around."

Selby watched its big chest heaving, its fur clotted in yellow tufts where its belly rubbed the deep snow.

"Maybe he's cornered a cat or a possum?" his wife said.

"It's lost. It saw our lights. Fierce bugger."

He went to check on his son, but the barking was muted on that side of the house and the boy slept through it. Selby picked up a shot glass from his son's bedside table. Its contents flamed bright fluorescent green. The SLIME had absorbed enough daylight to be successfully activated. He swirled the jigger until the sluggish gleam coated its rim, and then he put it down. The glowing substance seemed as miraculous as it was ridiculous, and Selby felt giddy.

He returned to his room and got back into bed. The dog barked. His wife rested her head in the crook of his shoulder. Together they listened to the dog's harangue; it was becoming familiar, an intimacy, a balm.

In the morning, Selby cleared his car windshield, then he walked around the house looking for any trace of the mysterious beast. The wind turned back and forth over the snowy surface where it had stood. Right then, a municipal snow plow went down the street. The vehicle was bright yellow from a recent steam cleaning at the city hangar. In the tight cab, beside the uniformed driver, was the buff-colored dog. Its tail brushed the ceiling as it nosed the driver's face in wild affection. The driver studied the curb as he lowered the blade. Selby watched the plow for sparks, but the driver was expert and took only the fresh white snow.

❖ PRINCE OF MOTOWN

That April, Marvin Gaye was murdered. Maurice
Greene, the father of Iris's six-month-old baby, went
to his old shooting den at the Linville Projects. In mourning,
he bought a spike and three hits of dope for the weekend. He
came home fully schmecked. His shoulder brushed the
doorjamb and pitched his torso the opposite way.

"You're gooned," Iris said. She watched him lift his feet
to fanciful elevations before dropping them down, picking
his way over to her as if he were negotiating cross ties in a
switching yard. His spinal column was unhinged, and Iris
knew he had put something in his arm, but Maurice exhibited a new and mystical flex, a curious exoneration: Gaye
was dead and Maurice was released from all his routine du-

ties. His part-time job at Benny's Home and Auto, his fatherhood responsibilities, all his tasks were shirked, while he paid whacked-out homage to the murdered singer.

For two weeks, Iris had watched Maurice crucify himself on piggyback needles, trying for a copycat ascension to mimic Gaye's transformation. High on tar, he spoke to her only in snippets from Gaye's discology, quoting lyrics completely out of context. *"I ain't got time to think about money or what it could buy, and I ain't got time to sit around and wonder what makes a birdy fly,"* he told Iris that morning as he walked out the door.

While Maurice was supposed to be working at the Home and Auto Supply, Iris left the older women in the apartment and instead of taking a cab, wheeled the umbrella stroller to the clinic. The clinic was nine blocks into town. Iris remembered to stretch a plastic dry-cleaning bag across the handles of the stroller for a windbreak, but even so, the baby's eyes were tearing from the cold when she arrived.

Her baby wasn't gaining. The clinic wanted to get a blood sample before Terrell could get his DPT shot on schedule like the normal babies waiting outside with their mothers in the Well Baby Room. Iris was never asked to wait in the cozy, divided area, which was well-stocked with bright toys and ladies' magazines. Iris heard the happy jingles and buzzers of a Busy Box, the cascading notes of xylophones, and taut plunking beats of skin drums. Above this din was the high warble of infants and toddlers amusing themselves, and the occasional singsong of their mothers. Iris was pulled into an examining stall as soon as she arrived. Her baby was scrawny. A nurse pricked his heel with a disposable stylet, which she then discarded in a bright red cylinder for needles and hazardous medical refuse. Next, the nurse wanted to test Iris and get her numbers. Terrell was fussy during the procedures, discomforted by the noisy sheet of crinkled paper on the examining table, and Iris lifted him off.

Afterwards she wheeled the stroller to Classical High School, where she tried to catch her old girlfriends when they came outside to switch classes. The girls huddled around Iris and the conspicuous lemon-lime baby stroller. They chatted on the walkway between buildings for ten minutes. When the bell sounded, the girls ran off in different directions. Sometimes, one of her friends brought Iris a drink from the cafeteria, where Iris wasn't permitted to sit down. Iris fancied a local Rhode Island dairy item called Coffee Milk, and her friends brought Iris an eight-ounce carton. They peeled the straw for Iris before trotting off to typing or advanced algebra class. Iris sipped the drink slowly, trying to make it last forty-five minutes, until the bell clanged and the girls reappeared from the classroom building.

Several Classical students had had babies in a wave the year after Lady Di had hers. When Iris's baby was born, her teenaged friends stood at the foot of the hospital bed and remarked upon his skin color. Iris held the infant in her arms and blushed at the contrast between them. The baby's skin was a deeper shade than her own. Someone said he looked just like the familiar sweetened coffee drink. Her classmates teased her. How many cartons of Coffee Milk had Iris consumed those nine months she was carrying Terrell? Their teasing reassured her—and she was pleased that they could still find the humor in her situation. Her friends told her that there was a big difference between Terrell and

the other mixed babies at the high school day care. Terrell
was lighter.

Iris didn't mind listening to their speculations as long as
she was still accepted in their circle. But when Iris and Terrell weren't admitted to the high school day-care program,
her friends started to avoid Iris during their chaotic lunch
period and at the city bus stops, where she sometimes
waited for them after school was dismissed. The novelty of
being outcast wore off. She wheeled the umbrella stroller
up and down the curbstones, bumping the nylon sling and
startling the infant; the plastic dry-cleaning bag whipped in
a mean wind, until he started bawling. By spring, Iris was
totally abandoned by her high school friends, and she no
longer tried to intercept them.

Maurice crossed the linoleum as if he were testing an
ice pond. His jeans were slipping off his hips and bunched
at his unlaced Cons. Maurice prowled towards her; his
weight lagged behind or tumbled ahead. His legs couldn't
align with his trunk.

"You're cranked," she said.

He twirled around and fell on the couch. They had
been forced to move in with Maurice's mother, Vicki, and
Vicki's sister, Estelle. Iris was tender meat for that pair of
harpies, and when Maurice was like this, he couldn't pro-
tect her.

Iris asked Maurice, "Answer me this. You give up
everything just because Marvin Gaye bought it off his own
father?" Her eyes were burning. She noted that her tears
were not the everyday drips but new and unplanned for,
brimming in huge and pitiful droplets. She wiped her face
with the heel of her hand and stared at her moist palm.

Its shiny residue did not directly reveal the exact nature of the new disaster she faced, and she rubbed her hand on her knee.

Maurice crumpled to one side of the sofa. She stood over him and raised her voice. "So what about me and Terrell? This is *our* life, you know. It's not just your life."

Maurice fluttered his eyes, trying to follow, but he never met her level of conjecture, which was a steep threshold, and he couldn't pull himself across its difficult lip. "My bro is gone," he told her.

"Fuck that. That's yesterday's news."

His eyeballs were tight. He flopped over on the sofa and stretched his legs out. He told her, *"We're all sensitive people with so much to give—"*

"What's this?" Iris said. "Is that Marvin Gaye? Is that him? You make me crazy."

"—Understand me, sugar," Maurice quoted the murder victim.

She smacked him. Maurice rolled onto his stomach and groaned with pleasure, which made her strike him again. His comic whimper alerted his mother and aunt. Iris started tugging his floppy arm and the whole household came apart.

Estelle pushed Iris away and she took off Maurice's shoes, which should have been Iris's chore. Maurice's mother, Vicki, yelled at Iris, grabbing her white wrist, pinching a pleat of translucent skin between her sharp, lacquered fingertips.

"You fixed him," Vicki hissed at Iris, blaming Iris for Maurice's nod. She said, "It's your mother's money that buys his dope."

"That's cash for diapers," Iris said.

"Shit. I guess he's goofed on Pampers."

"If he could, he would."

"He's had a shock and you're no help," Vicki told her. Vicki linked Gaye's sudden demise to Maurice's relapse, as if they were a chain-reaction phenomenon. "I've seen this for years. White girls enticing black men and making them crazy."

Iris went to get the baby into his plastic safety seat. Weeks before, Maurice had used a wire cutter to remove the rudimentary safety seat from a grocery cart that he had rolled four blocks from the Star Market parking lot.

"What do you think you're doing?" Vicki told her.

"I'm getting out of here."

"That's perfectly nice. You just put that baby down where he is."

Iris looked at the slender black woman talking to her; Maurice's mother was tense and muscled beneath an over-sized *Thriller* T-shirt with its solitary sequined hand. Vicki's features were sharp; her skin was sleek, honeyed Jamaican, but she wasn't attractive. She was a mean streak in its condensed, petite human form right down to her spiky eyelashes caked with military green mascara. Iris understood that Vicki, not Maurice felled on the sofa, was her real opponent.

Iris strapped the baby into the plastic seat.

Vicki said, "You go ahead. Go on back to your own mother, but you leave my grandbaby here. He's too sick to go out."

"He's not sick."

"Oh, honey."

Iris tossed her head. Her long hair whipped open like a golden saw wheel and Vicki backed up a few paces. Iris picked up her jacket and purse from the floor and crooked the baby seat on her hip.

"I'm saying," Vicki said, "you're not taking that child."

Iris said, "This is my baby. *Your* baby's lying over there. That one. That jab king—" She pointed to Maurice. Maurice's hand was dangling off the sofa, his fingers fully opened in his innocent, drenched sleep.

It occurred to Iris that Vicki was fourteen years older than Terrell's father, who was himself only fifteen years older than Terrell. Iris recognized that these three pitiful generations were set down in the world in not even as many decades. She wondered how many more repetitions might be introduced if she remained in that household.

Estelle watched from the kitchenette, where she was stripping a chicken carcass, nibbling tags of its chewy, burnt skin. She held its bony rib cage in her greasy hands. "I tell you, girl. Give that baby to his grandmother." She started to wrap the carcass in a sheet of foil, keeping the Reynolds Wrap box squeezed in her armpit. Iris watched the chicken fat glittering on her fingers.

Vicki pinched Iris, plucking a solitary dimple of baby fat and twisting Iris's cheek until the girl squeaked. An even greater affront to Iris was when she saw her own saliva dripping in a silver line from her skewed mouth. She pushed Vicki off and wiped her lips.

Estelle came over. She started smacking Iris on her head with the heavy Reynolds Wrap carton, sawing its serrated edge across Iris's face.

The strip of metal teeth was sharp and left deep cuts.

Dots of blood lifted in two intersecting ellipses lines. Iris wiped her chin and blood came off on the palm of her hand. "You cut me! You cut me!"

"Shit, why'd you do that?" Vicki asked her sister.

"Hey, I don't know," Estelle said to Vicki. She, too, was shocked at the result. Estelle pushed her hand in her apron pocket and found a pack of menthol cigarettes. She lit up and shook out the match. She offered the Kool to Iris but Iris declined. Estelle wouldn't take no for an answer and she tried to insert the filter tip between Iris's lips, saying, "Here, now, honey." Iris turned away. The two sisters retreated to the kitchen. Estelle shoved the foil into a drawer and picked up a dishrag, as if she might resume her household duties.

Iris adjusted the baby seat on her hip and turned the four dead bolts. She tugged the steel door open. Her cheek was stinging. At the elevator, she waited for the light to indicate the cage was coming. Nothing. She ran down the hall to the outside stairwell. It was the fifth floor and from that height she could see the mercury streaks of the Providence harbor reflecting engorged beams and gold puddles from the street lights and glowing ribbons of traffic on I-95. The wind was strong and it carried a rich, unrelenting scent from Narragansett Bay. She started down the cement treads. Blood dripped from her chin and she saw its tiny red stars and asterisks on every landing. The baby was squawking.

An hour later, Iris stood at the entrance of the Stop Over Shelter. The doormat was made from furred strips of common discarded tire treads and she instinctively wiped her feet on its waffle weave. No one came to answer the door. The women's center was in an Italian neighborhood west of Federal Hill, where the old-worlders were dying out and university professors, leftists, and do-gooders prevailed. Terrell was squirming and she released him from the baby seat and rested the seat on the stoop. She jiggled the baby on her hip to see if he would quiet. He wasn't consoled by her cooing or soothed by her touch; her brisk repetition of kisses across his wrinkled forehead only seemed to smart him. He didn't stop crying. Sometimes, when this happened, when the baby didn't respond to her efforts, she clutched his rib cage in both hands, extended her arms, and shook him to make him stop. His big head whipped back and forth on his narrow shoulders. His eyes pinched closed with the vibrations, then bloomed wide open, but he didn't shut up.

The baby cried. It was not a simple effort, but a complex, congested bawling, an inconsolable fusion of its wounded infantile psyche and its imperiled miniature body, between involuntary gasps for breath.

Iris shook her baby; her relief was immediate. She again held Terrell on her hip.

Iris depressed the doorbell and fiddled with the intercom at the front door. No one was coming very fast. A keypad to the left of the door regularly blinked, giving the stoop a green pulse. Iris expected to see someone's angry boyfriend lurking around, but there wasn't anyone. Her own Maurice might have followed her there, but he had not even shifted from his horizontal cloudscape when his aunt had attacked her with the box of foil.

For quite some time Iris knew that her home life had disintegrated past any saving grace. What had set the wrecking ball in motion was a public tragedy in the elite black music world, in that R&B nation to which she didn't belong and in which she therefore had no clout when Maurice went back to heroin. Iris started to think that she should actually praise Gaye's father for bringing it to a head. She decided, in a fit of pique, to send the murderer a thank-you card once she could find out the address of the security facility where he was being held pending a hearing.

After leaving the apartment, she had called the women's shelter from a Roy Rogers' Chicken, where she bought coffee. She tried to ask directions to the Stop Over Shelter, but a kid had just sunk a frozen block of drumettes into the fryer and the sputtering grease kept her from hearing. She asked the counselor to repeat the street number. "And you'll take my baby, Terrell?" she said. The counselor told her that the S.O.S. shelter would not take children into the program unless accompanied by a legal guardian. Iris could not just drop the baby off as she had planned to do.

"You can't take him?" she said. A crosscurrent of sensations prickled her when she pictured the baby alone. She pictured him in someone else's arms. First he is crying, then he is laughing. He's fat and healthy; he's a toddler; he's five years old; he's full-grown. She recalled the official medical expectations, and this halted her fantasy with a familiar, chilly relief.

In any case, she didn't plan to stay long in the Stop Over Shelter. She didn't wish to share her secrets with nosy counselors who might make her do housekeeping chores or force her to study for the GED, and she didn't like the idea of sleeping in a row of beds between bruised-up girls, hiding from their own mistakes.

The counselor told her, "We have twice as many cribs

as beds, but we're not an orphanage. We're set up for women who are seriously threatened in their domestic situation."

Iris explained Estelle's attack with the Reynolds Wrap box.

"Gee, honey, that sounds pretty bad. You come right over with your baby."

Iris remembered the last place she had fled to. There was a low paddock of babies holding filthy bottles of diluted apple juice as other tots warred over a few broken-armed dolls. The babies loitered around a community toy box with the manhandled remains of items issued every year by the Toys for Tots campaigns organized by local Harley-Davidson Owners Groups. That room of broken dolls and tattered games had looked like the littered, open-air rag-and-bone shops after hurricanes.

The woman at the Stop Over Shelter told Iris, "Our kitchen has a good supply of bottles, nipples, disposable nursers. We have Enfamil in cans and we also have the canisters of powder. Or, maybe you're breastfeeding?" Iris recognized the hopeful hesitation in the woman's voice, the same tone as the hospital's nurse-midwife who had tried to convince her to let Terrell suck while she was still on the delivery table. She was considering the task when another nurse grabbed the baby from her breast and scolded the midwife about having to take necessary precautions "with this one."

"Breast or bottle?" the voice asked.

"I get WIC coupons for Similac." Iris did not enjoy the telephone interview.

Iris read a sign over the glass transom: "Nothing Is Permanent But Change." The sign wasn't consoling. Iris didn't wish to keep having things change. For months, things in her life had been changing for the worse with malevolent precision. Events changed from unattractive to ugly, from monstrous to heinous, from black to pitch-black. She looked at the baby in her arms. His pinched features as he sputtered with discomfort did not encourage her. When she was pregnant, she had not foreseen the consequences of having this mixed child. She had escaped her suburban home, which she could not return to without arousing her lover's suspicions, or her own mother's hopes of a reunion.

Terrell was cute enough to encourage her close attention. Yet there were times she couldn't bear to lift him out of his bed, a tiny square of consistently damp foam she had cut out to fit an old bassinet. The streets were too rough to wheel Terrell after dark when she most desired to be away from her surroundings. She shared one bedroom with Maurice, the baby, and two of Maurice's younger brothers who had spread out into her space without even thinking. Stacks of disposable diapers had melted on the electric radiator; the pool of baby oil from the tipped bottle had never been tended to and had soaked a mound of laundry which she had left unsorted on the floor. The boys' basketball sneakers littered the room in various perches, like futuristic chicle sculptures.

Lilacs were growing in oddball droops on either side of the shelter's doorstep and she recognized yet another scent—sweet yeast from a bakery somewhere. The lilacs' perfume coupled with the tangy, fermenting dough made her want to put the baby down. She felt his weight in her sore wrists and elbows.

. . .

He was standing in front of the closet mirror in the half-dark. He ran the palm of his hand across his chest, down the hollow of his rib cage and over his stomach muscles. He rubbed the tight hillock below his waist where his navel should be.

He did not have a navel.

This curious deletion, a deviation from the normal anatomical references of the male physique, was a constant annoyance to him. His belly was a tight, empty plain. It had all the typical articulations of the external oblique muscles beneath a thinning zone of baby fat. His abdomen was firm and lean, gorgeous, yet it lacked the tiny, limned vortex of flesh common to his peers. As an infant his umbilical cord had become abscessed and it had to be excised and the tissue resutured. When the incision healed there was nothing to show for the fact that he had ever been attached to his mother inside the womb. He might have emerged, singularly intact, like a casting at a foundry.

In the high school locker room with the other teenaged boys he was sometimes called "Girl," as if his smooth, muscled waist—with its error in punctuation, its small grammatical oversight—spelled out a feminine trait.

He considered himself in the mirror; he wasn't girlish in any way. Proof of which, was his colossal erection reflected in the chipped silver plate. It was all or nothing. It was everything. But his masculinity sometimes seemed undermined by his smoother zones. His emerging sexuality, in its ambitious transit from childhood to maturity, was pushed askew by one tiny flaw: without the disruption of a navel, his stomach muscles formed a slight cleft which might somehow, remotely, resemble cleavage.

There was someone screaming outside in the street. He

heard her yelping and ignored it. He was stepping into his mother's half-slip and pulling it up over his hips. He was not "dressing up like a woman," but he wanted to feel the nylon fabric stretch over his cock, which, fully erect, pushed the polyester panel away from his body. He turned parallel to the mirror to measure how far the luxury fabric was distended; the half-slip was stretched taut by his hard-on, then it fell in a strict sheet from the secret projection, just like a table scarf. Next, he lifted the chilly hem over his cock and rested it there. He started. He waited. He started again.

The girl next door was screaming her lungs out. It was not unfamiliar to Rick and appeared to be a typical halfway-house scenario, not much different from the usual, yet her demonstrations were stubborn, and above her voice a baby's thin, staccato cries.

Rick lived with his mother, Carol, in a second-floor apartment next door to the women's shelter where his mother worked as assistant director. On the opposite side of the house was a bakery that specialized in pizza dough, just the dough, which they shipped out to local restaurants. The sweet odor of the rising dough curled along the windowsill of his room, and he didn't like smelling it at all hours, especially without the accompanying odor of the spicy sauce, without the sausages and other toppings. The smell of dough was a tantalizing *blank* smell, a tease, and at sixteen his whole life seemed similarly agitated by a swelling list of temptations which, like this virgin dough, had not yet been molded or completed.

The girl outside screamed for assistance. It was nothing new to Rick, who had lived in different women's shelters with Carol ever since his father was first arrested. She had always found them a place to stay. She would meet a new boyfriend, which was to say she became someone's mouse for a few months. When it fell apart, she left the man and took Rick to a new shelter, where he was attended to by grim, no-nonsense volunteers. These volunteers aided "women in transition," and, together with the victims, they drew up "contracts" based upon their individual goals. The women signed the contracts, placing their names, written in cursive, alongside the signature of the counselor, also in cursive. The filing cabinet in his mother's office had scores of these signed contracts.

Carol had taken an entry-level position at the Stop Over Shelter, volunteering to do the cleaning. Then she made the casserole dinners and learned how to shop for an uncertain population, remaining prepared and flexible for the unspecified drop-ins. Carol began answering the telephone in the office, and she took on other clerical duties. She learned to help with the intake interviews and she typed up the monthly reports for the executive advisory board.

Her professional duties quelled the tremors and aftershocks of her own violent history. By relating her personal experiences in a daily, instructive narrative for the benefit of the center's vulnerable residents, Carol believed that she purged herself.

Rick didn't enjoy living next door to the shelter. He was never free of its heavy moral scheme. The two buildings were separated by a tight alley, and his bedroom seemed directly annexed to the flow of moods coming and going.

The girl's voice evaporated in the complicated stagings of his sexual fantasy, which was typically about an imaginary girl who exhibited the collective aspects of all girls, including some of the bruised visitors next door, whom he sometimes viewed as they crossed the lighted stairwell.

He rolled onto his bed. He shuddered again, with a prolonged abdominal conclusion which radiated upwards from his pelvis and across the empty prairie where he had no tiny well, no navel to collect it. He lifted the corner of the shade to look out. The girl with the baby was being admitted into the house next door. His own mother was leading her by the elbow. Another volunteer took the squalling infant. He saw that the girl had beautiful blond hair like Darryl Hannah. Wavy sheets of platinum fluff, attractive for its unnatural tint, its supernatural loft. The baby wore a knitted cap with a gaudy pom-pom.

Rick's vigorous routine had provoked his asthma and he grabbed his inhaler. He took a few puffs from the plastic dispenser. His mother would be tied up for a while.

He stood up and pushed his mother's half-slip down until it circled his feet. He stepped out of it, and left it in a black ring on the floor. He pulled on his jeans and sweatshirt, remembering to return the slip to the hamper in the bathroom before walking through to Carol's bedroom where a portable TV rested on a chair. He lifted the TV, jerked its cord loose, and brought it into his own bedroom.

The baby was extremely agitated and Carol had difficulty appraising its general condition. Its eyes were puffy and its skin was blotchy from all its wailing. She opened a can of Enfamil and poured it into a plastic bottle. She put the bottle in a pan of water on the kitchen stove. The baby would quiet down with a feeding. There was something pitiful about the child which suggested some greater peril. Carol saw immediately that the young mother cradled her baby with the dumb ambivalence of a frozen peach tree holding a Sterno pot in its iced branches. The girl was already in flight, receding from her surroundings even as she sat there, across from Carol, writing her name on a form. Carol felt sympathy for the baby and for its mother, the other baby. Yet she had to write an accurate intake report. Iris's blank response to the shuddering bundle in her lap had to be documented. Carol wrote down exactly what she saw before her at that very moment, at 10:35 P.M.: "Mother exhibits no positive feelings for the infant."

"Thank goodness you had the foresight to come here tonight," Carol told Iris.

Iris nodded.

"You have made the right decision. It's a first decision. You'll have to make a lot more of them."

"Um-huh."

Carol said, "No kidding. It takes a lot of hard thinking, doesn't it? This is only the beginning."

Iris looked back at Carol. She didn't try to conceal her rising sarcasm, which tightened her mouth into a hard pink bud. "Shit. I guess I thought it would be the best thing to get out of a place where they were trying to kill me."

"A wise decision."

"I don't need to be Einstein."

Carol didn't smile. She showed respect for the seriousness of the attack. She had learned of many peculiar weapons used for their immediate availability. Table forks; nail scissors; snow shovels; wall phones; cast-iron door stops; any small appliance that can be hurled across a room. Carol told the girl, "You have to be more than Einstein. You have to time-travel. The future isn't something that waits for you. You have to walk towards it or else it pushes you around."

Iris nodded at Carol as if she suddenly understood the small feat she had accomplished. She had fled from her persecutors.

Carol said, "You got up and walked out of that apartment before your baby got hurt."

Iris looked down at Terrell. Never once had she thought of his safety as a catalyst for her departure.

A staff nurse had come back with a stainless-steel bowl of warm water to which she added a squirt of Betadine disinfectant. She pulled two gloves from a dispenser and their fine white powder drifted through the air. Wearing the gloves, she soaked a gauze sponge in the soapy water and dabbed it against Iris's face. Iris winced, but she didn't protest. The woman cleaned Iris's face, leaving the orange tint of the medicinal soap across her cheek. "I don't think stitches will help this." The nurse pinched the two-inch cuts together with her latex fingertips to see if they needed suturing. "These are probably going to scar one way or the other. Do you think she needs to get these stitched?"

"You won't do it?" Carol asked the nurse.

"No."

"I understand," Carol said. Carol leaned closer to Iris's face to look at her cuts.

"Are you a doctor?" Iris said.

"Do you want a doctor?" Carol leaned back in her chair.

The nurse peeled off her soapy gloves.

"I guess she's too spooked to stitch me up. Well, I don't give a shit about stitches," Iris said.

Carol reached up to her head and collected clumps of

her wavy hair, pulling it behind her ear. "See what I have here?"

Iris saw a raised scar at Carol's temple. The scar looked like pink piping edging Carol's hairline and upper cheek where her ear had been reattached, sewn a little off-center.

"He ripped it right off of me," Carol told her.

"He tore your ear off?"

"Just about did. I waited too long to get it fixed, that's why it looks like it does, kind of messy. Because I waited. That's a mistake. We're asking you what *you* want to do about your cuts. It's your decision. I told you, once you make the first decision there's a string of them."

Iris looked at Carol's ear. She turned back to look at the skittish nurse. "Well, don't stitches leave those railroad tracks? Like Frankenstein?"

"You don't want to go to emergency?"

"Not for now."

A resident came into the room looking for help. The nurse was relieved to have the excuse, and went out. Carol remained with Iris and walked over to the sink. She carefully emptied the sudsy water from the bowl and turned it under the tap. She saw her face smeared or constricted as she rinsed the shiny hip of the stainless-steel bowl. Her ex-husband assumed an important role in all her routine Stop Over indoctrinations. She brought him up at each intake interview, each time she pulled her hair away from her ear. The scars he had left her with were Carol's "tools of the trade." She pushed the cuffs of her sleeves past her elbows to show the new girl the ruddy burn marks on her forearms. "I got these burns from some Scottie-dog andirons when he tried to push me into the fireplace. You should have seen the blisters." She liked to describe these Scottie andirons to the girls—their absurd cuteness at that frozen moment. She opened her mouth to reveal a lopsided hump in the middle of her tongue. She had bit right through it when her husband slammed her against the hood of his car and her chin banged shut on the tough wedge of muscle. Repairs to her tongue required both internal and external sutures to reconnect blood vessels, nerves, and the pebbly surface where her taste buds were shunted, clustered on one side. She believed that this particular injury had a metaphoric resonance. She had to bite her own tongue before she could speak out against his infractions.

"That bottle's ready for your baby," Carol told Iris. Carol took the bottle of formula from the pan of tepid water and handed it to Iris. Iris followed Carol upstairs to one of the bedrooms. The hallway smelled of Murphy's Oil Soap and somebody's hairspray. Iris recognized the scent, a light alcohol odor laced with a sweet varnish smell. It was oddly reassuring; although she didn't use hairspray herself, she liked the fact that the other residents were far enough along in the game to be primping instead of swabbing facial cuts. Over and above the hairspray scent, the smell of fresh dough from the bakery, two doors away, added a sickening expectation to everything.

"In here," Carol said.

The room was small, with one single bed and a tiny baby crib, not a full-sized model, but good enough. "I get a private room? Why?" Iris was stung by her exclusion from the rest.

"You don't need to meet the other residents tonight. There's time for that tomorrow at Morning Meeting."

Iris didn't plan on attending any "meetings" or putting forth any effort.

Carol said, "Diapers are there. I think these are his size, right?"

"I guess he's wet. I should change him." Iris didn't move to check the baby's diaper. Terrell was already working at the bottle. His sucking was strong and consistent as if he were not only drinking the formula but losing himself again in its familiar contents. His shoulders heaved once, twice, until his back wasn't arched. His tiny hands opened and closed across the fat neck of the plastic nurser. His eyes were still dewy from his brutal course of tears.

Carol watched Iris to see if the girl herself took comfort in the infant's respite. The teenaged girl looked down at the baby with only a mild acknowledgment of the baby's level of comfort, which waxed in direct correspondence to the diminishing amount of formula left in the bottle. Carol saw that Iris had little available kindness after her turmoil and with the consistent stinging of the soap upon her bizarre cuts.

After another moment, Carol left Iris in the room and went down the stairs and out through the front door, leaving the house to the night attendant. She walked next door and climbed to her second-floor apartment. She heard the television going in Rick's room. When she looked in, he was asleep. The TV movie was reaching its conclusion and police sirens increased to a remarkable, sharp crescendo. She turned off the set. The abrupt evaporation of decibels caused her son to stir but he did not wake up.

Saturday morning the women had assembled in the downstairs parlor for their meeting. Terrell was happy in his crib, batting bright, felt zoo animals which hung from a dowel duct-taped to the railing. Carol brought Iris down to join the group. "If he cries you can hear him on the baby monitor. We've got two speakers downstairs." Iris followed Carol into the front parlor, where there was a coffee urn on the sideboard. Carol gave Iris a coffee mug. "This is your personal mug." Iris saw that each woman was holding one of these oversized cups with the S.O.S. logo printed in red script across the white ceramic. "Just wash and dry it for yourself and keep it with your personal possessions. Take it with you when you leave. It's a reminder," Carol told her.

Iris looked at the new cup in her hands. It was a token she didn't think she would cherish when she was ready to leave the shelter. She walked over to the coffee urn and turned the plastic handle. She filled her mug and spooned sugar over the lip, spilling the silky granules into the waffle place mat, where she couldn't sweep it up with the palm of her hand.

A woman named Leslie was explaining her week to the group, reviewing the final days before she came to the shelter to get away from her husband. She listed events in the order of their specific chronology rather than for their shock value. Her husband had whacked her across the chops on Monday—but he never touched her again. Tuesday, Wednesday, Thursday, he refrained from using his brute strength.

"You were waiting for him to hit you another time? You came here when you couldn't stand it anymore?"

"No. I think he was finished hitting me."

"Then what?"

"He started to say things," Leslie said.

"He said things," another resident underscored the detail.

"Sure he did," a third woman said. "The episode's not over without his verbal say-so. She's cornered and he can say whatever comes into his head. She can't get her back up about it."

"She's knocked down."

"He hates seeing the damaged goods."

"Yeah, with her tail between her legs."

"He can be as vile as he wants. Isn't that the long saga?"

"That's right."

Carol was pleased by how well the group was running itself. She no longer had to prod them. Yes, their mates have said terrible things. Neutral words, words that normally have useful and productive meanings, can be defiled. An ordinary verb can be transformed by an act of violence. Rick was just a toddler. She had not yet cut his hair, ever, and it fell to his shoulders in golden ribbons. She brought a scissors and a fine-toothed comb outside to the wading pool where the hose was still filling the tiny luscious circle on the first hot day of June. Just that morning Carol had purchased the plastic wading pool at Kmart, tugging it loose from a nested stack of preformed plastic shells. She set it up in the narrow, fenced backyard of the duplex. The surface of the water shivered as a light breeze shifted directions. Its chalk-blue disc looked irresistible against the newly seeded grass which already needed mowing. The water churned from the hose until the bright vessel was brimming.

Carol decided to let the water heat up in the sun before

she let the baby get in, so she started to cut Rick's hair, saving a few of his long curls in a number-ten envelope.

Her husband came outside. He had been sleeping in the dark living room and the bright sun annoyed him. He visored his eyes with his hand, in a frozen salute to his wife.

"What the hell is this?" he said, looking at the wading pool. "That's got to be bad for the grass."

"Do you think so?"

"It's too full. That's a lot of weight on my grass."

It was Carol, herself, who had sprinkled the seed mix over the shabby patches in the lawn. "Oh, you think it will hurt the baby grass?"

"Dump it," he told her.

Her husband had no landscaping interests. Carol recognized his mood; he was going to pick a fight if he could find a reason. The novelty of the little pool was an easy target.

"I'm not going to empty it yet. Rick hasn't been in it."

"Let's put him in for a second." He went over to the sand box and lifted the toddler.

"Wait, the water's still too cold," she told her husband.

He lowered the baby into the pool, until he was immersed to his waist; when he sat down, the water was up to his collarbone. The toddler squealed with the abrupt sensation. He started to wail, then changed his mind. He splashed his hands and chortled.

Carol glared at her husband.

"What's the matter? You have a problem?" he said.

She kneeled by the side of the pool and sifted the water through a plastic strainer to engage the baby. Her husband walked over to her and put his hands on her shoulders. "Got a problem?" he said. She didn't answer his question.

Her lack of a comment finalized her husband's half-formed idea. He pushed her face into the water and weighted her neck with his forearm. She struggled. He kept her head under the water. She opened her eyes and saw her baby's chubby legs and bottom.

He let her up once.

"I can't breathe," she screamed.

He pushed her under again.

She tried to sit up but he had his weight against her. She saw her husband's hand reach for the strainer and he stirred the water near the baby. Carol took a little water down her windpipe. She coughed and took in more. "Breathe," she heard him saying.

"Go ahead. Breathe," he told her again.

The water in her ears didn't entirely cushion his voice, and she tried to gauge at what point he was in his typical arc of madness. He allowed her to turn her cheek to the side to gulp air, before shoving her under again. The baby tugged her wet ropes of hair whenever it drifted near him. She reached for his tiny foot to reassure him.

Rick strolled into the room with two boxes of doughnuts. He opened the boxes and put them on the sideboard, slamming down some loose dollars. He flipped open the boxes and stole two crullers before going outside.

The women closed in on the sweets and returned to their chairs.

"My husband said terrible things," the woman named Leslie repeated.

The circle drank their coffee and nibbled the sweets with the unselfconscious, let's-get-down-to-brass-tacks poise of NASA specialists or a corporate think tank as they initiate the critical phase of a serious discussion.

But Iris sipped the metallic coffee and shrugged. She said, "Well, what *did* he say?"

The women turned to look at Iris. She was rushing into it. She should give Leslie's problem a little more skirt. "I mean," Iris said, "if you want to tell us what he said—we're all *ears*."

The women watched Carol to see if she took offense.

Leslie looked back at Iris and told her, "He says I'm dried up."

Iris said, "That's not bad. That's almost got manners."

"No, honey. He says I'm as dry as a *bone*. That's different." Leslie leaned forward. "Like a desiccated morsel. Like a freeze-dried breakfast berry."

Iris blinked but she kept her eye-to-eye with Leslie.

"After the change," Leslie said, "I got sore as hell. I started to tear. I was bleeding. I had to avoid Roy until I healed. Then it would happen again the next time."

Iris remembered the sign outside the front door: "Nothing Is Permanent But Change." She didn't think this was the reference Leslie was making.

A resident told Leslie, "You need a patch."

"What's the point? Estrogen isn't the issue. Why rebuild a bridge between warring nations," another woman said.

"For your own sake. A patch is good for your general health, your heart, your posture—"

"He really call you that? Freeze-dried—"

"—breakfast berry."

The residents looked at the floor in a stunned meditation on the simile.

Iris understood, at last, that the women were discussing the mysterious, unpredictable humidity of the female zone. Maurice often remarked on this bloom of moisture when he tested her interest with just a little talk, his fingers prowling her neckline, his lips sucking her collar bone, until he started biting the caps of her shoulders.

These women were discussing a time line Iris had not yet imagined, nor would she ever need to. She stood up and went over to the coffee urn. Suddenly, the women started shrieking. Each one screamed by her lonesome, as if cued, until they had all joined in.

A common brown bat had squeezed through a cellar floor grate before their eyes. It found itself in the tight, crowded room. It dipped from one corner to the other, circling the crouched women, eliciting individual shrieks. It flew out the parlor door. The group ran after it to see that it didn't enter their own rooms. It flew up the stairwell, where it became trapped in the second-floor hallway. It pumped its wings, a ratcheting, erratic W. It turned up and down in the confined space without touching lintel, doorpost, or ceiling. The bat's expert maneuvering seemed proof of its mysterious gifts. Its weightless reversals in flight were an attraction to the women; and yet, their attraction only heightened their repulsion.

Two of the residents were truly frightened and together had wrapped themselves in the full-length drapes, winding the fabric tight until they looked like a shivering cigar. Others locked themselves in their rooms and called out their nervous inquiries through the hinges. Iris climbed the stairs to her room and was laughing in her doorway. When the bat flew past her she tried to whack it down with a foam slipper.

It escaped past Iris and flew into her tiny room. It was clinging to the rolled window shade above the baby's crib. Iris wheeled the crib away and Carol stepped up to the window to remove the child-guard screening. She pushed down the window sash to release the bat, but it clung to the rolled vinyl. Carol saw its diminutive rib cage heaving as it breathed through its tiny nostrils. The bat didn't escape into the sunlight but flew back into the hallway. By the time they followed it out of Iris's room, it was out of sight.

"It's gone," Carol announced. The women protested. The evidence was inconclusive; they claimed they could not rest until they had seen it banished or had its actual carcass as proof. For another half-hour they sorted through the throw pillows, opened all the cupboards, knocked the tin wastebaskets, and carefully jimmied open bureau drawers. The flying rodent had vanished. Iris wasn't alarmed and she borrowed nail polish from an Irish girl in order to paint not only her fingernails, but the tiny gray wafers of her toenails. The glowing red polish had an artificial cherry scent. She told the girl who gave her the polish, "This is the first time in ages."

"Yeah. We forget we have toes."

Iris agreed. She had neglected these extremities, letting her nails blanch and chip, ignoring her cuticles until a thin membrane grew over the half moons on all her fingers. Having long fingernails didn't advance the diapering routine and interfered with other services she was constantly required to do for Terrell, whose own fingernails were difficult to clip. She had to nibble his fingertips to remove their ragged ends.

· · ·

Carol sent Rick to the True Value to buy some screening for the cellar windows. He spent Saturday afternoon in the alley between the two houses cutting measured oblongs from a roll of screen and tacking the mesh to the old casement windows. The cement walk was warming in the sun and he didn't mind lying down on it to tack the mesh to the hard-to-reach moldings. The window casements had substantial dry rot and dissolved into powder where he hammered. He moved the tacks around to find solid wood.

The women had opened the upstairs windows for air and he could hear their conversations, their kids chattering. He placed his Panasonic on the concrete beside him and turned up the volume. The station he usually listened to wasn't airing his New Wave favorites and was holding forth with "a full day of Gaye." He tacked the screen.

The girl with the blond hair stuck her head out of a second-floor window and said, "Can you shut that fucking thing off."

He sat up and leaned back on his hands to look up at her. She didn't appear as beautiful in the daylight as she had looked in the street light, but she was beautiful. She sat against her windowsill, her hip jutting over the ledge, her baby in her lap.

"You putting screens on those windows?" she said.

"Just about done," he told her, feeling his face glow. He looked down at his tools and lined them up another way. He waited to feel the heat in his face wash away before looking up again.

She was telling him, "You sure that bat is gone? You might be locking him inside instead of keeping him out."

"I'm doing what they want." He pointed to the office window on the first floor.

"Nobody saw that bat leave the house."

"I guess you'll find out."

She chuckled.

Rick recognized the idleness in her voice. She was enjoying her respite. Lots of these girls liked talking to him in the first days after they arrived at the shelter. They're chatty and friendly in their little oasis; then they get restless. If no one shows up to protest their absence, they think they have to turn around in their tracks. They start to miss their own surroundings and they run back home. This girl was dangling one leg out the window, swinging it back and forth, as if she was sitting on a school wall. Her baby was scrubbing his gums with a hollow plastic rattle like a tiny white barbell, teething on it.

"What's your baby's name?"

"Terrell. If he was a girl, you know, her name would have been Tammi."

Rick said, "No kidding?"

"Did you see *Essence*? It's all about what happened."

He told her, "That's a story, I bet."

"I hate Marvin Gaye," she told him. "I could write his epitaph. I'm just about a Motown widow myself."

Rick shrugged.

"It couldn't have happened soon enough for me."

Rick didn't punch the button on the radio and the music she loathed drifted up to Iris; it was Gaye's famous erotic anthem: *"Get up, get up, get up. Wake up, wake up, wake up."*

"I hope he rots in hell," she said.

Rick was surprised by her voice; its natural timbre suggested a plaintive, desolate truth. He looked up to the second-floor window to somehow acknowledge it, but she was gone.

Where the girl had been lounging on the sill, dangling her leg, her baby was left by himself, hunched in a jumbled position.

Rick stood up. Terrell was centered on the ledge, crumpled over in his terry suit. The baby appeared to be a complete amateur as he practiced the seated posture, his spine still too weak, and yet he didn't fall backwards or forwards. The baby held the plastic toy, hitching his fist up and down until Rick heard the loose particles inside the rattle. The noisemaker, alone, appeared to be the magical counterweight which kept the baby from falling.

Rick hollered up at the window but the girl did not come back to collect the child. He wondered why the child guard had been removed in the first place. There was nothing but open space between the baby and an entire spectrum of chances and fortunes.

Rick hollered again. No one came to the open window. Then, he watched the rattle fall from the baby's fingers and bounce off the siding. Like a white bone, it tumbled end over end, and hit the pavement.

He saw the baby tipping and Rick lifted his arms. He waited to intercept the bundle of chaos, to cushion the terry-clad icon of man's entire mortal profile, condensed in a split second, but someone pulled it off the window sill and slammed the sash. Rick stooped over to collect the plastic rattle. His heart was thudding. His chest felt tight and he recognized the sensation of his airways pinching shut. He walked over to the apartment for his inhaler. He sat on the edge of his bed and puffed the medication.

When he came back outside an hour later, he was just in time to see a familiar procession. The blond girl was leaving the shelter with her baby, accompanied by two other women. The women had arrived by taxi and they were helping the girl put the baby's safety seat in the cab. Rick still had the baby's tiny white barbell and he walked over to the car. He stood beside the taxi until someone noticed him. He handed the rattle to the nearest black woman, who handed it to the next one, who then handed it to Iris. Iris put the rattle in the baby's hand. One of the women wore the familiar *Thriller* T-shirt which Rick had seen everywhere that spring. Each time he saw the solitary glove, its disembodied hand modeled by all sizes and generations, the day acquired a forlorn tinge.

"Maurice is awake," Vicki told Iris, as if this was his ultimate gesture of a reconciliation.

Iris sat down in the backseat. She held an empty S.O.S. coffee mug on her knee. She saw Rick and called to him, "Hey, kid, can you give this back to your mom?"

Rick didn't want to be called "kid" when the girl was his own age, or younger, yet he sensed she was many dangerous miles ahead. He wanted to ask her why she had carried the cup outside in the first place, but he knew that Carol would gladly pass it on to the next one.

When he leaned into the taxi and took the mug from her hand, Iris could smell his breath, a tart medicinal odor which she found to be slightly disturbing. She recognized the scent from a previous trip to the hospital, when they gave her a drug and tested the congestion in her lungs on a Peak Flow Meter.

The taxi left the curb. The driver had tuned his radio to "a full day of Gaye," and Iris immediately recognized the iced crooner's sonorous murmur as he delivered his lyrics with silky pathos. This particular song had always crossed over the color line and was doing it again, tweaking her pink heart. Gaye whispered contrite, universal admissions to his female chorus, who replied in a breathy I-told-you-so singsong.

Rick was smiling at Iris, but she was riding away. The cab passed the entrance to the Stop Over Shelter and she read the sign with its foolish sentiment that seemed to openly misconstrue human failure for human promise. Such a banner was hurtfully misleading. Iris had told Carol during her intake interview, *"Change.* Find me something hopeful in that."

"Embrace it as your starting place," Carol had said, her eyes heated and luminous, as if lit by the pyres of the martyrs.

❖ EXCHANGE STREET

They were living in Providence again after spending the summer in Wildwood, New Jersey. In Wildwood, Stephen worked on a fishing boat, a deep-sea charter named the *Pied Piper*. It was a bad name for a fishing boat, since it made people think of rats in the water. Families and businesses hired the boat for reunions and other celebrations when their members wanted to reaffirm their brotherhood. Occasionally, someone brought his wife along and it was a sore spot with the others. After a couple of weeks on the boat, Stephen's burn turned deep bronze and he oiled his arms and chest every morning to enhance muscle definition.

While Stephen was on the boat, Venice worked at the

Acme supermarket, which was giving double pay for inventory; then she stayed on to stock the shelves there. She'd been working an act on the boardwalk but Stephen wanted her out of that line of work. Venice agreed it was better to stock canned goods in Acme than to earn your money as a spectacle.

They both had problems at their jobs. Venice wasn't careful with the Exacto knife when she opened cartons and she slit the boxes of cereal and crackers. Laundry soap sifted over the floor. Then she ruined crates of coffee and cigarettes and was caught when she tried to throw the damaged cartons in the Dumpster in back of the store. Stephen fared a little better in his job. He knew when to tell the captain to head in because of rough weather. He watched the clients getting queasy and they docked just in time, so that the people were seasick on shore instead of getting sick on the boat. He wouldn't have to hose the deck and gunnels. He didn't get along with the people who hired the charter. He was called a first mate, but they treated him like a slave. He had to fetch them cold beers, bait their lines, scale the catch, and the tips were sometimes insulting. At the end of the summer, just as the schoolkids started buying notebook paper at the Acme, Stephen and Venice left their jobs. They prowled the tourist attractions at Atlantic City before going back north.

Whenever Stephen was out of work he suffered an unpleasant mix of feelings. He had some anger about not working even if he himself had resigned, writing a short note to the boss, explaining that the work just wasn't his "cup of tea." Crewing for the *Pied Piper* was seasonal work, and when he was dismissed he took his freedom seriously and wasted none of it. He approached Venice three and four times a day, and when he wasn't in that privacy with her, he was leading her somewhere else, strolling down the tide line or through the alleys behind the hotels searching for another place where it would happen again. Atlantic City was a perfect town for him. Outside the glitzy façades of the boardwalk and betting parlors, everyone minded his own business. No one talked to them except for the occasional hick who had to explain his lucky streak to passersby. There were losers everywhere, and this gave Stephen a combined sense of doom and gratitude. He wasn't at the bottom. He was between jobs. He still had a wad of cash. After a week of roaming around, he got nervous again. He became cranky thinking about jobs. "I'd rather be digging a ditch than nothing," he said.

Then they were back in New England. They found a furnished apartment on the fringes of College Hill, where the rents edged down near the Chinese section. Stephen liked to blend with the dispossessed; it was live and let live, and he was happy not to see all the university students nosing around. They found immediate employment, both worked days and they had the nights together.

Venice worked at Industrial National Bank, in credit card operations. Her job was in the Customer Service Department and she was on the telephone all day. She retrieved credit card statements on her computer, consulted celluloid microfiche or daily printouts. The telephone was heavy in her hand, like a clot of hot tar resting against her cheek. The tendon of her thumb became sore after pressing the receiver to her ear for eight hours, and she often had to stop to wiggle her thumb as if she was playing "Thumbelina." Credit card customers called in to complain about their MasterCard accounts. A cardholder screamed at her about his trip to Mexico, where a hotel had submitted erroneous charges for numerous Papaya Softees and other blenderized drinks. He wasn't paying for drinks he never had. Venice listened to the customer, but she couldn't keep from questioning him about these Papaya Softees. What did they taste like?

Women called in to ask about charges on their statements which they couldn't identify. The charges might be for "Fantasy Phone," "Date Lite," or "Miss Paula," all dial-a-porn operations which the women's husbands or sons had contacted. Venice liked to advise her customers to have a "family powwow." "Bring it all out in the open," she told them. When her customers complained about their Master-Card errors, Venice told them to use cash instead of plastic. There was the matter of the finance charges: twenty-one percent, accrued daily from the day the charge is posted to the account, before the customer even received a statement. "With plastic you lose your dignity. It's out the window," she said.

Venice enjoyed finding the microfiche that had her ex-lover's statement. It pleased her to read the list of businesses and to see just where he was putting his money. She could tell by her ex-lover's purchases that he was certainly not someone to have second thoughts about, and the little bits of information revealed in the billing was affirming to Venice. She reported to Stephen that her ex had charged items at The Gentleman Farmer, a fancy garden-supply store for suburban types. "Shit. He's changed his stripes, you know that? He's scared himself completely into squaresville. He's backed into a corner."

They laughed about it. Sometimes her ex's new wife would make charges at clothing stores called Ample Beauty and Added Dimensions.

"His wife can't lose those pounds," Venice told Stephen.

Even with these few laughs, the job in the credit card department was bad and she was always looking for something better. Stephen was at Sears, in the key center. He made keys for housewives who had had recent close calls locking themselves out of the house or locking their babies in the car. They came in to get backups, and they watched him carefully to make sure he wasn't making a key for himself. Sometimes landlords Stephen recognized came in to get keys made. They said, "Are you still in town? Didn't you ever graduate from the university? You're at Sears?" When he wasn't making keys, he was in kitchen appliances; sometimes they even made him sweep something up. Stephen wasn't too happy about his position and together they looked at the Sunday paper.

There were always ads for couples in the paper. Couples were sought to run group homes and halfway houses for the retarded, for substance abusers, or for the elderly. Venice didn't like the idea because it usually required residence in a place and the shifts were three days on, then three days off. She believed that kind of a cycle was disorienting. "You have to keep an overnight bag all the time. You have to sleep there with those kids," she told Stephen.

"It's worse to eat with them. They slobber," he told her. "It's like living with monkeys."

"That's probably not for us, even with my experience."

He looked at her and smiled at her joke.

. . .

Before anything better came up, Venice had to quit her job at the bank. She couldn't sit at her desk after she had had some reconstructive surgery. She tried using a rubber donut, but the pillow didn't help much. She couldn't sit because of the stitches. Worse than the stitches were the spasms. The doctor told her the sphincter would take a little longer to heal. As it healed, the stitches would trigger spasms. He told Venice that her body was having a spastic response to trauma. "It's trying to tell you something," the doctor said. "The natural contractions of the colon are solely for expulsion, it won't tolerate invasive friction."

The urology intern wanted to consult with her and Stephen. He said, maybe it was time to take another step towards their lifetime investment. The previous year, when Stephen had worked as a dealer at Merv Griffin's Resorts Casino, he was able to put Venice on his insurance. Venice had some initial procedures done, implants and hormone therapy, but insurance complications postponed the final operation. Venice didn't qualify as a spouse. It was a catch-22. Venice needed further surgery before she was card-carrying.

Having had some more time to think about it, she wasn't a hundred percent certain she wanted it done.

The doctor who repaired her rectum told Venice, "In every law of engineering there's the female and the male, the outlet and the prong. Until you have the right connection, you're in harm's way. How long are you going to be a banged-up decepticon, getting it in your sore ass?"

"That's nice language," she said.

"My apologies. But, with more surgery," he told her, "you could have the correct 'receptacle.' "

"I can wait for that," Venice told the doctor.

"You're halfway there already," the doctor said.

"Just tell the boy not to jump me so much."

"I'll tell him to go easy for a while," the doctor said, but when Stephen came to visit her in the hospital, the urologist was missing. His shift was over.

Venice stayed home for several weeks enjoying the apartment, letting her hair air dry, playing solitaire on the carpet while the TV hummed at her shoulder. Now and then, she experienced an overwhelming, narrow edge of pain slashing the same few central inches. She fell, twisted on the rug, and tried to breathe, then it would pass. It happened less and less and she began to feel better.

Being out of work, she had time to cellophane her hair and she did a full body wax. She rubbed estrogen cream on her upper lip and applied it to her nipples, massaging in a circular motion. Being at home so much made her see the flaws, the grime and stains of the place. She started to think she should fix up the apartment the way other women might try to do. The wallpaper in the kitchen depressed her. The pattern had dark vines upon which small tobacco-colored leaves seemed to wither. It was an ordinary ivy design over uniform bricks, and it might have been meant to reflect autumn, but it suggested a wasted landscape. The wallpaper reminded her of an O. Henry story she read in high school in which a sick girl stares out her window at an ivy-covered wall. This girl is dying and as the ivy disintegrates and the leaves drift past her window, her days dwindle down.

"How many days do we have left?" she asked Stephen,

but he didn't go along with it. Alone, she counted the ivy leaves on the wallpaper. She jotted the figure on a note pad so that on the following day, when she counted the leaves again, the figures could be contrasted and verified. Each time, Venice had a decreasing number. "It's spooky," she said.

"You're crazy," Stephen said.

While she wasn't working, she borrowed a heavy book of wall-covering samples from a hardware store, but she didn't find a pattern she liked. There were outlandish daisies, harsh plaids, cannons and militia, historic emblems, and baseball-team insignia. Painting over the ivy design might be the thing, but when she asked Stephen, he told her she was crazy to think he was going to pay for fixing up the apartment. "We can't afford any face-lifts on our pad. Shit. We don't own this property. Come back and talk to me when you can tell me we own something."

It was disheartening to stay in the apartment all day. She got up with Stephen and poured cereal in a bowl, or she boiled an egg. Then he was gone and she had the whole day. She looked out the window, pressing her forehead against the cold glass. On the street, a neighbor was scraping frost from a car windshield. A cold daylight was ascending, a neutral illumination or off-whiteness Venice associated with views from inside institutions. Her neighbor finished clearing off his car and she watched him get behind the wheel, she followed the small hesitations the car made as he drove it away. Sometimes, her friend Jeannie would come by. Jeannie worked for a realtor and often dropped in if she was in the neighborhood. Venice made her tea and they talked about finding a decent job. They listed the pros and cons of working behind a desk or having to stand up all day like they did when they attended Top o' the Morning Beauty College.

"I can't wear more than a two-inch heel or my back starts to hurt," Jeannie said.

"That's right," Venice said, "beauty college ruined us for life—standing over those sinks."

"I only do Bobby's hair anymore," Jeannie said.

They looked out the window at the snow beginning to come down.

"Shit," Jeannie told Venice. "I have two signs to put up and it's murder when the ground is frozen. The posts have to be pounded into the ground or kids pull them out. In cold like this I can't drive them in."

Venice asked her if she wanted any help. She imagined hammering "For Sale" signs around the city. She believed that the brutal percussions of banging posts into the frozen ground might reverberate into her colon stitches. Her friend didn't think it would look right if Venice came with her. "Face it, Venice, you attract attention."

"I do not. I pass anywhere. Did I tell you I went to mass? Nothing. Not one double take."

"Maybe. But I remember the old days, I guess. When you were you."

Venice was feeling better and she took a part-time job transporting a carload of pets—cats, lap dogs, and several rabbits—to local nursing homes. Residents were encouraged to hold the animals for an hour, and after the hour was up, Venice collected the pets and put them back in their travel cages before driving to the next place. Venice accompanied a social worker who explained to her the purpose of the petting routine. "Stroking furred animals increases circulation, stimulates conversation, and generates a feeling of well-being. Holding a cat for just an hour every week can enhance short-term memory and cognitive function."

"No kidding?" Venice said. Before distributing each of the shaggy guests, she ruffled their coats. She figured she could use a boost herself.

Several residents in the nursing homes had had ministrokes and TIAs which left them confused and shaken. The petting routine worked directly on their neurological pathways, healing the damaged synapses. Venice realized that she, herself, often stroked her fluffy slippers absent-mindedly as she watched TV. She wondered if this provided the same benefits as the live animals.

Residents had specific names for the pets, but these names always changed. Fluffy, Whiskers, Snowball, Inky—residents named the animals for pets they had once owned. The MSW told Venice she should try to remember the correct names if she could. One rabbit had acquired more than twenty names; it was one of the original subjects. One favorite pet was losing its fur, probably from a skin disorder, but the residents blamed each other. "Don't scratch its withers like that," one woman scolded another. A resident told Venice that she didn't wish to hold the rabbit with "the sad ears."

"Which one is that?" Venice asked.

She had a nickname for her job. She told Stephen as she left for work, "I'm doing a shift at the Final Frontier." Yet there were one or two individuals at the nursing homes whom Venice enjoyed seeing. An eighty-year-old named

Abby amused Venice with her stories. She talked about her children with curdled disdain. If questioned about her offspring, she responded by saying, "They're inhuman. One-celled organisms. Termites, at best." It's remarkable, Venice thought, how Abby had come to accept the truth of her situation. Other residents made excuses for their children.

Her own father was in Florida. The last time Venice saw him, he was dressed like an ice cream vendor. White stretch-belt slacks, creamy socks, and white imitation gator-skin loafers. She didn't recognize him. She wondered if he would end up in a place like the homes she visited. She couldn't imagine her father holding a rabbit in his lap. He had success with cats because he ignored them and they couldn't stand his indifference. They perched on him like parrots. Yet, Venice couldn't imagine her father forced into a structured routine, petting cats because a doctor prescribed it.

Abby complained to Venice that there weren't any real cottontails amongst the pets.

"Cottontails are too wild for a petting zoo," the MSW said.

"Peter? Wild?" Abby said. "Peter Cottontail is a pansy. Ask my daughter, she married him." Abby cupped one side of her mouth with a papery, translucent hand. She leaned close to Venice. "My daughter says Peter can't perform. Well, I told her Brer Rabbit was the better one, but did she listen? God's gift to women, I told her. He had one longer than his ears—"

A neighboring oldster searched through the fur of her pet. "I can't find it," she said.

"You never could find it," Abby stung the wrinkled deb. Everyone laughed with an edge.

Abby told Venice, "I know about you—I won't tell anyone."

Venice described her job to Stephen. He smiled, but he told her she should resign. "It doesn't pay *shit*," he said, emphasizing that last consonant to warn her that he meant what he said. "It's for volunteers," he said.

Venice quit the job after receiving only two small pay checks. "It's not worth the glimpse into the future," she told Stephen.

Stephen kept on at Sears, and at first he didn't seem to mind being the only one holding a job. Maybe it was just her imagination, but Venice started to think he resented her time at the apartment. He came home from work and brushed by her, saying, "Kind of a mess. You could've done something."

"What's wrong with it?" She didn't see a crumb or a milky tumbler left out.

"It's a dump," he said. "I guess you're used to it."

"What does that mean?"

He ran his finger down the full-length mirror in the bedroom. "You're smoking too much. There's tar on everything."

"There's tar? Where?"

"Nobody should have to live like this," he said. He picked up her hairbrush and fooled with his short, blond hair. Venice looked at Stephen. Sometimes he seemed to mirror, quite perfectly, the overall costume of a white supremacist. His cornflower eyes, his fine profile looked chilling. He had a perfect crease in his trousers, which he pinched between his thumb and forefinger to keep fresh. This mannerism disturbed her more than any other.

He fell back on the bed. He arranged both pillows behind his head and he looked at his fingernails. She didn't know whether she should lie down beside him, since he had taken both pillows and perhaps this was significant. She sat on the edge of the mattress and looked at him.

"Why don't you clean the bugs out of that lamp?" he said. "It's disgusting."

She looked up at the dark plate of insects on the ceiling fixture. She was embarrassed by the sight of it, but it was just another thing for him to mention. The frosted glass revealed small bodies and exaggerated wings. Venice found these winged corpses repulsive. "Those bugs were there when we moved in. I'm not touching it."

"I'm saying, clean it out."

"You think when I get rid of my gear I'm the housewife? You wash it yourself."

He was reading the job opportunities out loud to her. There were several openings in local jewelry factories. "That's all assembly-line stuff," he warned her. "You might have to insert itsy-bitsy earrings onto little squares of cardboard all day long, or maybe they'll make you sort links of chain. Millions of links. Also, there's some chemical hazards. Epoxy. Epoxy is wicked shit."

"Okay, okay," she said.

"You're not desperate. Not yet," he said.

She didn't like it when he said *you're* not desperate. Shouldn't he have said, *we're* not desperate?

When they didn't have the capital to invest in a Payless shoe-store franchise, Venice suggested the Del's Lemonade truck idea. She thought it would be pleasant to drive around the beaches and sell frozen lemonade; the citrus SnoCones reminded her of the Papaya Softees she had learned about at the bank job. She had always liked the Del's vendors she had met. They stood at the window, tanned and friendly, with a little white swatch of zinc oxide across the bridge of their noses.

"It's the middle of winter," Stephen said. "Wake up to reality." He didn't often use such clichéd speech—*wake up to reality*. He was shooting her a signal, implying that she was dipping to a low level in his eyes, she was bottoming out. She deserved these phrases.

She went for an interview at a fish-processing plant down in Newport. It was a half-time position, dependent on when the huge offshore boats came into port to offload, but the salary was above average and they said she could work day or evening shifts, however she wanted. The plant was right on Narragansett Bay, where there was a nice view of both the Newport and the Mount Hope bridges, and she thought that working by the water might be invigorating after being in the apartment. A woman gave her a tour of the plant, which was built right against the shore where they could suction seawater into the operation and spew it out at the other end. Fish kept moving up and down fast-moving belts. The job didn't appear difficult. She would arrange fish fillets in plastic trays and prepare them for freezing. Venice was ready to accept the position. The interviewer told Venice that, of course, all her initial medical costs would be reimbursed.

"You mean I get back on insurance?"

"We pay your medical appointments the first six months."

"Just six months?"

"Most people don't have too much trouble after the first few weeks. We pay for any prescriptions you might get."

"What kind of trouble are we talking about?"

"It's normal until you become desensitized."

"Shit, what are you trying to say—"

The woman sighed, she saw she was losing her candidate. "Just a rash. A rash from the brine. Even with rubber gloves, you'll get some kind of reaction. But after you get used to the brine, it's clear sailing."

Venice had jumped at the news there might be insurance, but it wasn't to be. The processing plant would pay for office visits and cortisone cream, nothing more. She didn't want to arrange fish in plastic trays if it meant her skin was going to erupt. When she told Stephen about this, he looked at her as if she had made up the story about the brine.

"I'm not lying," she said. "You think I don't want to get a job? I want to work. I want to bring in money, but not if it gives me a rash—"

"Maybe you have an allergic reaction to anything that's *nine-to-five*." He might have been teasing her, but he walked away. With his back to her, she couldn't tell if he was finding fault with her or not. He came back into the room and took her hand. He led her to the bedroom, where they lay down together. He wanted to enter her where her stitches tugged her sphincter together like a sausage casing. Venice told him, "I'm probably going to faint, you understand?"

"You're not going to faint." It wasn't a reassurance, it was more in the nature of an order. He rested the heel of one hand on her tailbone as he fitted himself inside her, then he gripped her hips. She felt the first slicing motion, then the full progression of his disregard. He weighted her upon her own pain and placed her worth in it. She permitted it to happen and believed in its judgment.

The lounge at the Marriott had solid brass doors. Venice had to polish the tarnished metal with industrial-strength paste. The lounge had a slimy fountain. Two cherubs squirted a few gallons of stale water to which Venice had added a half-cup of bleach to cut down on the algae. It wasn't a great place to work, but she was making tips along with the free stuff she crammed into her oversized shoulder bag. She was waiting tables in the lounge and pushing the carpet sweeper over the floors. A vacuum would have done a better job, but the carpet sweeper was more discreet.

The hotel was always busy with conventioneers since it was located only a couple of blocks from the Providence Civic Center. Washington Street whores had duplicate keys to the rooms, which caused the chambermaids trouble because the cleaning personnel were the first to be accused of any thefts. This was bad enough, but it was also the hotel where the New England Patriots stayed on the nights before home games. They showed up in their limousines and sports cars at the last minute before the curfew. They had to follow a pregame diet of some kind, but they often took racks of ribs into their rooms from House of Bar-B-Que and left a big mess. They came into the lounge for fruit juices and Cokes; they weren't allowed to spike their drinks when it was a pregame countdown. The lounge filled up with Pat fans and groupies leaving their fingerprints on the brass doors she had just finished buffing. These trashy women ordered drinks but tipped cheap in their search to glimpse a quarterback.

Venice had been doing well there for over a month. The hotel had a big carve-up of the city's local ass peddling, and once or twice she was mistaken for a business girl. She sympathetically declined, pleased to see she was passing. Once or twice someone had her number. A man said to his pal, "Look at the grand duchess behind the bar." Venice was peeling the rind from limes and lemons to make twists. Her fingers were long and delicate, but her hands were just too large, and despite her pretty face and all her toil and grooming, it was usually her hands that told the tale.

They had the Providence *Sunday Journal* and their pencils. They didn't talk to each other as they read the tiny print and marked the descriptions of possible jobs. Venice looked over at Stephen and watched his eyes descend one column and then another.

"Here's something," Stephen said, and he brought the newspaper up close to his face.

"What?"

"This sounds good. It's right down the street. We could walk to work," he said.

"We can walk? Walk where?"

"It's a management slot."

"That same Walgreen's ad? They still want assistant managers?"

"No, the Cheaters Club on North Main. It says here, 'Couple wanted to manage club.' "

"That strip joint wants a couple?" she said. "Isn't that the place with the runway right up the bar? It has a wrestling pit with hoses and a drain?" She watched his face.

"They probably need people to manage the bar. You know, ordering liquor. The back room has video games, pool tables I think. We would have to keep that up. It's a small setup, really, it'd be okay. It would be mostly nights, don't you think? You'd have to miss *Letterman*."

"That place? Shit, that place is buzzing in the morning, for God's sake. They're loitering around in broad daylight. You ever been there?" she asked.

"A few times," he told her.

"That's a straight bar. I didn't know you ever went in there. Is that a twenty-four-hour place?"

"Hey, I looked in from the sidewalk," he said. "Tell me you haven't looked in."

"Never. I'm not interested in those 'happy girls.' Are you?"

They decided to go see the place before applying for the positions advertised.

Venice said, "I think I'm being pretty flexible, aren't I? Speaking for myself, I'd say that's an understatement. Shit, I'm burned out with sex clubs, aren't you?"

"Say the word, we won't pursue it."

She didn't say the word. She wasn't going to be a prude about it. "I'd like to talk to the talent," she said.

"Talent?" He laughed. "Shit, this isn't your premium drag palace, honey. Lower your standards. This is just a flesh room. These are mostly college kids who flunked out of their pastry arts class at Johnson and Wales cooking school. They're going to get more cash from one lap dance than they would get in their food service careers. These are wised-up Kelly Girls."

"And you want to be their boss?"

"They're self-governed."

"The ad says they want a couple?" she said.

"We're a couple. Since when aren't we a couple?" he asked her.

He knew what to say to her, but she was glad to hear him say it, just the same.

He told her, "Look, the mom-and-pop thing is just what these stripfests need to keep an even keel. We could do it. With your stage experience and my bartender's certificate, we're perfect. Like any bar, the money's in the alcohol. Difference being, the girls are walking around in thongs. It's just a public-awareness problem. We could improve that."

Venice didn't care about any girls wearing tired old thongs. She was curious about Stephen's sudden mood shift. The managing opportunity had electrified him after weeks in the doldrums. In order to decide what she felt, she needed to *see him* seeing the strippers. She wasn't ashamed of this.

The clientele was enough to make Venice turn right around. Pods of men wore orange hunting jackets and camouflage overalls as if they had just come in from the woods after blowing away a herd of deer. Venice sat down next to Stephen at a small table near the runway. She noticed her lover remove his jacket. He put the jacket in her lap. "Hold this," he told her. This alarmed her. He was settling in to watch the girls. He looked as if he were giving in to something, to an old ache. Once or twice he lifted his arms over his head to stretch, as if he was trying to curb his anticipation.

They drank some house bourbon. "This is like a razor," he told her. "I'll order something smooth for our regular stock." Then he pointed to an imitation Tiffany lamp that hung over the bar. "It's cracked, see? We'll have to replace that."

She put her arms in the sleeves of his jacket, but the lining was icy. Then the house lights dimmed and Stephen's face deepened. A spotlight fell on the stage and washed over Stephen's profile and farther into the crowd. The pale blue light reminded her of Atlantic City where she had performed at the Exchange Street Bar. She had been famous for her eclectic concentration of blondes: Carol Lynley, Jean Seberg, Tippi Hedren, Piper Laurie, Eva Marie Saint, even Peggy Lipton. She preferred the svelte examples and avoided cows like Monroe and Mansfield. Every night after her show, she went with Stephen as he shopped for boys on the boardwalk. Stephen trailed the local coin collectors who strutted their stuff until a juvenile curfew drove them inside. Venice watched their young faces change color under the purple bug lights—their skin looked unnaturally radiant and fuzzy like velvet pictures of Elvis. Stephen took his time with the kiddies, buying chances at arcades and shooting galleries, pinging a line of severely perforated targets to win jackknives and neck chains for the teens. He could pick and choose. Venice knew Stephen's routine as he slipped another trinket deep into a boy's pocket. Next came the cash, flashed open and closed like a dinner napkin, and the boy went home with them.

. . .

The show started. A girl executed a slow and delicate cartwheel onto the runway and into the circle of blue light. She was wearing a United States Olympic Team sweater. She danced to the right and to the left and then she did some somersaults. She made gestures like a swimmer and then she pretended she was throwing the shot put. She pulled the sweater over her head, and her breasts lifted higher and higher until the sweater was off and her breasts jiggled back to their appropriate level. The girl folded the sweater neatly and placed it to one side of the runway. She was naked except for a transparent g-string fashioned from ordinary panty hose.

"She's cute," Stephen said.

"Sort of," Venice said.

"No, I like the idea."

"What idea?" she asked.

"The Olympic theme."

"That's an old standard."

"If it ain't broke don't fix it."

Stephen was watching the stripper as if she was already in his stable. Her eyes seemed blank, like in archive photographs of sweatshop girls sitting at their sewing machines. She smiled haphazardly in one direction or another, into the dark. Soon the men started to give the stripper money. They inserted dollar bills in the girl's elastic g-string. Wary of paper cuts, she assisted them when they tried to poke the crisp bills in her muff. She stood at the edge of the bar and turned her back on the men. She bent over, touched her toes and waited. A man rolled a twenty into a tight tube and tucked it in her crack, but she had a glittered cork in her ass and he couldn't sink it.

Venice had expected to see just what she saw, but she

couldn't help reminding Stephen that in all her months on stage, she had never stooped so low as to be a mere coin slot.

Stephen was making a business appraisal, but Venice thought he should still hand this girl some cash. Her months on a runway gave her a feeling of solidarity with the plain-faced coed on stage. She didn't want the girl to think Stephen might be trying to get something for nothing. When the music stopped, the girl walked off the stage. There was scattered applause and a wave of lewd discussion about her. Stephen applauded the stripper. He said to Venice, "That girl is making a living."

"No kidding."

"I mean, she's doing something. *You* could work this hard for your money. *You* could do what she has to do," he told her.

"Hey, it was your idea for me to get out of it. I was happy at Exchange Street, but I don't want this end of it. I don't want to sightsee."

"You'll get used to it."

"I don't think so. I'm finished with these gropers and oglers."

"Well, I could do it on my own," he said.

"You want to work here every day for a living? It's not my idea of a real life's work." She looked at him. He was trying to look back at her, at her face, but he followed the next act. Then he turned to look straight at her. He told her she didn't have to be part of the plan, she might not be included in his decision making. He wasn't forcing her into it.

Venice recognized a threat. Since her surgery, she had lost her resilience to his icy warnings, they were harder to brush off.

"I have to use the ladies' room," she said. He nodded his head at her. He fondled his chin and rubbed his shave as he watched a new girl on the stage. He smoothed his palm over his face in a new dreaminess she hadn't seen before.

On her way to the lavatory she passed the dressing room, where the girls were arranging their scanty costumes. One of the girls looked up at her and smiled.

"Where's the john?" Venice said.

The stripper told her how to get to the lavatory and she warned Venice that one of the toilets didn't work. She told Venice which toilet she should use.

"We all use that one toilet," another girl said.

Venice thanked the girls, wondering at her inclusion in such an odd, protective detail. One stripper helped another get dressed. She used a pliers to tug a zipper. "Getting it up is one thing, getting it down is a scream. Every guy has to give it a shot," the girl said.

"Can they get it down?" Venice asked.

"Only after I'm stuffed with loot. Then I decide when."

"Oh," Venice was smiling, "it's a trick?"

"A technological miracle," the stripper said, "that's what I'd call it."

"There's a lot of science in this," one of the other girls said.

"It's not just bump and grind. It has to do with centrifugal force. Centrifugal force is behind every move you make."

Venice laughed, remembering that her basic high school science didn't prepare her for what really lay ahead.

"I bet you'd like to try it," one of girls told Venice. They all turned to watch her face.

"Maybe," Venice said.

"There's a cash advance if you decide."

"An advance?"

"Henry will give you a cherry popper. Two-hundred-dollar stipend on your first night."

Venice smiled at the word *stipend*. She recognized how these initiates might want to whitewash their everyday commerce with fancy words.

"In a little while, Cindy takes a shower."

"You take a shower out there?" Venice asked.

"About ten times a night."

"Hence the drain," Venice said.

"That's right, the drain. Who needs Liquid Plumr?"

"Forty dollars, they can soap us up. That's forty dollars *per customer.*"

Venice said, "I guess you really clean up."

The girls had heard this a lot.

Venice enjoyed the farce.

The one named Cindy unscrewed the cap from a big bottle of Spring Green Vitabath. She invited Venice to sniff the fragrant contents.

"That's nice."

"It costs me, but it's extra emollient. Five showers in here and your skin gets chapped. We have to look out for ourselves."

In the lavatory, Venice noticed the roach tape along the baseboards. She saw it the way an accountant follows the diagonal line through graph paper. For some reason she could not urinate. That part of her body wouldn't open. Her whole pelvic triangle was tender. She stood over the sink. A tiny mirror framed only her eyes. Seeing her eyes like that, without the rest of her face, was unnerving. Her eyes revealed something which her mouth, her lips would have erased with a quick smile.

She sat down beside Stephen. Another girl had climbed onto the runway. She said her name was Pepper. Pepper had red hair. She wore a minuscule g-string and she had combed her red frizz over the tight border of nylon. The men were calling her "Spicedrop" and "Fireball" because of her red hair. The men kept proposing new names relating to the combustion metaphor, drifting over to an arson theme, and everyone laughed. Venice thought of the rabbit with the twenty names. Stephen was laughing with the crowd, a short, disciplined bleat that was easy to discern.

She walked back to the dressing room. "Well. Where's this Henry guy?"

"He's in Atlantic City."

"No kidding? I was there last summer."

"So, you want to dance tonight?"

"That's right."

"You need to change into something. There's a rack of stuff in here."

Venice pulled the hangers across the rod until she saw a prom item, a floor-length gown in peach-colored satin.

She tugged the dress over her head and borrowed the lip pencil and mascara left out on the table. "You need one of these thongs," a girl said holding out a wastebasket full of panty-hose sashes.

"I don't need it," Venice said. "I'm wearing a string, à la Calvin Klein."

"You're all set?"

Venice was ready. "I'll go next," she said.

The music churned on. Venice flounced down the runway, swinging her hips and paddling the air with her forearms, breaking her wrists in haughty birdlike gestures just like Bette Davis. The audience seemed stunned by the sudden shift from the continuous nude mural to this higher plateau of *entertainment*. They chided the new "actress," for stalling. The men yelled at her to disrobe.

Venice started to peel the satin neckline off her shoulders, then tugged it back on. She rolled her shoulder free, then covered it up again. This went on for a while. She searched the bar rail for Stephen, but the tables were too dark to see him. She minced up and down the stage. Her fluid gait perpetuated a pendulum effect; she allowed her hips to slip left, then lock, slip right, then lock. She tossed her hair, wiped her bangs from her forehead with exaggerated pathos, like the crone in *Sunset Boulevard*. Again she looked for Stephen to see how she should proceed. Behind the runway, there was a screen with projections. Slides of sandy beaches alternated with slides of pinto horses. A single moth followed the cone of light back and forth, dipping from one end to the other. The insect landed on the screen, fanning its wings. Once it became the white eye of a horse, then the slide flipped and it was gone in the foam of the sea. The moth pulsed forward again. Instinctively it climbed the smoky column above Venice and its shadow grew monstrous against her.

❖ ASBESTOS

I t was dark at 5:00 P.M. The streetlight churned with large, boxy snowflakes like erratic frozen June bugs. Peterson watched the snow until buildings lost definition. He was meeting a client and waited in a company truck, a new wide-bodied 4×4 that made him feel pleasantly self-conscious. He was working for his brother at Dover Environmental Consultants. At his brother's request, he affixed a Dover sign to the passenger-side door, knowing it would leave an outline of adhesive when he removed it.

Last winter he had the snow-removal contracts for food franchises on Route 202 north of Wilmington. Then he worked on a crew clearing the Delaware Memorial Bridge. He plowed nights, driving back and forth across the double span, raising the blade at the little hitches at each expansion grid. Using guardrail posts as checkpoints against the dark industrial skyline, he knew when to elevate the blade and when to drop it back down.

The client was scheduled to meet him outside of the Glenside United Methodist Church. She would stop by on her way to work. She was hostess at the Fairfax Supper Club and had to be there by six. It might be just as well if she was a no-show, because the woman sounded a little too fired up; she wasn't going through the proper channels. His brother instructed him, "If she doesn't have anything on paper, say goodbye."

A car pulled in behind his truck and he was surprised to see it was an old Caddie, salmon pink. Then he recognized it, one of those used Mary Kay Cosmetics sedans; the chrome rims of the headlights were rusted out and lacy as garters. A rock must have hit the right side of the windshield leaving a shattered web a good foot in diameter. He watched her in his mirrors as she locked her car and walked slowly across the white scrim. She was wearing spike heels that didn't grab the snow. She walked carefully, with a delicate wobble, but she didn't seem threatened by the unpredictable surface. He focused ahead as she came up beside him. The snow was still light but it had a funny, gluey look as it touched the truck's glossy hood and layered the smoked windshield.

She tapped on the truck window. He turned, his breath rising on the glass. He was out of the truck shaking her hand in a quick tingling motion.

"Mr. Peterson?" she said, when he dropped her hand.

"No, not *the* Mr. Peterson. I'm his younger brother."

"And, your name is?"

"Peterson," he told her.

"Of course. How stupid of me," she said. She looked over his shoulder for a moment then looked at him again. "Angela Snyder. Angela," she said.

"Angela? That's nice," he told her. "Root word being *angel*, I guess." He looked the other way.

"Just another cross to bear," she said.

At the Halloween party at the firehouse just a couple of months ago Peterson had seen a little girl in a white satin costume. Her mother had written across the skirt with a gold glitter pen: "Daddy's Little Angle." Hardly a soul noticed the spelling error. Who was going to break the news?

"So it's Peterson, plain and simple?"

"Right," he said. He knew she had expected him to give his first name, but he wasn't happy to tell it to people. He was named after a middle child who had died in the cradle. He didn't trouble her with the story, but throughout his whole childhood he had to visit the cemetery and stand before the marker with his own name chiseled on it. He went by his last name only. The one name.

"No first-name basis?" she said.

He stared at the whorls of snow which collected and condensed momentarily into reassuring shapes, cartoon cats and rabbits, and then dispersed, sifting right and left.

"Well, I understand these things," she told him, "names are such a grab bag." She looked as if she was trying to decide if she was going to accept him instead of his brother, the certified inspector whom she had spoken to over the telephone. "You're an expert? Like your brother?" she asked him.

"My brother couldn't make it tonight. I can do the job, same as him."

"The big thing," she said, "is how to get inside. Just look at it, will you? This church is spooky when it's empty—sort of Gothic." She looked up at the high windows, which were an impenetrable slate-green.

Peterson said, "There's no one here to let us in? I thought it was funny not to see anyone. I don't know about this."

"It's locked. But it's to our advantage that there's no one here. You see, they think I'm a nuisance. I'm sort of eighty-sixed."

"You asked us to come out here unannounced? The place is dark."

"It's always dark somewhere. At any one time, half the world is dark—did you ever think of that? Does that stop the professionals?" She looked at the empty building. "This is the fellowship hall and the preschool wing. I know where the lights are once we get in there."

Peterson said, "Let's see if I understand this. There's nobody in the building? We aren't expected tonight?"

"No. But, Christ," she snapped at him, "it's not exactly an ice cream social."

"We have a problem here."

"Can't you get the samples?" she told him. "You don't need the pastor for that. Let's just take the dust and say no more."

"We told you we need something in writing before we take the samples," he told her. He noticed how he had switched to saying "we." He decided he wouldn't let that happen again.

She, too, changed her tone; her voice became more solicitous, girlish but firm, like a waitress running out of patience when sometimes he was too sleepy making his breakfast order. "Look, is it the money?" she said. "I'm going to have all the parents chip in once I explain the situation to them." She shook a tight leather glove from her left hand, using her teeth to tug it free. "Do you want me to pay now? I'll pay you in advance. I don't have anything on me, but I can get an advance from my boss at the Supper Club. I'm hostess there. I can get something like a down payment."

"Money isn't the first consideration. The problem is," Peterson was telling her, "you don't own this building. Am I right?"

"Correct."

"Need permission from the owner," he told her.

She lifted her shoulders and tugged the collar of her coat higher. She walked in a small circle before him. He watched her profile one way, then the other. There was something feral in the way she shifted back and forth before him. She was wearing a cranberry leather trench coat, open at the collar. Beneath that, she wore a deep V-neck sweater, something like mohair. The fluff against the crisp leather upset him. His sister-in-law sometimes wore sweaters like this, the feathery hairs rising and falling with her breath, or she'd wear a quilted satin bathrobe. Certain fabrics hitched and draped around a woman's curves— these odd textures, mohair or pillowed satin—made his abdomen clench.

His brother and sister-in-law took him in after his trouble at the dog track last spring. He had been hired to clean the pens. It was tedious work, scooping the loops of waste into a barrel and hosing the cement. He cleaned the drains, running a snake rather than using Liquid Plumr. Chemical solvents caused fumes to permeate the kennel. Kennel maintenance was the only work he could get after he had wrecked a big Massey-Ferguson plow and his urine test turned up a profile of cannabis-related enzymes.

He had worked at the dog track only two months when two men came into the barn. They walked directly into the pen with the ex-champion, Believe Me, a veteran brindle greyhound. The dog hadn't been winning for a year. Peterson was at the far end of the barn, teasing the string open on a bag of garden lime. If the men saw him, they didn't much care. He figured they were up to no good. The dog was overinsured. Its time was coming up. He heard one of the men talking to the doomed mutt, punctuated by the other's bitter chuckle. When Peterson walked over there, he saw a man cutting silver duct tape from a roll while his partner straddled the dog, resting one knee on its withers to keep it still. He pinched its muzzle as the other wound the duct tape around the dog's delicate, dished face until its chops were sealed shut. He wrapped the tape around its narrow snout, pressing a sticky strip across its glistening black nostrils. The dog reacted immediately, bucking loose from the man's legs, whipping its head right and left and pawing its face with its dewclaw hooks. The men turned away and lit up smokes. Peterson walked up to the pen. The men looked right through him. He was invisible. They were so secure in their fiendish system, they didn't expect interference. Not from him. The dog had fallen back on its haunches. Its eyes rolled back in its head, then refocused once. It quite suddenly reclined on its side and convulsed. Peterson started for the greyhound, but the men flicked their butts to the cement. One said, "Don't touch anything."

Later that summer Peterson was arrested for possession

of marijuana and his brother bailed him out of the city jail. His brother gave him work at Dover Environmental. Peterson took the job and tried to move to his own apartment. His sister-in-law went to inspect the rental property and found it unsuitable for him. His sister-in-law had the final word as surrogate matriarch or warden. He had to watch her drift around the house in her nightie and polish her toenails in front of the TV, bending her knee and resting her foot on the ottoman until the soft, creamy bulge of her inner thigh was revealed. She wasn't aware of him. He was nothing to her but a delinquent foster child.

He looked back at his client.

Her bare skin, the fluff, the leather. These gradations. Then it was the snow. The snow melted in a ragged necklace across her bare breastbone. She didn't seem chilled. She looked slightly overheated; the snow dotted her shoulders like the tepid icing on hot cinnamon rolls.

And she didn't dress like women who typically worried about the environment. He thought those women usually wore hiking attire or the floral Indian prints of hippie fashions. This Angela Snyder was wearing a tight skirt, above the knee, and a bright blue sweater, dense as rabbit fur, just like the hostess at a steak house was expected to look. He noticed that her hair was loosely permed—at home, inexpertly—and frosted in uneven patches. Her mouth, touched with pencil, made her lips oddly defined, dingy at the edges.

She pulled up from her circle and said, "Can you tell me one thing? Peterson, who owns a church? I mean, who *owns* a church?" She smiled. Waited. She looked utterly merry stating her point.

"You think it's funny?" he said. "Who owns a church?

It's like a knock, knock? Some kind of punch line? You should have squared this away before you called me out here."

"You? I thought it was going to be the other guy, your brother. He seemed to have some experience."

Peterson turned to get back in his truck. He opened the door and rested one foot on the rocker panel, lifting his hip so it rested against the high seat.

"Oh wait," she said, "I'm sorry. I'm not fooling around. I don't have the faintest idea who owns this church. It's some kind of congregation, right? Well, what about these asbestos fibers? Invisible. It's my little boy. It hasn't exactly been a picnic. Three years at the Fairfax Supper Club. First I was at Steak & Ale, now I'm at the Fairfax. One pay stub. I'm on my way to work now. Right after this. The hours. You should know my hours. And now, this *hazard*. This *risk*. I mean, maternal instincts. Instincts have a life of their own—" She kept talking until her explanation became wholly monosyllabic.

Peterson noticed how her breast heaved lightly after she was finished. Her delicate respirations suggested her feminine triumph. Her words coming fast, clipped, until it was severe litany—then her breathless calm. She had him going for a moment. He extracted a toothpick from its delicate white wrapper and poked it through his bottom incisors and sawed it back and forth over his gums.

"There's usually a board of trustees," Peterson told her. He was putting his key in the ignition and the dash lit up like a hospital wall. "Get in here with me and I'll tell you what I need before I go in that building," he said.

"Oh, really?" she said. She walked around to the other side of the truck but skirted the open passenger door. "Who do you think I am?" she said. She walked over to the front door of the church and tugged it with her bare hand. She put both hands on the brass pull and rattled the heavy panel.

He jumped out of the cab and told her she had misunderstood him. Then he saw she was laughing, pressing her one gloved hand over her teeth. Her teeth against the leather made a tight, squeaking sound.

He watched her while twirling the toothpick against his tongue, using his thumb and forefinger to keep it turning. "Shit," Peterson said, "I was going to explain the legalities. A church like this probably has a board of trustees. We need their consent before we can enter the premises and take away incriminating samples."

"They'll never let you."

"Sure they will."

"Trust me," she said. "It's now or never."

She started to walk away in the snow, following the slight troughs and indented lines on the sidewalk. He followed her around the building to the back. He saw the small playground, which faced the old church cemetery. He never imagined these two worlds could exist in tandem, one beside the other, the tiny jungle gym for toddlers and, twenty feet over, the rough, flinty slate of antique graves. Were these first and last groups harmonious or indifferent? He felt his scalp sting when he imagined the relationship might even be some kind of malevolent entanglement.

"See this playground?" she told him. He was already staring at it. "It's not up to standards, but I found out where to get free sand. The sand is supposed to be four inches deep to make a good cushion so the kids won't get hurt."

Peterson noticed the high ridges of sand, dunes of it,

capped with snow. He toed the sand and saw it was gray and gritty, like the stuff he'd seen at municipal ball fields. Flaked rock that got into your socks if you had to slide into base.

She said, "That's Vulcan's washed screenings from Vulcan Quarry. They give it away free to nonprofit organizations."

"You had them deliver it here? These washed screenings?" The name for it sounded absurd.

She told him, "The truck had a hard time getting around the gravestones to dump it here. The load was so heavy, they thought it might roll over an unmarked pocket—you know, a grave. The dirt would cave in. It was one more thing for the church to bitch about." She turned back to look at the dark building. "These are the classrooms, here, in this basement wing." She pointed to the preschool rooms. "These windows push out from the inside. I'll find one that isn't locked and we can pry it open," she told him.

"We're not going to destroy any property to get in there. If it doesn't come easy, that's it for me," Peterson said.

"Look, you say you're an expert? Well, you should know how important this is. All these babies, some still on the bottle, rolling around in asbestos."

"That's your guess, anyway," Peterson told her. "Why don't you find another day-care center for your boy? Why are you making such a hassle for yourself?"

"Do you have kids?" she said. "If you had some kids, you'd know."

"Who says I don't?" He didn't like her making these grand assumptions.

She told him, "Let me tell you something. Listen to me. When you have children, it's cash on the line."

"You make it sound rewarding," he told her.

"I mean it. I can't afford to pay professional day care when I already pay a sitter who comes five to twelve each night. You know what that runs? Plus the two-liter bottles of Coke she has to have. I'm just trying to steer my own ship. These asbestos fibers. You should know. Microscopic."

"You can't be sure it's asbestos, it's not proved yet," he told her, but the way she described it made him think of a barge with a hundred babies drifting into a sea of monolithic chrysotile structures.

Until this time, he had not experienced the subtle pressures of his job at Dover Environmental. His usual routine consisted, singularly, of light tasks. Cutting chunks of friable asbestos insulation from heating ducts and plumbing, brushing particle samples together, sealing them in plastic bags and shipping them off to a state-certified lab, where the materials were tested using transmission electron microscopy. Some days he set up the large three-horsepower fans for aggressive air samples. He wasn't involved with the testing procedures or the subsequent discovery of the facts. He never once envisioned a personal consequence, it was always general. It was for the health of the general public, the general upkeep of industry.

She told him, "This tile is probably thirty years old. It's totally abraded. Like cake flour, dense and weird. You'll see once we get in there."

She was checking the windows, trying to insert her fingernails under the aluminum moldings so she could tug. Everything was tight. Then she found a window that wasn't fastened. On the inside pane, yellow construction-paper ducks were taped in a neat row. She pressed her cheek against the glass, trying to inch it free; Peterson saw the little ducks behind her face. Peterson went over and jerked the window open. The entrance was at a hard angle and was hardly enough room for her, let alone for a man his size.

"I can't get through that," he told her.

"No kidding," she said, turning to look at him square. "Of course, I don't expect you to come through this window. I'll squeeze inside here, then I'll go around and let you in the door. You get the red carpet and don't have to rip your pants."

He walked a tiny, almost imperceptible box step when she spoke those words. When she turned away, he looked at her, following her legs until they disappeared at the hem of her coat. Her hair was loose and knotty beneath a melting crown. She looked back at him, making the okay sign with her thumb and index finger. He studied her but the snow started to come heavy, like a glittering fiberglass curtain between them.

He raised his voice to mask his rocky feelings. "Be my guest," he told her. "Climb in that window. It's not up to me. Breaking into a house of worship. Not every day I witness this sort of thing."

"Oh, don't be such a priss," she said. "I'll get in, and then you can come through the proper door. It's on my shoulders then, right?"

He rubbed his hand down his forehead and over the sharp, freezing tip of his nose. He was getting into something. Peterson tried to figure how he could run the tests at the lab without his brother knowing. He struggled to ignore the children, the way he pictured them, on the swing set beside the tombs, or on the drifting barge.

Perhaps it was the snow, the ice specks pumping around the streetlight that gave everything an unnatural surge. He was excited by the first weather of the year, and by this woman, who seemed to have put him in an obedient trance. He started to trust it.

As she climbed through the window, her coat snagged on something and the leather was gouged. She cursed, rubbing the hide between her fingers in the near dark. Then Peterson lost sight of her as she moved away from the window to find a light switch. He was out there in the churchyard, alone. He thought about Believe Me, the silver tape locking its muzzle shut. After ten minutes the men had gone back into the pen to unwind the metallic strips. They used a terry-cloth rag to carefully clean the short fur and whiskers on its refined, scooped face, to remove any telltale adhesive.

He heard Angela calling his name. He walked up and down the length of the building, trying to find her voice, his boots sliding through new ribbons of snow. Then she was taking his arm, pulling him through a side door. She led him down the hallway to the playroom, which was pitch-black, but he could smell the dust. He heard her as she patted the cement walls with her palms, trying to find the light switch. She touched it and the fluorescents fluttered on.

"See, it's everywhere." She twirled slowly in the center of the room. She pointed to the dusty corners, the glazed toys and tricycles. She ran her fingertip along the window ledge and showed him the lemon-yellow powder. "It's even in the light fixtures. They ride the trikes and it rises up this high."

He squatted down and rubbed the palm of his hand over the floor's surface. "Christ, this tile's completely abraded, porous."

"There's asbestos in this kind of tile, am I right?" she asked him.

"See that over there?" he told her.

"What?" she said.

"Those old shuffleboard inlays. You never see these anymore. That's from the 1950s. This is some old linoleum."

"Asbestos?" She looked at him. "Well. What are you waiting for? Get the samples. Get everything we need," she told him. Her eyes were glossy, triumphant and desperate in one halting gaze.

He suggested going for drinks. They had finished scooping up dust from little drifts around the legs of the playhouse and from underneath the foam mats near the wooden slide. "Let's go have something when we're done here," he told her.

She acknowledged his invitation. Her eyes rolled around once and returned to a businesslike squint. She pushed the side of her hand along the floor, making pie-wedge swipes through the dust. He was closing a plastic bag, turning a twist tie until it was secure. "How about it?" he asked her, but he didn't want to look at her to see if she rolled her eyes again. He was thinking that he had been ut-terly professional in his handling of the situation up until that very moment. Other than the fact that he was tres-passing, and stealing property, he was on the level. When she didn't answer him, he returned to the same, worn-out declaration, "I don't like taking these samples without the proper consent. In writing."

"Shit. The Lord is with us," she said, but she didn't say it with any reverence. She sniffed loudly and rubbed her nose with a bony knuckle, and he could tell she wasn't even thinking about God. Maybe the dust was making her eyes itch; her eyes looked accentuated, watery. Her eyes had that darty, intense style of watching him without seeing him.

Peterson told her, "This is enough dust, these four bags, but we've got to cut a sample of the tile. A sliver about an inch square."

He scored the linoleum and shoved it loose with the flat edge of the knife. She was bending down to watch him. Her lips looked bitten, crosshatched, when he saw them up close.

He put the plastic bags with the dust samples and the sliver of floor tile in his breast pocket. They left the basement of Glenside United Methodist Church, making sure the window was closed and the door was locked behind them.

She started to show her relief; her teeth chattered lightly as if, at last, the cold had touched her. They were sitting in the cab of his truck. She told Peterson, "He was breathing it, pretty as you please. It was everywhere. All over the trikes and Hot Wheels. You saw it. Not the best thing for a child."

"No, that's true," he told her, trying to calm her down. He turned the heat on full blast, hoping she would quiet, but she raised her voice over it.

She said, "I went to the preschool director. A fluff-brain. Then I met some church guy, whoever, and he said anytime there was kids, you had dust. He said, 'Kids make dust.' He twirled his finger in the air, you know, like a Dennis the Menace cartoon with the little whirlwind. Shit. Kids can't make this kind of dust. Thick as Bisquick, you know, like pulverized rubber."

"That's degraded linoleum. It's vile." He didn't know what else to say. He was embarrassed by her gratitude, the sudden, breathy hitches in her voice, strange tri-level inhalations which were new and wonderful to him. Perhaps he would tell his brother to step over the line and send the samples to the lab. Disrupt procedures. The business had to have a social conscience, didn't it?

Her teeth clicked together as she shivered. Her coat didn't fit her right, leaving her breastbone naked to the cold. He wanted to tell her she should dress for the weather. Instead, he took her coat and tugged it together, he folded the lapels, one over the other. Then he took the ends of her leather sash and yanked them tighter.

She looked at him. Her face had a strange expression. She looked like a person who was waiting to see if what she expected might happen. "Thank God you got the samples. This will prove it," she told him.

Peterson touched his Exacto knife to the shellacked oak bar at Emerson's Lounge, twisting its point until the wood flaked upwards in tiny resinous specks. His loose, black hair shifted back and forth when he jabbed the knife. He traced her hand with the blade, making a yellow line in the veneer between his beer bottle and her tumbler. She didn't move her fingers as he cut, leaving a wake of waxy dirt around her hand.

"Watch it, will you?" she told him.

The girl behind the bar came over to complain, but the mark disappeared with a swipe of her soapy rag. Peterson put the knife down and pushed it away until it rested on the rubber netting where some glasses where drying.

"So, we're here," he told her.

She didn't say anything, but her shoulders lifted and fell in comfortable acknowledgment.

He poked her arm with his pinky finger.

She twisted on her seat to shoot him a complicated look. An unfathomable expression—impatience tempered by bliss?

"When I asked for an asbestos consultant, a certified expert, I didn't expect to get you. The younger brother—what d'ya call it? The apprentice," she said.

"You're lucky I came out. My brother wouldn't touch this with a ten-foot pole. You don't have the correct papers squared away. You should be happy."

"I am. I really appreciate your help. That's why we're having this drink. In appreciation. I'm showing my appreciation pretty damn sincerely, am I right?"

"Well, it means something to me," he said.

She asked him if she could see the little plastic bags of dust. He placed them on the bar and she arranged them in a row and then in a diamond formation like miniature bases for a softball game. The girl behind the bar looked worried, as if the samples might be miscellaneous contraband, but Peterson explained. After a few moments, Angela allowed him to put the samples back in his breast pocket.

She was sipping scotch with small, reserved kisses to the rim of the tumbler. Peterson leaned against the bar and drained a bottle of beer, his third. Peterson stood up behind Angela's stool and saw an opportunity to insert his arms through hers. He took hold of her around the waist. He asked the bartender to make a pitcher of margaritas. Angela looked over her shoulder at him. "I have to go to work," she said.

"Go."

"Goddamn you, Peterson." She wasn't smiling, but she closed her eyes and didn't get off her stool.

Peterson wanted this woman to win her battle at the church. He wanted more time with her. These desires had no corresponding strategies. Each of these goals both heightened and impeded the other. If he didn't get the tests to the lab, he could ruin his chance with her. "You have to get those permissions from the church, we need the church consent," he told her. "What we did tonight was like the cart before the horse. We need a letter—"

"Oh, we don't need a letter now," she said.

"Do," he said.

"What are you saying?" she said.

"The lab won't run the tests without signatures."

"Can't you sign something? Now that we have the actual samples, can't you sort of send it through carte blanche?"

Peterson told her, "The dust remains a mystery. Mystery dust without the signatures."

"Mystery dust? What are you talking about?"

"Limbo," he said. "The dust is in limbo." He was touching his tongue to the hoary circle of salt on his margarita, dense, kosher crystals, a delicious mortar.

She lifted the glass out of his hand. "Are you saying you can't have these tests done, you can't put that dust in the electron microscope like your brother explained?"

"That's right. We can't send it through the lab without an official Bombs Away from the Reverend Four-Eyes, or whoever, at the church. But who says we can't go over there right now? Why can't we get someone to sign something for us? Tonight?"

He tried to imagine finding the right church official, rousing him from sleep or waiting until morning before knocking on the door, scooping up the man's morning newspaper and greeting him like that. How would he approach such a task? What would he say to enlist the fellow's support? He could describe the swing set beside the graves, the barge adrift in a chrysotile sea, this woman's torn coat, the pale hollow of exposed flesh where her lapels wouldn't close.

"Don't worry," he told her, seeing her tears cling, then slip from her lashes which were dense and skewed with dark violet mascara. He drew her close, moving her bar stool counterclockwise with her weight still on it, until he had her perched before him. "I'll take it straight through. Myself. Don't even blink—it's done. I've done it already, is how you should think. The results are in by tomorrow P.M.," he said.

"You will, really? Are you saying you'll get the tests?" she said.

"Transmission electron microscopy. Case closed."

She was drinking some of the lime concoction, pale as

dishwater and stronger than the usual. She thanked Peterson, thanked and thanked. He refilled her glass, soaking the bar with spills from the pitcher. She was leaning against him, her arm curled around his waist with her hand pressed into his back pocket. "We'll close down that fucking school until they get it cleaned up," she said. "We'll make them get new linoleum. All because of you, Peterson."

"If it was God. If it was just God we were dealing with here, the permission slip would be written," he told her. "Across the sky: *Proceed immediately with all four samples for possible asbestos content.*" That's all I would need, he was thinking. One measly sentence. Signed by God.

She was late for work when she drove away from Emerson's, heading for the Fairfax Supper Club. He stood in the snow and watched her Caddie fishtail too close to the parked cars before she got centered. "Take it slow, take it slow," he called after her.

He drove his truck back to the church. He saw the sign panel which announced the times for church services but it was covered with snow. He got out of the truck to brush off the glass. The snow felt wet, it wouldn't last through the next day. He read the faded letters naming the Sunday sermon: "Ancient Lessons for Modern Families." Beneath the sermon's title was the name of the church pastor: "Rev. Charles D. Moffat."

Peterson drove to the 7-Eleven and bought a paper plate of cheese nachos that microwaved too runny. He set it on the roof of his truck until the chips firmed up and the cheese gelled. He looked through the telephone book at a pay phone until he found an address for Reverend Moffat. It was just three blocks from the Glenside Church.

He parked on the street in front of Reverend Moffat's house. A small, well-kept colonial with an immaculate yard and new brick borders around the empty flower beds. The front door showed three tiny descending panes of glass, none of them eye-level. Peterson waited through a song on the radio, but its bass line was irritating and he shut it off. The snow was letting up. He looked in the rearview and wondered if his day's beard was coming in too dark and might give a wrong impression. He watched the reverend's home and saw a curtain flutter, but sometimes a furnace kicking up might ruffle the curtains, you could never be sure. Then, a man was coming outside and walking over to the truck.

He stood beside Peterson's window the way a teacher asserting discipline might lean over a desk in grammar school. The man had a neutral face, without a touch of personal worry or internalized regret. His expression was one of steady expectation interrupted by an irregular wince, a tic of some kind. His forehead was symmetrically etched in even lines, as if drawn with a protractor. These surface lines had no apparent link to the reverend's intimate life and seemed related only to the tiresome situations of others. Peterson recognized these features, he'd seen this face on twenty-year police veterans.

When Peterson stepped down from the truck, one foot slid out from under him and he unconsciously gripped the reverend's elbow. Together, they shifted, lurching back and forth for balance, trying to keep from pulling one another down. Peterson straightened up and after adjusting the shoulders of his coat, he shook the reverend's hand. "About the dust," he told him. "I need a signature."

"Yes, yes. Miss Snyder."

"That's right, Angela," Peterson said.

"Did she contact your company? Hire you to come over here?"

"I just need a simple John Hancock. I can write it up, a description of the test, the TEM, on a piece of paper. It's scrap paper, if you don't mind? I forgot my receipt book. This once I don't have the official form, but this will be serviceable enough. Okay with you?" He tore a sheet of paper from a spiral notebook and wrote a sentence explaining the dust samples, naming the appropriate tests. He told the reverend, "You word the permission. Dictate to me whatever you need, and then you can sign on the dotted line." Peterson waited with the pen firm on the paper. "Shoot," he said. "Go ahead." He waited for the reverend to tell him how to word the permission.

"I'm afraid you came out on a cold night for no reason," the reverend told him.

"Excuse me?"

"It's Ronald Doyle. He'd be the one. He's chairman."

"You say I need this other man, Doyle?"

"That's right. He's chairman, but he spends his winters in Sarasota."

"Florida?"

"He has a little emphysema," the reverend explained, crossing his arms and massaging his elbows in the palms of his hands as he talked.

"Long way to commute to church," Peterson said, but it wasn't sounding so good. He didn't figure this Doyle came and went too often. "Well," he said, smiling big, so his teeth felt the chill of the air, "you'll have to sign in his absence. What do you think?" Peterson noticed the moon going down over the west-side roofs. The snow was over, and Peterson stopped to think that the moon was probably there, behind the snow, all along, throughout his night with Angela Snyder. At that official minute it looked alarmingly crooked, a partial crescent eroding at the center.

Peterson said, "Are you saying you can't do anything for us? Aren't you the kingpin at the church?"

Reverend Moffat explained his situation.

"You say you are *and you aren't*?"

"It's not in my capacity," Reverend Moffat said.

Peterson said, "This Sunday, you're going to find the nerve to talk about the modern world?"

"You have the wrong man," the reverend told him, touching Peterson's sleeve, plucking the nylon shell as he talked. An odd, unconscious, and girlish gesture. He said, You Have The Wrong Man, enunciating each word as if he believed Peterson did not have English as his first language.

Peterson leaned back against the great, solid bulk of his truck, which he could drive, if he wished, right through the small white door with the postcard-size windows. He listened to the reverend's side of it. You'd think it was the sabbath. Peterson heard the familiar, overstated assurances. As he talked, the reverend touched his fingertips together and closed the heels of his hands as if to create a tiny room—the children's playroom. Its hazard: simple conjecture. Its remedy: unwarranted. Either way, it was out of his realm of duty.

The reverend returned to his house, closed his front door, and switched out the light. For a moment the reverend's face reappeared at the door, framed in one of the small, waist-high accent windows. Peterson got behind the wheel and looked at the reverend's snowy lawn, smooth and squared like sheet cake. In fact, the frosted brick borders had the sugary gloss of wedding-cake decorations, rosettes and peaked dollops. He steered the truck over the curb and faced the house. He tugged the stick into neutral and revved the big V-8. His palm felt the buzz in the knob. It opened up. It roared. A clean, fully lubricated growl which echoed off the little house. Moffat came back outside and stood on his stoop with shoulders lifted in pantomimed inquiry, his blanched hands leveled before him as if he held a laden dinner plate. What was he asking? For understanding? Peterson put it into four-wheel drive and artfully worked the gas pedal and clutch making the truck jump forward, advancing in tight, halted progressions like a mammoth predatory beast rehearsing its pounce. The jerky accelerations tore up the sod beneath the wheels. Moffat appeared suddenly convinced by Peterson and he went inside and slammed the door. Again his face bloomed in the tiny window until at last he must have moved to the telephone to dial 911.

I could drive through a house, Peterson was thinking. It would be the least he could do. Instead, he steered the truck around the front yard, riding a figure eight through the thick, slushy surface. The wheels climbed over the low brickwork, riding in and out of the geometric garden beds at both corners of the yard. The snow muddied beneath the tires. The second time around, he spun out a little harder, leaving deep gullies. He flicked the high beams to study the surface flecked with random grass divots and long mud sashes which had peeled loose from the tire treads. It looked complete, this small suburban ruin. Peterson knew the lawn could be reseeded or measured for new rolls of sod. The church congregation would foot the bill in pity for their pastor. He turned back onto the pavement; the slush lifted in a heavy wave.

Everything was melting as Peterson drove across town. He cranked the window open and rested his hand on the side mirror. The tires made a hushing, mothering singsong over the asphalt. He took the particle samples from his breast pocket and arranged them on the dash. Using his teeth to tear the plastic, one packet after another, he extended his arm and released the contents. The branny grit settled to the wet street, but its toxic powder flared level with the truck in parallel clouds, ghosting the taillights. Instantly, it cleared, aspirated by the opposite traffic.

❖ RIDERS TO THE SEA

Bell was fighting a sex hangover as he fixed a fried egg sandwich. He was feeling unsettled and wanted to line his stomach before he resumed his evening schedule at the Narragansett. He scored the egg with a spatula; the gold pillow wobbled, then steadied, its lacy albumen white as a doily.

His knees turned hollow and tensed back each time he remembered the CVS girl from the other night. They had parked at the Cliff Walk. He let her out of the passenger side and she came right along, with just her fingertips alert in the palm of his hand. Her jeans had zippers at the ankles and she ripped each tag, one cuff, then the other. The twilight lingered, reflected on the sea. She made him acknowledge his first view of her, the labia's pink crest, sudden, symmetrical as a tiny valentine.

He adjusted the toaster. The electric twists glowed. Then a neighbor kid ran past the window, notching left and right and screaming in crimped bleats. Bell snapped the dial on the stove and went outside. Some neighbors had stepped onto their lawns to see whose boy was having the trouble. Bell looked down the string of white clapboard houses which ended on First Beach; nothing had changed much since he was small. He tucked the spatula inside the mailbox and followed the people down to the water. A group had assembled at the edge of the sea; a few men waded in ankle deep. Thirty feet out, a windsurfer tacked back and forth in silent, accurate swipes.

The woman was face down, her chestnut hair filtered forward, then pleated back in the calm water. The waves came in like clear rolls of Saran before puddling on shore. The sea hardly tugged her. A wreath of suds, pearly as BBs, surrounded the body and tagged the rocks. He couldn't see her face or guess her exact age. She was wearing a cocktail dress stitched with fancy beadwork. Sewn in undulating lines over her hips, the beads reflected the sun in shifting gradations of light, like the contrasting whorls in polished marble. This marble effect made her look like something that had toppled from a pedestal. The woman rode back and forth in six-inch increments over the pebble sheet. Bell saw it was the agitation of the brine, the brine forced through the cores of the miniature beads on the woman's dress which had created the foamy scud on the surface of the water.

.   .   .

Bell was living at home again with his mother and his sister, Christine, coming back to Newport after three months in a Navy brig at Portsmouth, Virginia. He had hoped to wrangle some duty in his hometown. He asked for the Construction Battalion Unit, where he could do his hitch building piers or grouting the swimming pools on base. Instead, he had been assigned to the Naval Supply Center in Norfolk. He never shipped out. He worked on a terminal in the bowels of a warehouse, cataloguing dry goods and food supplies for the carriers. He couldn't tell the weather, what clouds scumbled overhead, tinting the sea. All day he was under the fluorescents.

He began to do some pilfering. It wasn't much, just what he could get into his Plymouth once or twice over weekend liberty. Mostly it was cases of cigarettes, which he sold to Richmond Vending. After his time in the brig, he wasn't surprised by the general discharge. Its abrupt language was stinging, even without being accusatory. In just two lines of print it was all over.

He tried to adjust to hours in his mother's house—scents from the kitchen, yeast cakes soaking, knotted rolls swelling like broken knuckles, the floor always gritty with cinnamon sugar. He hated to hear the same low thump of the radiator building with steam, the pipes knocking room to room, and then subsiding. All of his old haunts flipped before his eyes like lantern slides or stereoscopic pictures: the old Viking Look Out Tower, the Mount Hope Bridge with its green lanterns, then the Providence skyline, the State House with its needle spire injecting the horizon. The vision of the drowned woman was a refreshing surge, washing through the ordinary furnishings and clutter in his childhood house.

. . .

The crowd on the beach had adjusted to the visual impact. One man questioned the idea of an actual drowning—the woman could have been dumped. Someone said she must be a Boston whore down for the weekend. Bell knew that there were always illicit odd jobs during the off-season, when summer boutiques fell back on drug trafficking. Motel bars hired girls to do some modeling; they arranged elevated runways by just lining up three or four billiard tables. One or two video pioneers manufactured hard-core tapes, working out of the Sheraton, and the same up at the Ramada. Bell's stomach was still empty, but he wasn't hungry. He felt weighted, almost sleepy; the abrasive slushing of the waves over the beaded dress was hypnotic. Because the woman had washed ashore so close to his house, he couldn't resist thinking it might be a commentary on his arrival. He studied her body. Bell saw she had a little mole halfway up her thigh, just at the hem of her short dress. He saw it, then flicked his gaze farther out. It was restful to study the horizon, letting it snag and scurry. Then he looked back at the woman.

An emergency vehicle drove up the beach. The paramedics flipped her over and tried to revive her, by rote theory, before lifting her onto a gurney. The wheels of the gurney left tiny furrows in the sand, but the tide was coming in, erasing wide crescents. Bell was impressed, but he couldn't figure out what left him astonished. He envied the woman's anonymity. Her suspended identity enriched his ballooning awareness: the world was full of nobodies.

He thought of a bar trick he liked to perform for the girls. He could do it all night with just a pack of Salems and a sixty-five-cent Krazy Wand bottle. He takes a calculated drag and exhales smoke into a soap bubble. It drifts into the tables of ladies. It pops. The smoke is released.

When he returned to the house, his mother was in the kitchen stirring a pot, her hand making a figure eight, then tapping, then twisting. The spoon on the enamel rim resonated on the spinal nerves and Bell walked over and took the spoon out of his mother's hand. She took it back. Divorced from his father for years, she was still upset if she sometimes saw him on the street. She told Bell that she had met his father at one of the rotaries and they had to steer around the circle together for a few moments, jockeying for position. Bell told her to pretend that his father doesn't exist. She reminded Bell that they lived on an island, after all, and they couldn't always avoid each other, could they? "Quite a scene on First Beach," he told her.

"Did we know the girl?" his mother asked him.

"Probably not."

"You didn't recognize her?"

"I said no."

Then he heard his sister, Christine, drive up the oyster shells with her boyfriend, Miller. Christine worked days at Raytheon. She seemed different since his discharge from the Navy. It wasn't anything he could put his finger on. Her face looked both expectant and sullied. As if expectancy itself was what tainted her. Bell didn't imagine she could have changed too much since high school. She maintained a serious, collegiate aura although she didn't go on to college. She had a habit of biting her lower lip, organizing her thoughts with her teeth clamped down on the same red swell. In Bell's absence, she had joined the local Latin League, going to monthly potlucks with some steeped-in-culture oldsters and scholarly kids interested in the Roman lifestyle. She tried to explain to Bell about the Saturnalia. Then, she was a new member of the Newport Community Theater, where she had been asked to star in a one-act play. She showed Bell the flyers advertising the production: "Kristine Bellamy in *Riders to the Sea,* by Irish playwright J. M. Synge."

Her name had been spelled incorrectly with a *K.* Bell approved of the change, telling her he never liked the word *Christ* in her name. He saw that she carried a spinning wheel back and forth to the rehearsals. The first night he was home, he watched his sister leave the house with the little wooden contraption, a wheel and a spindle. It gave him a start. Yet she was still wearing her David Bowie tour jacket, scuffed leather, scabby at the elbows, a relic of the seventies. The spinning wheel lost its clout against the rock-'n'-roll souvenir, and the contrast pleased Bell.

"This is Miller." Christine introduced Bell to her new boyfriend. "I met Miller at the Community Theater."

"I change the colored spots and move the flats back and forth with the kids who don't get the parts they want. Idle brats," Miller called them. Miller came often to the house to prompt Christine and help her rehearse her lines for *Riders to the Sea.* Bell wasn't pleased to have Miller around when he wanted to settle in with his mother and sister.

Bell told Christine, "I found a drowned girl on the beach."

"You found her?"

"Actually, I was second in line." He waited for her reaction. His sister looked at him. She saw he was evaluating her, so she didn't say anything. His mother went next door to discuss the news with her neighbor, who had signaled to her through the facing kitchen window.

When it was just the three of them, Miller admitted that he wished he had seen the drowned woman. "Nothing like a body in the surf," Miller said.

"What do you mean, nothing like it? Are you crazy?" Christine asked.

Bell squinted at Miller, trying to see where this was going and he pushed it along. "Miller's right about that. It's a seventh wonder."

"An impressive sight, isn't it?" Miller asked. "More lyrical than a body on dry land. Like a message in a bottle. There's a mysterious connection, a romantic spell, like a tryst between the victim and the person who finds her. Who found the woman?"

"A kid."

Miller said, "Yeah, well, but you were down there. You had a part."

"I felt that," Bell said, "like I'm initiated."

"Exactly! It's a tingle," Miller said.

"She was like some dish from Atlantis," Bell went on, teasing his sister.

Miller discussed local catastrophes, boats going down, a couple of notable shootings, Sunny von Bülow, and the six or seven yearly leaps from bridges.

"Hey, who writes the Crime Report, is it you?" Christine rolled her script into a tight tube and pointed to Miller who had seated himself at the kitchen table.

Miller talked all that time but never looked directly at Bell. He talked about the drowned woman as if he was teaching a class on it. Miller looked too old for Christine.

He had stiff ashy hair that formed three or four stalactites across his shoulders. He smiled at Christine, showing teeth that were harnessed in clear plastic fencing, some kind of invisible orthodontics to correct an overbite. A progressive decision for a man his age, he told Bell. Miller slouched with his legs extended deep under the kitchen table, a posture, Bell believed, that should be reserved for family members only.

When Miller stretched his arms over his head, Bell glimpsed a peculiar device belted at his waist. It was some kind of hospital gizmo, a tiny box, the size of a pack of Winston Kings. A small display screen shimmered as an emerald dot pulsed to prove the battery pack was A-okay, or to provide some other light-coded information. Bell tried to remember what he knew about modern medical technology. "What is that you've got there?"

Christine said, "That's Miller's insulin infusion pump. It regulates a steady flow of insulin through a little tube taped to his abdomen."

The explanation disturbed Bell; he wasn't alarmed about the man's problem, but he realized Christine had been privy to this tube inserted in Miller's belly. Bell saw that this high-tech medical toy might be an attraction for Christine. Her lovers seemed to have chronic maladies, a skin condition or a joint replacement. Then she dated new arrivals, Cuban boys and Cape Verdeans with English as a second language; there was always some obstacle she enjoyed tackling.

Her current squeeze: a diabetic stage technician. For someone suffering a condition, Miller appeared self-assured and arrogant. Thin and sallow, he looked utterly confident in his underweight condition. His smile, reinforced with plastic brackets, had a sinister depth. He had Christine up against the GE, kissing her, the buzz of the freon increasing. Bell took the keys to the car and looked back once, hoping his sister had disentangled, but she wasn't rushing for his sake.

He drove his mother's car the full perimeter of the island. He went up West Main Road, watching the late sun touch long ribbons on the bay, wakes from tankers and little frothy bows behind pleasure boats. He came back on East Main, seeking blue splints of the Sakonnet all the way down. He drove out Ocean Drive, where breakers crashed against the jetties in bright crescents, glassy as chandeliers. He loved the spectacle of the sea, the ornament of its lighted spray against notches of granite. After seeing something like that, he sought the smeary ambience of a tavern. It was the tiled bar at the Narragansett, black and white inches of cracked ceramics like a littered shoreline and stale spills puddled around the table legs.

"They're all gone now, and there isn't anything more the sea can do to me." Christine was just coming in the door, home from Raytheon. She was in character, the keening voice of an Irish matron whose sons have all been drowned. Her authority always surprised Bell. She took the spinning wheel from the closet and went into the living room. Bell watched as she placed it on the floor and the wheel revolved slowly. It was like something he might see at the helm of a small ketch. She wanted to rehearse while spinning a snag of yarn and she asked him if he would read the lines and cue her.

"This play is in Irish?" he asked her.

She told him, "Don't be stupid, of course it's English, but it lilts. I'll show you." She recited a phrase, an insistent querying dirge. "Everything sounds like a question," she told him. "The words go up at the end, the sentences just keep ascending like climbing switchbacks."

"No kidding?" he said.

"*There's someone-in after crying out by the seashor-ir,*" she recited. The words were echoey, lifting at the final syllables.

"Okay," he said.

"*He's gone now, and when the black night is falling I'll have no son left me in the whar-ald,*" her voice climbed and faltered, climbed again.

Bell read from the script like a mechanic running his eyes over a parts-and-service ledger in the metric system, rubbing his chin with the back of his wrist. Christine enjoyed his shyness and she let him founder.

"*Riders to the Sea* is supposed to be a tragic play," she told him. She wanted to share the winey taste of the lines, and she told him the words should feel exciting on the tongue, like capers or wild mushrooms.

He asked her, "Why are they doing this one? Why not the usual *West Side Story*? What about *Hair*?"

"This is a real play," she told him. "You know, there are just two themes in life. No musical soundtracks necessary."

"What themes?"

"Love and death."

"When did you decide this?" he asked her.

"We're all born with the secret," she told him.

Christine wasn't just teasing. Her remark emerged whisper-smooth, the way a U-2 submarine rises all glossy and serene in the middle of a giant swell.

"Real drama," she told him, "is pain kept brewing all the

weeks before the curtain goes up, so that no one can misinterpret pain as performance. It's supposed to be pain *alive*."

He wanted to get out of the house. Christine was tilting something. She looked pale and eerie, but maybe this was from working deep in the windowless complex at Raytheon.

He cued her lines. It was a depressing story. All the men drown and the women are left weeping before a rough-hewn coffin. "This is a little hard to swallow," he told her.

He told her that he was happy she was just practicing for a performance when sooner or later it gets dark on its own. "Don't ask me what I saw in jail. Not just the crowd on the inside, I'm talking about the families who come to visit. Talk about the sad truth."

Christine nodded, she was trying to picture the unhappy relations queuing up outside the prison doors. "I would have visited you, Bell, if it wasn't Virginia. Didn't I come to see you all the time at the Training School?"

"I'm not complaining," he told her. He was wondering. Maybe acting in a tragic one-act play can make a girl responsible and wary. "This Miller dude," Bell told her, "what's the story with him?"

Christine turned her face to the window to secrete her grin. The beach light touched her profile as it reached into the house, splicing through glass curtain pulls and lifting the grain on the woodwork. Bell saw that Christine was pleased he worried about her; or, perhaps she was pleased, simply, to think of Miller.

She began again. This time her voice was too high, the singsong of leprechauns. She halted mid-sentence and started over. Finding the right pitch, she recited a long passage and tried her best to keen at an appropriate octave, with the complexity of a vibrating cello string, the way her director had explained it should sound.

He was in the first booth at the Narragansett Tavern. He liked to watch the door sweep open and ratchet slowly back. He glimpsed the harbor outside, a dense stand of masts like a glaring aluminum atrium. The girl from the CVS drugstore was rolling a ballpoint over the curve of his knee, inking a burning dot on the stiff denim of his line-dried jeans. The other week, he had found her sorting the magazines in the front of the store. Stacking the older issues on a trolley. He asked her what she did with the old issues. Do they get recycled? He took a heavy issue of *Computer Shopper* out of her hands, thick as a phone book. She didn't say anything as the weight was transferred. She looked back in a steady, instinctive perusal of his face the way a bird and its worm exchange a moment of awakening.

"We send them back on the truck," she said after a while. She looked pretty young. But youth is a pie with many slices. She told Bell, "I can punch out for an hour at about seven-thirty. Come get me if you want. Or do you just want one of these periodicals?"

"I'll be back," he had told her. He was smiling. He liked the way she had said "periodicals," as if she were some kind of librarian. No names were exchanged. He didn't tell her his name was Bellamy, Bell for short, and she seemed just as happy to stand, unidentified, in the center aisle, surrounded by waist-high stacks of glossies.

She finished writing her telephone number along his inside seam and he told her, "You could have spared my mother the annoyance. Besides, I have a photographic memory."

"Really? Well, what's my number, then?" she said. She flattened her palm against his eyes.

He recited the telephone number.

"God, that's scary," she said. She didn't look scared.

"Lucky try," Bell said. It was easy to please this girl. He didn't have to encourage her. She sat next to him, pushing her cuticles back as if her fingertips were a key to everything. She wasn't like Christine, who might get bored without conversation. Christine might demand to play cards or challenge him to match historical data with highlights from the last three decades of rock-'n'-roll. Christine had said, laughing, "Rock stars are noble primitives. They have their roots in ancient culture, like the Saturnalia."

When he was in the company of a thriving slut like the CVS girl, why was he thinking about his sister, trying to nestle her image against the drugstore clerk? The CVS girl already failed to intrigue him beyond his first inspiration, which was never a thrill for long. He might go with the CVS girl again. For a couple of hours, park on a side street near the Cliff Walk. Relief, without an immediate rekindling of tension, is often a disappointment.

Never calling it forth, still he saw the dark fleck on the drowned woman's thigh. Its tiny circumference seemed to recur in his vision like a vitreous floater or a snag in the retina. He faced his companion. She wet her lips and waited. He spoke and her eyes squeezed shut in tight winces of approval. She agreed. It didn't matter what he was saying.

. . .

His father was standing in the kitchen holding a heavy paper bag. The bag was leaking from its bottom folds and Bell could see from its dripping mass that it must be some two-pounders. His mother had the big speckled kettle whining on the stove. Christine was peeling the wax paper from a pound of butter. She put the pale block in a saucepan and adjusted the gas until the flame steadied. She set the burner very low, using her expertise so that each flame kept separate, lifting from the jets like the beads of a blue necklace. The butter started to slide in the pan.

"To celebrate. You're back home. Man of the house," his father announced.

Bell looked at his mother, but she didn't seem put out by the intrusion. She accepted his father's presence in her kitchen now and again, the way she was tolerant of plumbers, electricians, painters, anyone she had to incorporate into her household for small allotments of time until maintenance was complete, a repair job finished. She showed no familiarity, yet she tried to stand at ease, without knotting her apron too tight as she might do in moments of distress. Then again, she didn't confirm the notion that, by default, Bell should be "Man of the house." She didn't seem to want anyone in that role.

"Supper is a surprise," his mother said.

"Are you staying to eat, then?" Bell asked his father.

"Oh, no. I just brought these over for you and Chrissie. Your mother's got one there, if she desires."

Bell lifted a heavy lobster out of the paper sack. "This one's mine," Bell said, trying to keep the talk going. "And for you, Christine?" Bell reached into the bag and pulled another one forth. "This one's seen it all." Bell held the lobster high so everyone could admire it.

"His big claw looks funny," Christine said, seeing the lobster's aggressive, thumping arms, its large, palsied claw.

"It's a fighter," his father said, looking back and forth between his son and daughter. "Vinnie Pazienza."

"The Paz." Bell was smiling.

"Twelfth round," Christine said, "*ding!*" She lifted the lid off the big pot.

The lobsters went in the kettle and the water stilled for a moment before churning back. Bell's father said his good-byes. "Come over any time," he told Bell.

"When?"

His father shook his head. He wasn't good at calibrating dates and times, and he didn't land on any specific day and hour.

Bell walked him out to the street and drummed the trunk of the car as it rolled away. When he went back in the house, Christine was arranging newspaper over the kitchen table, opening the sections and layering the wide sheets. "Look at that," she said to Bell, her fingertip touched the newsprint. It was a picture of the drowned woman at First Beach. The photo was from Con-Temp, a temporary office pool where she had been on the roster for a year. The woman's name was Kelly Primiano, from Medford.

"Irish-Italian," Bell's mother said. "Where was her luck that day?"

"If she's half-Italian, that cancels out the luck factor right there," Bell said.

"Says here she wasn't drunk. No bones broken." Christine read the print. "Her parents say she was a good swimmer. They taught her in Marblehead every summer."

"You can be an excellent swimmer, but if it's too far to swim, you might as well not know how," Bell said.

"Are you saying she tried to swim the cove?"

"Maybe she was pushed off a skiff," Bell said. "Anything."

Christine read some more: "There wasn't any fluid in her lungs."

Bell dropped his face down to the sheet of newsprint. "Shit. She didn't drown, then. See what I'm saying?"

"She wasn't *dressed* for the beach; it must have been something awful. Maybe she just slipped and hit her head on the rocks," Christine said.

Bell looked at the face in the newspaper. Her hair was twisted in two elegant braids high over her forehead, as if she were going to the opera. He thought she looked "lace curtain" but must have crossed the tracks at some point in time.

"Says here she was engaged," Christine said.

Bell said, "Is that so? Who was the lucky guy? Her fiancé was Davy Jones? Man-of-war in her trousseau. Honeymoon cruise on the *Titanic*." He listed the possibilities until his mother set the lobsters in the center of the table. Bright shells steaming, long red whiskers tilted at odd angles like extra-sweep second hands on a tourist clock.

Bell discovered that a Navy friend had been reassigned to the Naval Underwater Systems Center in Newport, a good job in combat research and electromagnetics. The assignment came with a pretty duplex in relandscaped naval housing. Bell left messages for his friend, teasing him about his fat job, but none were returned. He thought he would drive over there, and he decided to take Christine and

Miller. Maybe they would be sandblasting a destroyer at Pier I and Christine could take a look at that. He drove his mother's Buick and Christine pounded the center armrest closed so that they could all sit in front. Cracker crumbs and stale cookies sifted over the vinyl, and Bell wondered why his mother's world was always defined by bread stuffs, a branny litter of sweets and biscuits.

Miller complained about the sweets and he teased Christine, accusing her of trying to tempt him.

"You can't eat a cookie?" Bell asked Miller.

"It isn't the best thing for Miller," Christine said.

"If he wants a cookie, give him a cookie," Bell said.

"Maybe he doesn't want cupcakes and candies. Maybe he wants something else. What should I give him?" Christine was electrified, giggling each time Bell turned the wheel and his elbow knocked her. Women love to be centered between two men.

"You sure are on top of the world," Bell told his sister.

Now and again, even with the motor humming, Bell heard a blip from Miller's tummy pack.

He turned into Gate 17, but the MPs were checking stickers and wouldn't let him come on base. An official Bronco tugged around the Buick and headed down the road leading to Coddington Cove, but Bell was directed to turn his car around.

Slow flushes bloomed and receded, bloomed again, starting at Bell's throat and climbing over his cheekbones. He didn't give the fellow his name or rank, or bother with explanations about his past connections with the Navy. He turned the car around and drove away. Christine cleared her throat. She tried one small apologetic cough to relieve a collective indignant feeling, but it didn't help.

Miller said, "Anyone drives on base, what's the problem, Bellamy?"

Of course it had nothing to do with Bell's general discharge. There was probably some reason why they were sending people away. They might have the pot-sniffing dogs going around, or maybe they were spraying grass seed on the lots or painting the curbs. Bell told them, "Do we care? Do we need this crap?"

"Let's forget it," Christine said.

Miller said, "I don't understand. Since when do they send people away?"

Christine tried to shush him, but he stopped on his own and fiddled with the lapels of her blouse. Bell tried to ignore Miller's hands on his sister. It was jokey and innocent, but it irritated him when Miller went on for too long. He drove through town and stopped in the Almacs parking lot. He got out of the car and walked across to the CVS. He came back with the girl. She trotted behind him, removing her gray smock. She looked bewildered but pleased, shaking her head, letting her curls flop side to side. She scanned the parking lot to see who might acknowledge her. She was leaving her job for this impulsive, hotted-up guy, and it must look interesting. She told them she had been collecting the expired Easter cards from their Plexiglas bins, then sorting and inserting new cards for Mother's Day.

She started right in. "I hate working the card display. It takes me forever. I have paper cuts. See these poor fingers? You know, the envelopes—they're like fucking razors!"

Christine and Miller shifted to the backseat. The CVS girl took her place beside Bell. Bell revved the engine and thumbed the radio dial as everyone settled in. He turned out of the parking lot onto Bellevue Avenue. "Well, what do you want to do?" he said, but he was just being polite.

"What about the Green Animals?" Christine said.

"Christine, how many years have you been going to see Green Animals? Every single year of your life, am I right?" Bell said.

"It's beautiful there," she told him.

The CVS girl said, "Are you talking about those sculpted bushes? I've never been up there to see those."

"Forget it," Bell said.

They drove past the famous mansions, most of them acquired by the Historical Society. Bell slowed the car as they approached the driveway where an heiress had steered a sedan over her chauffeur as he opened a gate. The murder location gave them a giddy surge as they left Bellevue's heavy arbor and the street jogged onto Ocean Drive. They were out of the proper town and snaking up the shoreline. The sea's white light washed through the windshield.

"Well? How many times have we driven out here? Only a zillion times," Christine said to Bell, but her remark drifted. They were looking at the first glimpse of the sea at the turnaround at Bailey's Beach. There was a strong, sweet scent coming in through the open window. It was the narcotic spell of early plankton blooming. The scent made his lust grow razory, his daydreams intensify, wavering through harsh stages of melancholy. Bell recited from his high school botany text, "The plankton bloom is a biological phenomenon having to do with chlorophyll and photosynthesis, a simple process impelled by the sun." Yet, each season, Bell felt indirectly involved in the event, as if the sea's rejuvenation triggered second chances for everyone.

"A sign of spring," Bell went on, trying to subdue an explosive coronary rhythm which started to crush the breath from him. The scent was so luscious, he rubbed his hand over his face as if dusting sugar from his lips.

"It intoxicates me," Christine admitted to Miller. "You never think of the sea as a kind of garden, all floral like this."

"It's peaking," Bell said, "like a thousand water lilies—"

"I don't see lilies, where?" the CVS girl said. Miller leaned over the front seat and tapped her shoulder. She turned and shrugged in benign agreement. She wrinkled her nose once, puffed in and out, trying to track the scent that Bell was describing. "Everything smells like Giorgio to me," she told them. "A lady was spritzing it on herself at the counter."

They parked the car in the empty lot at the Beach Club, a private string of pastel cabanas still boarded up for the winter. There was a stiff wind, but the sun felt strong, falling in broad plackets of peachy light. The sand was extraordinarily hot for a day in mid-spring, and the heat rose to shin-level. They walked four abreast, the women in the middle.

"He basically *kidnapped* me!" the CVS girl told Christine.

"God, what did your boss say?"

"What was she going to say? Bell looked intense," the girl said. "But I didn't think we were going for a walk on the beach. I would have stayed where I was. I make four seventy-five. That's an hour," she confided to Christine, but she punched her small fist into Bell's side, digging her thumbnail into his ribs and cranking it a quarter-turn.

"Here," Bell told them. He climbed onto a grouping of boulders and granite formations that made a natural break-water into the sea. Giant ledges of rusty shale ascended like drunken stairways right and left. The surf sliced over the misshapen pillars and sloshed into its hollows, dragging ropes of effervescent foam. Sudsy lines extended far out. The water was so aerated, the place smelled of extra oxy-gen. A central configuration of rocks formed irregular bleachers around a deep chamber where the sea crashed in-ward, doubled its pressure, and shot upwards through a narrow fissure. The small opening was like a whale's nostril. The place was called Spouting Rock, a local perch for teens who used its unpredictable force for threats and dares.

Christine sat down beside the blowhole. She rubbed her fingertips over its stony lip, inserting her pointer to the second knuckle. She looked distracted by something far out on the water as she fingered the blue-black opening. Her fingers probed and swirled over the slick rock until the men couldn't hide their discomfort.

The CVS girl pulled her jersey over her head to feel the sun. She was wearing an underwire bra and its ribs rode up until her breasts were sliced across, making four even lumps out of two. She tugged the bra back in place and threw her shirt at Bell. He caught the jersey before it fell into the water. Christine looked at Miller to gauge his reac-tion, or she was trying to find her own response. She un-buttoned her top button and lifted her shirt off. Bell thought she was just trying to keep up.

He didn't want to stare at her and he studied the water. A large bank of waves was coming in and it would cause some action at Spouting Rock. It was so utterly familiar, these procedures. He saw the undertow pull back and the surface flatten. For a few seconds, nothing. The swell ascended in frothy notches, wobbled and shuddered in a dead halt before beginning its advance. Building a high curl, its wall looked green and corrugated as a carport awning. Bell thought of the drowned woman, her beaded dress, variegated and marbled like the rocks, as if she herself might have broken off this reef and washed onto First Beach.

"Here comes," Bell shouted, pulling his sister to her feet. The sea crashed into the trough, smacking the planes of rock like pistol shots. The level ascended, rising up until the full force of the wave exploded from the crevice where Christine had been seated. The spray shot up twelve feet, feathered left and right in different tugs of wind. The girls squealed as the men yanked them out of its circle. Miller touched his hip to see if his insulin pump was wet. It had been spared. The CVS girl saw it; she recognized the box. "Hey, I've seen one of those at work," she told Miller. "Is that one of those electronic blood-pressure kits, is that it? Have you got hypertension?"

Miller started to explain to the girl. He walked her over to the craggy shale ladders. He put his arm around her bare neck, letting his wrist swivel on her shoulder as he talked. He strummed her hair away from her eyes and pulled her close, into his medical confession.

"He's telling her his symptoms," Christine said.

"What are his symptoms?"

"Weakness, blurred vision. He could go blind, you know."

"He just looks lovesick, if you ask me," Bell said.

Christine watched her boyfriend with the other girl. Christine was smiling. Bell admired this. He didn't feel like walking over there to claim the CVS girl for himself or to get Miller back on her account. Christine walked out on a tiny natural bridge to another huge boulder. Bell followed her out. She was reciting lines when he came up beside her. The wind erased her words and she turned around in the other direction. She faced her brother.

"They're carrying a thing among them and there's water dripping out of it and leaving a track by the big stones."

"Don't you know your lines by now?" Bell had to yell.

"Leaving a track by the big stones," Christine repeated.

"Must you always—"

She was laughing. *"The big stones*—just like these," she said. She toed the granite with the tip of her sneaker.

He watched her profile, the wind lifted her weft of blond hair until it flared level.

"What are we doing here with these people?" Bell asked her. "These geeks? What are we doing here? With them?"

"Oh, Christ," she said, looking out at the water. She was trying not to listen.

He squared before her. He put his arms around her waist, crossing his fists at the small of her back. He cinched his wrists tighter and held her without the imprint of his hands. She was beneath his chin. "What are we doing?" he said.

"Meaning?" she said. Her eyes looked startled, the pupils swirled open, but she kept her face level, steadied. The slight translucent down at her hairline was electrified by the sun; her eyelashes blazed like tiny welders' arcs.

She bent her knees and crawled out from under his

arms. She laid her palms flat against his biceps and shoved him lightly across the rock. She told him, "You're just getting adjusted to home. Shit. Everything's a three-ring— that's what you used to say."

Miller was calling to them. He was having some sort of panic spasms and his arms windmilled in two directions.

Bell went down to where he was standing.

"She's fucking with me, man," Miller said. "She's took my insulin pump and won't let me have it."

Christine descended carefully from the boulder. She reached under her shorts and tugged the elastic leg of her panties, letting it snap. "So you took it off? Are you supposed to take it off? What happens to your blood?" she said.

"I was showing it to her," Miller said.

Christine said, "Since when do you disconnect it?"

"Wake up, Chrissie," Bell said.

"What do you mean, wake up?" She looked at her brother and back to Miller. She saw Miller was wearing his Nike sweats inside out.

Miller said, "It was nothing, Christine. Just nothing."

"Not worth the effort?" Bell said.

Miller didn't protest the assumption.

"Since when do you take it off for that?" Christine said.

Bell examined his sister. Then he looked for the CVS girl and saw her leaning against the car in the beach parking lot. Her arms were crossed tightly at her bosom, the way girls fold their arms when they're ready to go home.

"Is that your gizmo? Right there?" Bell pointed to a rocky ledge where the girl had propped the insulin pump. He lifted it off the granite niche and tossed it to Miller. It fell in a weightless arc and landed in the water. The little box drifted back and forth in one of the frothy gullies between land and sea.

"Nice," Miller said. "That's just wonderful. Just what am I dealing with here? Do you have the hard cash to replace something like that? That's what I'm asking—"

"Did we ask you to get undressed?" Bell told him.

Christine looked over at the CVS girl and waved. The girl knew it was a snub; she shifted her legs and looked in the other direction.

"Maybe you can get the box," Christine told Miller.

"That's crazy," Miller told them. "I've got insurance. Let's just travel. I'm ready."

"Tell you what. I'll race you for the cost of that thing," Bell said. "Swim out, touch the mooring at Bailey's, turn around, come back. Ten minutes. If you win, I pay for the machine. Even-steven. Time us, Christine." He pulled his jersey over his head and the wind snapped it until he wadded it down.

Miller turned to Christine, but her eyes were squinting and unreceptive. Her face showed a refined acknowledgment of something. Miller said, "Does your brother want me to race him to that mooring? Is he serious?"

"That's the request," Bell said.

"Sorry, my friend," Miller said. He tried to edge past Bell.

Bell put his arm out. He grabbed Miller's throat, half-serious, pinching the windpipe with his thumb and middle finger. Bell wiggled the ribbed cartilage left and right, like a toilet paper tube, until Miller started coughing. Bell might be reaching his maximum capacity for self-control and the other man recognized that Bell was nearing this boundary.

Miller pushed his sweats down and stepped out of

them. He marched around the ledge of rock, searching for a way down into the trough. The water was rough. He turned back. "Fuck you," he told Bell, but he was looking at Christine. "I'm not going in that Mixmaster to please you."

"What about Christine? Here's your chance to make it up," Bell said. He was marching Miller backwards on the ledge.

"You want me to jump in that icy water?"

"Does he have to?" Christine said.

"It's a free world," Bell said. "Do whatever you want." He turned away from Miller and let the two of them discuss it.

A retired couple, exercising their dog, arrived at Spouting Rock. The dog climbed the boulders, its nose brushing side to side for mollusk scents. The couple were surprised to see Miller without his clothes.

"The Polar Bear Club, are you?" the man asked Bell. He had to shout over the surf.

"That's right," Bell told him. "The initiation stage. It's a closed session, try not to gawk."

The man stopped coming when he heard Bell's tone. He watched from a distance. Bell's grave, no-nonsense dementia was beginning to show. He was shifting his legs, stepping in place. He clenched his fists at intervals, and some surface veins had engorged along his pectoral ledge, his dark nipples flared. The stranger steered his wife by her elbow and they walked off. The dog raced ahead.

Christine found her shirt and slipped it over her head. Bell looked at his sister's lover; his penis was screwed close inside the scrotum, his teeth were clacking, an inaudible chatter of strikes and pauses as he pulled the fleecy side of his sweatpants right-side out.

"Pants on, pants off. Can't decide what to do with it?" Bell said.

"You're sick!" Miller said, shivering in large, convulsive shrugs as he dressed. Bell looked out at the sea. A tanker was coming in by Brenton Reef; it was carrying a full load and rested flat as a domino. Closer in, there was something in the water. A pale form rolled on the waves, taupe-colored, like a raincoat. Bell watched the waves fill the fabric in fleshy billows before shooting past. He remembered the way the dead girl filled his thinking, devoured that entire morning when he found her, and kept eating into his mind, even now, days later. The garment surged forward on a swell, took the curve of a hip, then flattened as the wave eased underneath.

"What is that?" Miller said.

"Something or somebody?" Christine said.

Bell said, "It's just a sailcover. A tarp, I guess. It's trash. This is becoming a nautical waste heap. Jesus—what comes and goes in the water. Things wash up, and you don't always need dental records to figure it out." He studied the ragged sheet as it opened and folded, accenting the voluptuous depths that carried it forward. He was taking his shoes off, toeing one heel loose, then the other. He pushed his jeans down.

"What are you doing? You can't swim today," Christine told her brother. "The water's too cold."

Miller said, "Oh, but it was okay for me—"

"I'm going in." Bell removed his jockeys and dove from the rocks into the sea. Christine picked up his briefs and collected them in her right hand. She walked to the end of the jetty to keep sight of him. He was swimming towards the mooring, but he swam right past its rusty sphere and shifted in another direction. He headed towards the mysterious cloth. He swam in smooth, aggressive strokes, as if he could swim a long time, perhaps he could swim far beyond any return to land. He wasn't trying to worry his sister, but he knew she waited. He felt her longing like a vibration in the water. It seemed to help his rhythm; his kicking was silky and powerful, but he was getting tired.

The scrap was a loose-weave sheet used to repair drift nets, something makeshift and discarded. Its grommets were knotted with nylon wire that feathered in the surf like a colossal hydra. Bell circled the torn square as if it were marker for a particular disaster in a man's life. Its ghost outlines flowered, palpitated, and contracted in mockery of the living. He tried to sink it. Free it from its endless float. He shimmied onto the netting, but it disappeared under his weight, retreated to the deep like a frightened pneuma. The mesh wrapped his ankle as he kicked, fanned out behind him like a train, then swirled to the surface again.

The Irish girl floated, lofted in his retina's mirrory sea. Seeing that kind of thing once was plenty. Her body, its helpless curve against the shore, everything, even the tiny decals on her fingernails. Glossy as a photograph. Her body washed in, it conformed to a few general expectations, but her spirit collected or dispersed—where? He couldn't imagine. He had no imagination for that. Ordinary silver nitrate could never etch a picture of heaven. He preferred to think of the live girl, her summers at Marblehead. What was her line of work? Was she in the profession? Did her innocence seize up, suddenly, or was it a natural decline?

Bell tried to gather the unmanageable netting and tow it in to shore. Despite its transparency, its coarse knots, the sheet was too difficult to maneuver and he had to leave it.

He worked to get back to the rocks. The rip current made swimming hard. When he pulled himself out of the water, his flesh was pink from the effort, he felt a tingle of sweat beneath the crystallizing salt scum. He picked up his jeans and put them on, forgetting his underwear. Christine twirled the waistband on her pointer finger and let them sail. Miller tried to lead Christine back to the car. Her dramatic handling of her brother's briefs made Miller question out loud his luck with women. Why did Christine have to insult him with such inventive gestures? Miller told Christine, "I want to leave. Now. Fish or cut bait." She waited for Bell to lace his shoes.

Christine looked at her brother and smiled. She started to recite her lines, her voice silky and true to her role. *"There does be a power of young men floating around in the sea—"*

Miller rubbed his forehead with the back of his knuckles. "Jesus Christ. You're a sad story. The two of you. You're both really sad."

At the car, the CVS girl climbed in the backseat with Miller and Christine rode in front, beside her brother. The girl wanted to return to her job and Bell let her off at the drugstore. He drove down Memorial Boulevard. He watched his sister's profile and he bounced the heel of his hand on her knee. "Christine. Green Animals?"

"The topiary? You want to go there? You're not just being nice?"

Bell told her, "I'm giving it another chance."

She smiled and turned her face the other way. "Look, there's Pop," she said, pointing to a car in the next lane. She started to wave but her father didn't see her. "In his own world," she said.

"It's the same world," Bell said.

"Just let me out here," Miller said. He jumped out at the next intersection and left the car door swinging. Bell watched the light change, then he tapped the gas pedal just-so until the door came back and the lock caught.

❖ ABOUT THE AUTHOR

Maria Flook has published two novels, *Family Night*, which was awarded a PEN American/Ernest Hemingway Foundation Special Citation, and *Open Water*. She has received a National Endowment for the Arts Fellowship and a Pushcart Prize for Fiction. Ms. Flook teaches in the core faculty of the Bennington Graduate Writing Seminars at Bennington College. She lives in Truro, Massachusetts.